PRAISE FOR JANICE CANTORE

Janice Cantore is in a league of her own and at the top of her game with her newest razor-sharp procedural, *Edge of Truth*. It is unputdownable and a must-read for fans of romantic suspense and crime thrillers!

JESSICA R. PATCH, bestselling author of the FBI: Strange Crimes Unit series

Be prepared to do nothing until you've finished reading this masterful suspense novel! I took a peek at the first page and couldn't stop until the last sentence.

DIANN MILLS, bestselling, award-winning author of *Canyon of Deceit*, on *Every Deadly Suspicion*

A thrilling read full of heart-stopping tension and great twists. An awesome blend of suspense and romance. Don't miss *Every Deadly Suspicion*.

DARLENE L. TURNER, *Publishers Weekly* bestselling author of the Crisis Rescue Team series

Janice's books are always something I look forward to reading. She hooks you from page one. I highly recommend you hide somewhere fun to read this book because you won't want to be interrupted.

LYNETTE EASON, bestselling, award-winning author of the Lake City Heroes series, on *Every Deadly Suspicion*

Cantore draws on her real-life experience as a police officer to write compelling thrillers that accurately portray cop life and also offer a deep thread of faith, along with interesting characters.

LIBRARY JOURNAL on *Every Deadly Suspicion*

This timely police procedural from a twenty-two-year veteran of the Long Beach, Calif., police satisfies.

PUBLISHERS WEEKLY on *Code of Courage*

In *Breach of Honor*, Janice Cantore tells a complex tale of deceit and backroom deals that leaves you wondering who the good guys actually are. . . . I could not wait to get to the end and see how it all tied together.

HALLEE BRIDGEMAN, bestselling author of the Love and Honor series

Janice Cantore has crafted an adventure filled with brutal crimes, heartbreaking injustice, shocking twists, a gentle romance, and hard-won faith. Words like page turning, breath stealing, and pulse racing, while accurate, don't begin to do it justice.

LYNN H. BLACKBURN, award-winning author of the Dive Team Investigations series, on *Breach of Honor*

A complex tale of murder, deceit, and faith challenges, complete with multifaceted characterizations, authentic details, and action scenes, even a subtle hint of romance . . . [all] well integrated into a suspenseful storyline that keeps pages turning until the end.

MIDWEST BOOK REVIEW on *Lethal Target*

EDGE OF TRUTH

EDGE OF TRUTH

A NOVEL

JANICE CANTORE

Tyndale House Publishers
Carol Stream, Illinois

Visit Tyndale online at tyndale.com.

Visit Janice Cantore's website at janicecantore.com.

Tyndale and Tyndale's quill logo are registered trademarks of Tyndale House Ministries, registered in the United States of America.

Edge of Truth

Cover design by Faceout Studio, Spencer Fuller

Interior design by Brandi Davis

Published in association with the literary agency of Books & Such Literary Management, 52 Mission Circle, Suite 122, PMB 170, Santa Rosa, CA 95409.

For information about special discounts for bulk purchases, please contact Tyndale House Publishers at csresponse@tyndale.com, or call 1-855-277-9400.

Library of Congress Cataloging-in-Publication Data

A catalog record for this book is available from the Library of Congress.

ISBN 978-1-4964-8797-1

Printed in the United States of America

32 31 30 29 28 27 26
7 6 5 4 3 2 1

Don't let sin against you produce sin in you.

J. C. RYLE

Take care, brothers, lest there be in any of you an evil, unbelieving heart, leading you to fall away from the living God. But exhort one another every day, as long as it is called "today," that none of you may be hardened by the deceitfulness of sin.

HEBREWS 3:12–13

PROLOGUE

Officer Lainie Jensen yawned as she patrolled her downtown Long Beach beat. The early morning darkness had a hypnotic effect when the police radio was quiet. Her partner had called in sick, so she would be alone for the entire shift. It was the first time in her brief career that had happened.

At first, fears of inadequacy about performing her job without having that safety net of an experienced officer next to her threatened to overwhelm.

What if something crazy happens?

Will I make the right decisions should I need to act fast?

Will I do my job right?

But in the squad earlier, when the teasing started, she knew she'd be fine.

"Hey, rook, you want us to put some training wheels on your cruiser?"

"Maybe give you the nice, quiet academy beat?"

Lainie still smiled a bit when she recalled the jibes. The ribbing in squad meetings didn't bug her. The older, seasoned cops only wasted their teasing on peers. Though technically a rookie until the next academy class graduated, she was off probation and a peer now—a part of the team.

Once seated in her black-and-white, nervousness spread through her gut like melted butter on dry bread. But it was an okay feeling. It meant she was alert and paying attention. Her duty was to search for trouble—and head straight for it. Lainie wanted to keep a little edginess.

The novelty of being by herself wore off quickly. Being solo on graveyard patrol meant she was a Robert car—a car dispatched only to report calls, of which so far there had only been four. She wrote some tickets and assisted on a few calls, but overall it had been a boring, uneventful night.

Around 6:00 a.m., with two hours left in her shift, more traffic began to roll as early risers headed to work. Lainie felt more alert, hoping to write some traffic violations before she went EOW, end of watch, to the station.

She'd imagined that a career in law enforcement would be a little more exciting than it had been tonight. Training officers warned recruits that real police work was not like what they watched on television—95 percent adrenaline and 5 percent downtime—but rather the reverse. Once field training began, Lainie learned right away how true that was. Officers on cop shows hopped from one hot call to the next. Real-life police work just didn't move at that frenetic pace.

Still, Lainie wouldn't be doing any other job.

After a few circuits around downtown, even ticket writing didn't pan out—everyone was driving according to the rules. Today was her Friday, so she considered heading in early. Then a black Lincoln Town Car ran a red light right in front of her without even slowing.

Lainie activated her light bar, turned right, and accelerated after the vehicle. It wasn't speeding, and she caught up in about half a block.

Ignoring her lights, the driver continued rolling, running a stop sign.

Though adrenaline surged—a vehicle failing to yield could be a stolen car—her instincts said the guy was probably drunk. He didn't seem to be evading per se; he just wasn't stopping. She grabbed her radio mike and asked dispatch to run the plate for wants and warrants.

"Robert 8, 28/29 on license plate 4-David-Tom-William-987. Northbound Chestnut Street approaching 7th."

"10-4, Robert 8, stand by."

They continued rolling north, and the vehicle ran another light. Lainie beeped her siren and got no response.

"Robert 8, 28/29 returns no want or warrant, application in process."

Lainie groaned. It wasn't stolen, but *app in process* meant she couldn't know who the car truly belonged to. Time to let everyone know the guy wasn't stopping and that she thought the driver was drunk.

"10-4, be advised I'm following the vehicle north on Chestnut, just crossing 10th. He's failing to yield, probably deuce."

She hoped her voice was steady. Her adrenaline had ramped up, but she didn't want any of the older guys accusing her of being hysterical. Traffic stops could always go wrong; every training officer had instilled that lesson.

"Any unit in the area to assist Robert 8 with a vehicle failing to yield, northbound Chestnut crossing 10th."

Lainie muttered her standard prayer, "Lord, I pray for wisdom and safety—for all involved in this stop."

Several units answered up to assist.

Lainie turned her siren on, hoping that a bunch of units didn't show up just to watch her wrestle with a drunk driver.

The siren had no effect. The Lincoln continued north without even pausing at intersections. Thankfully traffic was light, and they were in a residential area. Maybe he was heading home.

The car came to an abrupt stop. He didn't pull over; he simply stopped in the middle of the street. As if all of a sudden he saw the cop car behind him.

Lainie jerked to a stop as well, shutting down her siren but leaving the emergency lights on while she notified dispatch. "Robert 8, the vehicle stopped on Chestnut just north of 10th Street."

Another unit pulled in behind her, and she heard them tell dispatch that they were on-scene, 10-97. It was Jason Griggs and Sara Green, both from her class. That was good; an officer with more time in patrol might jump in and take over.

This is my chance to handle something from start to finish on my own, Lainie thought as she stepped out, staying behind the door, never taking her eyes off the Lincoln Town Car.

Sara came up on her left and Jason took the cover-officer position on the passenger side.

"What'd he do?" Sara asked.

"It's just traffic. He blew a couple of lights and a stop sign. Like I said, probably a deuce."

Sara nodded knowingly. This time of the morning, drunk drivers were not uncommon.

Lainie stepped from behind her door and started for the driver's side of the Lincoln, moving cautiously. Eyes on the back of the driver's head, her adrenaline still running high, she worked hard to fight off tunnel vision.

Pausing at the trunk, she placed a hand on the lid to make certain it was closed. The vehicle's motor still rumbled, and that bothered her. The back windows were darkly tinted, and she couldn't tell immediately if anyone else was in the car.

Flashlight in her left hand, right hand on the butt of her gun, Lainie approached the driver's door, stopped just at the doorpost, and shone her light at the driver.

The window was down. Behind the wheel was a white man, maybe forty, squinting in the beam of her flashlight. He wore a button-down shirt with a black necktie partially untied, as if he'd begun to take it off and then stopped. He craned his neck and peered back at Lainie with bleary gray eyes.

Definitely drunk. A nasty, jagged scar ran across his left cheek.

He held up a hand to shade his eyes from her light. "Is there a problem?" A pungent odor of alcohol wafted up toward Lainie when the man spoke.

"Can you turn off the car please?"

"What did I do?"

"Please turn the car off."

He mumbled something that sounded like a curse, but he complied.

"You ran a couple of red lights. Do you have your license, registration, and proof of insurance?"

"It's not my car."

"You're driving. Do you have a license?"

"I'm almost home."

"Sir, I need to see your license." Adrenaline dissipated in a cloud of annoyance. Drunks were rarely easy to deal with.

Lainie leaned forward, shining the beam of her flashlight around the car's interior. Someone was lying down in the back seat, but Lainie left that to Jason. She needed to concentrate on the driver, grateful she had backup with her.

She asked one more time for his license.

"Officer, you're making a huge mistake. I'm almost home." He had both hands on the steering wheel, and he now stared straight ahead.

"Sir, can you step out of the car please?"

"*I said,* I'm almost home."

She shoved the flashlight in her sap pocket to free up her hand, then pulled on the door handle and opened the door. "I need you to step out of the vehicle." Lainie had clear probable cause to administer a standard field sobriety test.

Anger flashed across his features. This time she heard the curse loud and clear, but he climbed out of the car.

The odor of alcohol grew much stronger now, the stench rolling across her nostrils in a noxious wave. He stumbled and she caught his arm. Sara stepped up and grabbed his other arm.

"What is this?" He stiffened. "You guys are wrong, wrong I tell you." His words were slurred. He attempted to pull away, but they both held on tight.

"I smell alcohol on your breath, sir. How much have you had to drink tonight?"

"You will regret this. It's wrong, I tell you, wrong." Like most drunks, he repeated himself. He tried to jerk away again, but his balance and coordination were almost nonexistent.

As she and Sara guided the drunk back toward her patrol car, Jason stepped up to help.

"We got him," Lainie said. "Can you check out the person in the back seat?"

He nodded and returned to the Lincoln's passenger side.

Lainie and Sara guided the driver to the hood of the black-and-white. Lainie had already made the determination that she had enough objective symptoms of driving under the influence to arrest him without the balance test.

"Do you have any weapons on you?" She began to pat him down.

"I've got nothing to say."

Lainie felt a wallet in his left back pocket and then the butt of a gun in his right front pocket.

"Gun!" She grabbed his right wrist and twisted it behind his back while Sara did the same with his left arm.

"Ow! Stop it," he cried as he resisted.

Recharged with adrenaline now, Lainie held on tight and quickly reached for her handcuffs. Once he was secure, she retrieved the gun. It was a small semiautomatic handgun, probably a .22. She handed the gun to Sara and then retrieved the wallet.

"Lainie."

"What?" She turned to Jason.

He looked pale in the glare of the flashing red-and-yellow light bar. "You have to see this."

"Okay. Let me get him in the car first." She flipped open the wallet. The drunk's name was Dallas Vine.

"Mr. Vine, you're under arrest for driving under the influence. And for carrying a concealed weapon."

He said nothing.

Lainie finished her pat down and found nothing else on the man. With the gun and the wallet on the hood of the car, Sara helped Lainie slide Vine into the back of the unit and strap him in. He was tight-lipped, maybe sobering up a bit. Once she closed the door, she turned to Jason. "Show me."

They walked to the Lincoln's rear passenger door, and Jason opened it.

A woman was sprawled across the back seat, half dressed.

"She's dead."

Lainie stared at Jason. "You checked her pulse?"

He nodded. "She's cold, Lainie. Been dead awhile. Bullet hole in her head. You got more than a drunk driver."

Had she arrested her first killer?

CHAPTER 1

FIFTEEN YEARS LATER

Tuesday, just before noon, on a beautiful spring day, Detective Lainie Jensen and her partner Mike Pepper left the courthouse and faced a gauntlet of reporters and news cameras. After a twelve-month investigation, they'd just closed the book on a serial rapist, so the attention was expected. The case had gone to the jury first thing this morning, and they only deliberated three hours.

"Detectives, do you have a statement for us?"

"Was the verdict satisfying?"

"Did the quick verdict surprise you?"

"What about Hammer's claim that the DNA sample was planted? That he is, in fact, innocent?"

Lainie had to stop for that one. She searched the group for the voice. Callen West, a local reporter for a Long Beach weekly. West was a vocal activist for what he called "bail reform," but in Lainie's opinion, he espoused not arresting anyone for anything, meaning no one should ever go to jail.

"What about it? The evidence proved that Cory Hammer was a serial rapist. We caught him in the act, and his DNA tied him to thirteen other attacks. The jury was spot-on with its verdict. I would have expected nothing less."

"You profiled him! It's not a stretch to think that you planted evidence."

Lainie started to head toward West, but Mike grabbed her arm and kept her walking toward the car. Lainie let him. If she got in West's face, she'd get herself in trouble. And she'd already been in enough trouble at work—she couldn't afford any more.

They continued through the crowd, ignoring the rest of the reporters' questions. West's gaze shot daggers at her. He would never be called a friend to law enforcement.

Once in the car, she blew out an aggravated breath. "That guy."

Mike chuckled as he started the engine. "He sure knows how to rev you up."

"He sat in the courtroom; he saw the evidence and heard the testimony." She shook her head. "Still, he thinks the guy is innocent. Or worse, that we fudged the evidence."

"It gets him clicks."

"Humph." Lainie was just happy to be done with court. It was, of course, essential, but with their caseload, it felt like lost time. She was eager to be busy with police work. Lainie had wanted to do this job since she was seven, when her best friend, Jaycee, had been kidnapped in front of her house.

The police had found and rescued her seven hours later. The picture on the newspaper's front page of Jaycee cradled by a large police officer, her arms wrapped around his neck, was indelibly inked in Lainie's mind and heart. The incident fomented a desire to be a cop herself, to be a dragon slayer and a rescuer.

"Thanks for the save, by the way."

Mike shrugged. "That's what partners are for."

After the trouble she'd had with internal affairs, Lainie was lucky to have Mike. An inch taller than her, five foot ten to her five nine, he was well-built and fit, having dabbled in boxing and MMA before he became a cop. He kept his head shaved and wore a bushy black mustache. Mike was devoted to his wife and their special-needs son. He was thirty-six, the same age as Lainie, though she'd been a cop a year longer, so technically she was the senior partner. But they played to each other's strengths, and there never was a power struggle.

Mike drove and headed for their predetermined lunch spot. Lainie pulled out her tablet to review the details of their next case, now that the rape case was over and done. As violent crimes detectives, they handled assaults, rapes, serious domestic violence, and just about anything short of murder. At times the work weighed on Lainie—they couldn't save everyone, and some of the victims' stories were heart-wrenching. But she rejoiced in victories like the one they'd had in court today.

The radio crackled on and off with routine police traffic, and she half listened to the happenings in the city. Her best friend on the force, Sara Green, worked day patrol, and Lainie picked out her call sign, 2David23, from time to time.

Beep beep.

The emergency tone caught her attention, and she looked up from the iPad.

"All units and 2David23, incomplete 911 call, possible domestic violence at 345 Elm Street. Respond Code 3."

Lainie glanced over at Mike. They were about to turn into the restaurant lot, but they were only two blocks from the address. On the radio, Sara's voice answered that she was en route, and her siren blared in the background.

"Hey, you up to helping on that? Sara's without her rookie and we're close."

He gave a half shrug. "Sure, we'll get the case anyway if it's a domestic." Mike swung the car in a U-turn and activated the plain car's lights and siren.

Lainie turned up the radio a bit as the dispatcher continued.

"Before the call disconnected, the calling party stated that her boyfriend had hit her and was now threatening her with a knife . . ."

Mike turned the corner on Elm and slowed—at the other end of the street a black-and-white rapidly approached.

Since the emergency tone would keep beeping until someone called Code 4, Lainie advised that they were on-scene so everyone would be aware that the beat car had backup.

Sara had exited her vehicle. By the way she moved, Lainie had to believe she heard or saw something dangerous. Mike saw it too because he sped up and slammed on the brakes when they were one house away from the address.

They both got out and hurried toward the dispatch address.

"Drop the knife!"

Sara clearly faced a threat.

Lainie sprinted up five stairs and saw a courtyard to the right. Sara's back came into view. She repeated the command to drop the knife.

Lainie saw a man holding a woman by the hair. She was on her knees, face bloody, and in his free hand, the man held a knife, a big one.

"I'm not going to prison."

When he spoke, Lainie recognized him. He was what they called a frequent flyer. Someone every beat cop in the city had interacted with at some point. She'd arrested him for burglary when she was in uniform and had noted his name in several reports now that she worked violent crimes. Hank Bucshon.

He jerked the woman's hair and raised the knife.

"Taser, Taser, Taser," Sara said as she deployed the less-than-lethal tool.

The prongs hit the target, and the knife fell to the ground as Bucshon stiffened and fell backward, toppling like a tree. The Taser delivered electrical currents meant to overwhelm the central nervous system. When it worked like it should, it totally incapacitated a suspect long enough to get him cuffed and secured.

All three of them surged forward. Sara secured the knife and the man, while Lainie helped detangle the woman's hair from Bucshon's clenched fingers. She and Mike moved her to the side as gently and quickly as they could.

The woman sobbed, in shock. Lainie requested paramedics and knelt next to her, comforting her until they arrived.

✦

Later back at the station, after the woman had been admitted to the hospital, Sara called Lainie from booking.

"This guy wants to talk."

Lainie shrugged, not really concerned. After all, they'd witnessed Bucshon while he was threatening his girlfriend with a knife. They didn't need a confession. "I'll be around to talk to him after he's booked."

"No, you don't understand. He wants to talk now. We found some receipts on him. He works for Dallas Vine."

Lainie sat up straight. Sara had her full attention. Dallas Vine—a name Lainie would never forget. The first big arrest of her career. And the first crushing disappointment. "What?"

"He sounds legit. Bucshon's saying he's got inside knowledge, and he wants to spill. He doesn't want to go to jail again; it's a third strike for him."

"I'll be right down." Lainie ended the call, and Mike shot her a quizzical expression.

"Come on, I'll explain on the way downstairs."

Lainie finished telling Mike in the elevator.

"He's totally pulling our legs," he protested as they exited in the basement. "No one rolls over on Vine." Mike shook his head. "You of all people should know that."

"We can talk to Bucshon and figure it out. It's worth a few minutes of our time."

She could tell he wasn't sold.

"What can it hurt?" She went to push open the door to booking, and he stopped her.

"Lainie, you were sued by Vine for harassment. Your obsession with him almost ended your career."

"Ahh." Lainie closed her eyes, brought her palms to her forehead. "Mike, that was years ago. I've stayed away. Other than reading the occasional news article about him, I haven't been watching him or searching for evidence against him."

She opened her eyes, lowered her hands, and held his gaze. "Bucshon dropped right. In. My. Lap. All I want to do is see if he's on the level."

Mike said nothing for a few seconds. "Five minutes." He pushed open the door.

Sara met them in the holding area with Bucshon cuffed to the bench. Hank was a rat-faced guy with a slight build. The burglary he'd committed when Lainie arrested him was a window entry. Wiry and flexible, Bucshon had no trouble getting in and out of small windows. She'd caught him in the alley coming out of one when he tried to run.

Now, he sat on the bench, subdued. Taking a Taser shot tended to do that to people. He'd been checked out by medical personnel and was okay to process.

"You still want to talk?" Lainie asked him.

"I don't wanna go to jail."

"I can't help you there. We saw you about to scalp your girlfriend. I can't make that go away."

"You can keep me out of county jail, can't you?"

Lainie considered this. No one liked going to county jail. Especially those men with small builds and no gang attachments. Hank was only tough when it came to hitting women.

"I'll listen to what you want to say, then it's up to the DA."

He nodded. "I work inside with Vine. I can give you Vine, I promise. Catch your big fish, let the little one swim away."

"Get up."

They walked him to an interview room.

As they sat, Lainie's phone rang and she silenced it. As a matter of form, she advised Bucshon of his Miranda rights and then unhandcuffed him so he could sign the waiver saying he understood his rights and wanted to talk. Once he signed, she recuffed him, hands in front.

"What do you do for Dallas Vine?"

"A little bit of this, a little bit of that."

"Specifics?" Lainie tapped on the desktop with her pen. Mike shot her a look that said, "waste of time."

Bucshon brought a handcuffed hand up to stroke his chin. "I know he ordered that hit two weeks ago on Martin Straight." He held Lainie's gaze with washed-out gray eyes.

She fought to keep her face blank. Straight was not her case, but she knew about it. He was a legitimate businessman, unlike Vine. Straight was well-liked and a vocal critic of Vine's business practices. He had been murdered in his driveway when he pulled in after work. The team working the case had zero clues.

"How do you know?"

"Guys who did it were from out of town, Chicago. They're back there now. Skiff and Charles are their names. Now, that's all I'm giving until I get some assurances."

Before Lainie could answer, someone pounded on the door.

"We're busy right now," Lainie called out.

Then Mike's phone rang. He checked it. "Lainie, it's the chief."

She stared in disbelief. The knock on the door sounded again. "What is going on?"

They both went to the door. Frustrated, Lainie threw it open. "We're in the middle of an . . ."

Standing on the other side of the door was a tall, dark-haired man in a suit, not a uniform. His appearance fairly screamed "Fed." Lainie looked up at him and words fled. He could have walked off a movie set he was so perfect. Sharp blue eyes cut into her. He held up an ID that confirmed he was, in fact, a Fed.

Special Agent Benjamin J. Isaacs, Federal Bureau of Investigation.

"You need to cease and desist. I'm taking Mr. Bucshon into my custody."

"What? He's our arrest." Sara was in the hallway, and she jumped in before Lainie found her voice.

"Not anymore."

Everyone turned as the voice of Chief Mackall entered the fray. He stepped off the elevator and strode in their direction. "Officer." He nodded to Sara and then to Lainie. "Detective. You all did great work." He motioned for Lainie and Mike to step out of the interview room, and he closed the door.

"But Agent Isaacs is from the Bureau. Seems you all have unwittingly stepped into the middle of an FBI investigation."

"What investigation?" Lainie found her voice as anger overwhelmed the shock.

"I'm not at liberty to relay details," Isaacs said. "Suffice it to say, Bucshon is part of it. I want him in my custody."

"He asked to talk; he signed a Miranda waiver."

"Has he said anything important?" the chief asked.

Lainie wished she could say yes, but she couldn't. Her gaze bounced from the chief to Isaacs and back again. "We just got started."

"We'll be able to do more with what he has to say than you will," Isaacs said.

"You don't know what he wanted to talk about. Besides, we saw him almost kill his girlfriend and you want us to let him go?"

Heat rose in Lainie's face. Now over the initial shock of seeing Isaacs, there was no way he would take away her chance to nail Dallas Vine.

"Chief, Bucshon works for Dallas Vine and he wants to talk. Are we going to let the Feds just take him?"

Chief Mackall gave her a sympathetic gaze. "I'm afraid we have to."

"I'm not going to release him," Isaacs said, "if that is any consolation. He will answer to your charges, just not immediately."

"That's no consolation at all." Lainie folded her arms, livid now, hating being condescended to. "This is *our* arrest. No one asked the Feds in on this. How did you even know he was in custody?"

"That information is on a need-to-know basis. I'm sorry, Detective, you don't need to know." Isaacs's keen cerulean gaze was almost hypnotic. Then he softened his tone. "Detective, all you want is Vine behind bars, right? Does it really matter who pounds the nails in his coffin?"

Lainie wasn't sure how to answer. "We had a clear shot" was all she managed, and even to her it sounded weak and pathetic.

Later, after Bucshon was gone, the chief pulled her aside. "Lainie, everyone in the department knows your history with Vine."

"Chief, I—"

He held up a hand. "I know this was a random happening. But your history with Vine is problematic. Good work helps people forget black marks. And your work since your last contact with him has been exemplary. Please don't do anything to refresh people's memories, clear?"

She bit her bottom lip to keep from saying something stupid. What he said was true and wise. "Clear."

Later, when she and Mike were back in her office, Lainie brooded.

"Get over it, Lainie. Why are you taking this so hard?"

"I wanted another crack at Vine. Bucshon seemed like an omen or something. Dropped right into my lap after all this time. Why is the FBI involved anyway? Vine is a Long Beach criminal; he should be arrested by Long Beach cops."

"He was only saying what you wanted to hear. You don't even know if what Bucshon had to say would have been actionable."

"If it wasn't, why did Isaacs swoop in and take him away?"

Mike had no answer and Lainie kept brooding. She busied herself with writing the names *Skiff* and *Charles* on a notepad. Were they first or last names? She logged on to her computer and decided to do some searching. When she came up with nothing on those names, her thoughts turned toward Agent Isaacs.

She wished she had a photo of him to put on her dartboard. Her first official contact with the FBI and she hated the agent she'd met.

CHAPTER 2

The Federal Bureau of Investigation was methodical in its investigations, sometimes taking years to finish a case and make arrests. They wanted to be certain all their t's were crossed and their i's dotted so they wouldn't lose in court.

Ben wanted to explain all of that to Detective Jensen. If their roles were reversed, he would have been just as upset as she was. There just hadn't been time.

She'd asked what they were investigating—someone she knew well. Dallas Vine. He'd hit federal radar a year ago and was one target amid a large multistate investigation into human trafficking and money laundering. Ben and his partner Efren Gomez had been assigned to a growing task force six months ago. They worked out of the Los Angeles bureau office.

They knew Bucshon was connected to Vine; they weren't certain how much he knew or how close he was to the top. His name had been flagged, so when the arresting officers entered it into NCIC, the National Crime Information Center, the federal team was notified. Bucshon's arrest opened a door for them to talk to him, hopefully without Vine being alerted. Since Bucshon beat up his girlfriend, it shouldn't leak back that his arrest had anything to do with the investigation into Vine.

The last thing they wanted was LBPD spooking Vine at this juncture. Especially Detective Jensen. Her heart might be in the right place, the guy was a vicious criminal who needed to be taken off the street, but a city PD did not have all the resources a federal agency had. Even with their resources, the team heading the investigation was frustrated. Vine was careful, and he seemed to have a sixth sense about investigators. He was as slippery as he was evil. Ben was confident they'd get their man.

Ben hoped they had enough leverage on Bucshon to get him to spill something that would help move their investigation forward.

He contacted his boss, Mark Gentry, as soon as he secured Bucshon in the back of his vehicle and before Ben got in the driver's seat. "I've got Bucshon."

"Did he say anything to LBPD?"

"No. I don't think he had time. I'll be at the office in about twenty minutes."

He climbed into the driver's seat and started the car. While he drove, Ben considered Detective Jensen. He knew who she was because of her history with Vine, and Ben knew everything about Vine, but this was the first time he'd seen her in person. *Formidable* was the first word that came to his mind. The second was *stunning*. Dark-auburn hair and vibrant hazel-green eyes caught his attention immediately. And she was one of those women who appeared feminine even in conservative cop clothes.

Ben hadn't known what to expect when he was notified about Bucshon. Jensen was not the arresting officer. Meeting her was a shock to the system—in a very good way.

It tweaked him that now she probably hated him.

She'd arrested Vine when she was a rookie—impressive. Her arrest report almost read like a crime novel. They were serious charges. It was not her fault that he'd skated on everything.

Vine was released. Jensen shadowed him, staking out his office, his businesses, and his home on her own time, trying to find evidence connecting him to the murder of Daphne Sparks. Evidence that would put the man in jail for good. But she wasn't skilled in surveillance. Apparently, she showed up on Vine's radar one too many times. A lawsuit got Jensen reprimanded and suspended.

Word through the grapevine now, years later, was that she had grown into a good cop. Ben was acutely aware that if she had been able to stop him from taking Bucshon, she would have. Determined people made good cops.

She was someone Ben would like to sit down and have coffee and conversation with. The first question he'd ask was, what drew her to law enforcement? He'd bet it would be a good story. Ben himself had gone into law enforcement unsure if the profession was really for him. His father and grandfather were both retired US Marshals.

Ben felt pressured to follow in their footsteps and thought for sure he'd hate it. But when he and Efren first became partners and they rescued several boys, girls, and women who had been trafficked into the country, Ben knew he'd found his calling. He wanted to help people; he wanted to make a difference.

"Hey, where're you taking me?" Bucshon spoke up from the back. "This ain't the way to County."

"I explained to you that you are in federal custody now. I'm taking you to the federal lockup in LA."

Ben hoped the guy would stay quiet. He wanted to interview him, sure, but he wanted a controlled, recorded environment.

"Just as long as you don't send me to County."

"Not today." *But I'm not making any promises.*

Bucshon settled down and in the quiet, as Ben navigated traffic on the 405 freeway, he let his thoughts drift back to Detective Jensen and Dallas Vine. Vine had been a small-time crook when she'd arrested him fifteen years ago. Ben could only imagine what a rookie felt when she discovered a dead body on a car stop. Unfortunately, the body could never be connected to Vine. The gun on his person was not the murder weapon, and the car was borrowed. The woman had been murdered elsewhere and placed in the car. Vine claimed he'd never seen her before.

One quote from the report had stayed with Ben because it was emblematic of how Vine got out of jams. *"I just borrowed the car. I didn't look in the back seat."*

Every bad act was always blamed on someone else. Like a greased pig, Vine slipped out of every arrest.

All he got after the smoke cleared was a slap on the wrist for drunk driving and illegally carrying a concealed weapon. That would upset any self-respecting law enforcement officer.

If the unjust situation wreaked havoc with Jensen's career, it also affected Vine. His MO changed after that arrest. He became more careful, more circumspect. He began to insulate himself with high-powered attorneys.

One odd fact in the report stood out to Ben: Vine had no online presence at all. No social media, no website, nothing online that could be monitored. He didn't even use credit cards.

In Ben's estimation, Vine had been humiliated, and a man like Vine hated to be humiliated. As a result, he'd worked hard to become Teflon. So far, he'd been very successful. In the last several years, he'd grown into a virtual recluse—a recluse king of crime. The FBI became involved when evidence surfaced that Vine was part of a large multistate human-trafficking operation. He was part of a much larger puzzle.

Ben and Efren were small parts of the larger task force. They'd just finished another case when they were assigned to gather intelligence on the money-laundering portion. Efren had gone undercover, infiltrating the Vine crime kingdom to try to find connections to the larger operation and evidence to nail Vine.

Efren was the reason Ben had swooped in to take Bucshon from the stunning Detective Jensen. Efren hadn't checked in at the prescribed time. He was now four days overdue.

As Ben drove, he clutched at a straw that the filthy little man in the back of his car might be able to give him a little hope concerning his partner.

Please, Lord, let Efren be okay, just delayed.

CHAPTER 3

Anger.

Obsession.

Fixation.

Axe to grind.

Those had been some of the things said about Lainie after Vine escaped being charged with murder and was released. They were all true back then, and it not only almost destroyed her career, but it also nearly destroyed Lainie. The city took a dim view of a rookie cop costing them money because someone like Vine filed a harassment lawsuit. Thankfully, the chief had recognized that her hard work had dulled, if not erased, the dark-black mark on her career. That she'd made it to detective status was evidence that she had succeeded. Hard work made up for a rookie lapse in judgment.

It was late. At home, she still brooded. She sat at her desk and rummaged through the top drawer. Near the back, she found the photo and pulled it out. It was a picture of Daphne Sparks, the woman she'd found dead in the back of Dallas Vine's vehicle. Memories of that night were still vivid and came to life in her mind. Vine had thoroughly unsettled her. An aura of evil surrounded him.

They had almost reached the station when he'd spoken up from the back seat. "You're making a mistake."

He'd barely said anything since the arrest. The only other words he'd uttered were when he refused to take a Breathalyzer test. Lainie had to take him to the hospital and have his blood drawn. By then, he was stiff and uncooperative. It surprised her when he sat quietly for the blood draw. Lainie wanted to advise him of his rights and question him, but the homicide detective on call had asked her not to. That was their job.

Lainie aspired to work homicide one day, so she followed their instructions. Vine had spoken first, so she answered him.

"I don't think so. You're drunk, you're driving, and you're carrying a concealed weapon, among other things."

"I'm so much bigger than you know. You're too small and insignificant to stop me."

"That so?" She glanced at him in the rearview mirror as she made the turn to the booking tunnel.

His gaze pierced her with a cold, deadly stare. The stony gray eyes and the jagged scar on his cheek made his mere appearance malevolent. He gave her the creeps. All of her instincts screamed that he had murdered the woman in his back seat. She prayed that he'd volunteer something incriminating.

The prayer was not answered.

"I'm bulletproof" was the last thing the smirking man said when she released Vine to the jailers.

At the station Lainie learned a little bit more about him.

"Whoa." The booking sergeant stared down at Vine on the bench when Lainie brought him in. "I know this guy."

Vine scowled at him and cursed, then spit on the floor.

The sergeant chuckled. "This guy was in a vicious bar fight a few years ago, over a woman if I remember right. Cut the other guy up so bad he bled to death. Then he gave a sob story at his trial, kept his scar uncovered, and gave the jury puppy dog eyes. Got acquitted." The sergeant turned from Lainie back to Vine. "I knew you'd be back. Hope it sticks this time."

That night, Vine didn't speak to the homicide detectives either. Then he avoided being charged with anything serious. He pled guilty to two misdemeanors, paid a fine, and did forty hours of community service.

The murder of Daphne Sparks had never been solved. It was now in the cold case file.

Lainie had taken that miscarriage of justice personally. She tried hard to solve the case. It took nearly two years for Vine's plea agreement to make its way through the system. When it did, Vine was free and clear.

She couldn't let that stand, so she began to follow him. Her off time was consumed with trying to prove that the man had killed Sparks. He lived in a big house on Appian Way, in the Naples section of Long Beach, on the water with a dock for his yacht. She was down there often, documenting the comings and goings. He also had a cigar lounge on Pine Street and an office at the harbor for a time. She visited those locations often as well.

Like an addict, even when she was told to back off, Lainie kept after Vine. In hindsight, she realized she was acting on raw emotion and not thinking clearly. When the lawsuit came, even though the attorneys negotiated a settlement, it was only her friend and training officer Max Beck that saved her. He stuck up for her to all the brass.

Max had always told Lainie she had promise.

"You're a good cop. Vine is a dirtbag. He'll go down because of good, solid police work; they always do. Don't let him goad you into destroying your career, clear?"

She had listened to Max, and so had internal affairs. Over the years she had watched the Vine crime empire grow, paying passing attention, but kept her distance. He'd been indicted twice more only to be acquitted both times.

She studied the photo of Daphne Sparks, a smiling, bright, attractive woman. When Lainie had first glimpsed her in the back of the car, blonde hair splayed across the seat around her head like a halo, she looked unreal, like a mannequin. It wasn't the first dead body Lainie had seen, but it had a profound effect on her. Daphne appeared defenseless, innocent, and she was young, very close to Lainie's twenty-two years.

Later, when Lainie had read about Daphne's mother, her heart broke for the woman. A picture popped into her mind of Daphne's mother at the funeral. Losing her daughter had destroyed her. Two months later she had a stroke and died. In Lainie's eyes, Vine was responsible for both deaths.

She wanted so badly to put the killer behind bars. She'd learned so much since then. How she wished she could apply her knowledge to arresting that man and making it stick. Today it seemed as if she'd been given another chance.

And Ben Isaacs had stopped her.

Frustration twisted her gut into knots, and for some reason Lainie thought about texting Glen. He was a man she'd flirted with in the past, dancing up to the line but not crossing it because he was married. It was such a non sequitur she let out a burst of nervous laughter. The only good thing about Glen was that he would let her vent. He was good at listening. No matter how bad things got, there was no excuse to call Glen.

She fiddled with her phone and saw that her sister, Evie, had called earlier. She hadn't left a voicemail.

Groaning, Lainie put the phone down. The last thing she needed tonight was a lecture from her sister about how Lainie should be back in church.

Evie was the oldest and the perfect child. She led worship at church, had a voice like an angel. Their brother Archie was the youngest, and while he'd struggled in high school, he'd eventually found his path as a youth pastor and was now on track to get a master's degree in theology.

Lainie was the middle child and now a decorated violent crimes investigator. While her siblings embraced church life, she'd become a Chreaster, a person who only attended church at Christmas and Easter. Lainie liked to tell people that she'd flown under the radar all her life. Evie got all the accolades and Archie got all the lectures. Nothing was left for Lainie.

She got ready for bed as the oppressive feeling of guilt settled down on her like a shade. Lainie had been raised in the church. When she was a new officer, she'd stayed involved with her fellowship. She'd taught Sunday school, attended prayer meetings and a Bible study for police officers.

The incident with Vine infected Lainie with a bitterness that ate at her soul. Cynicism colored everything. Christian activities seemed less important, useless even. She had been content to use work as an excuse to avoid church and Bible study. Her schedule would change, and she'd drop out, try to find something else, then her schedule would change again. She gave up trying to find the time to attend church activities and, finally, gave up regular attendance as well.

Police work was important, and even more so because of the memory of Jaycee, Lainie knew that she'd need to clean up her act if she ever wanted to move to homicide. Because homicide handled kidnappings. She needed to be dedicated to police work, and she had been. Two years in a row she'd been named investigator of the year by the California Peace Officers' Association. Training to be the best cop became her church. She was a master at weaponless defense and a marksman who'd won several statewide shooting competitions.

Lainie wanted her work to shine so when an opening came up in homicide, the spot would be hers and nothing in her past would keep her from it.

She'd eventually put her cuffs on him again and it would stick.

No one was bulletproof.

CHAPTER 4

"I really need to shoot something," Lainie spoke to Mike as they headed for their car.

"Have anything in mind?" Mike asked.

"Right now, I'm not particular."

He laughed. "Good thing we're due at the range."

The morning had been busy with court; now they were scheduled for the range. The department required all officers to qualify with their duty weapon four times a year. While some officers saw the qualification as an interruption, Lainie loved going to the range for any reason. A member of the PD pistol team, she was classified a sharpshooter—a 100 percenter.

Shooting helped center her thoughts and shut out stress or issues that bothered her.

"Hey, Lainie, Mike, how are you guys doing?" The rangemaster greeted them when they stepped inside the range office.

"Happy to be here today," Lainie said as she prepared her target.

She and Mike were the only two officers at the range to qualify, so after their targets were ready, they stepped up to the firing line. Officers qualified with handguns through a fifty-round course of fire, starting from the twenty-five-yard line, moving to the fifteen-yard line, then the seven-yard line, and finishing at the five-yard line. Each stage was timed.

They used a two-handed grip except at the fifteen-yard line, where they switched to one-handed shooting, first with the strong hand and then with the weak hand. A score of 80 percent was mandatory.

Lainie hadn't shot below 100 percent in five years. Mike was usually between 85 and 95 percent. When they finished the handgun course, they moved to the other side of the range where a handgun/shotgun course was set up. This was Lainie's favorite. The course configuration changed every other quarter.

Today the emergency simulation was set up with a parked black-and-white patrol car at the start. Officers began the course seated in the vehicle. When time started, they had to unlock the shotgun, get out of the car, fire four shotgun rounds at metal targets, set the shotgun down, draw their handguns, and hurry through the course, using cover when it was provided, then fire at fifteen more targets, some of them moving.

Being timed bothered some people; Lainie knew that Sara didn't like it. But Lainie loved the challenge and the *plink* sound when bullets struck the metal targets. The instant feedback when she hit every target was very gratifying. Again, she aced the course.

"Great job as usual, Lainie," the rangemaster said. "She sure is carrying you there, Mike."

Mike laughed. "Don't I know it."

Lainie felt better after qualifying, but she forgot to call Evie back. It wasn't until the weekend that her first Saturday off in months rolled around that she remembered. Lainie slept in, not rising until nearly noon. Evie came to mind while she was in the shower. Head under the shower steam, water as hot as she could stand it, Lainie tried to think. Why would Evie call except to ask her to some church thing?

Have I forgotten a birthday? Evie had twin boys. No, their birthday wasn't for a couple of months.

Guilt rolled over her in a heavy wave. Though she and Evie had been close in the past, they didn't talk often lately, and that was generally Lainie's fault. She remembered that it was Evie's anniversary month. For the first time since Evie had married Stan Moffit, they had the money to take a nice trip. Lainie had heard that her sister was over the moon. Evie probably called from Hawaii to gush with excitement over the trip.

Why else would she be calling while they were on vacation? Worry dissipated.

I'll call her when I'm done here.

She dried off, dressed, and started a pot of coffee. Just as she picked up the phone, it buzzed with an incoming call. She read the caller ID, hoping it was Evie. It wasn't. It was Stan Moffit, her brother-in-law.

Lainie's mind sputtered, Stan and Evie should be happily vacationing. Lainie and Stan would never be described as close.

Uneasiness spread. He was not one of her favorite people. That he was reaching out could not be good news.

Reluctantly, she answered. "Stan?"

"Lainie, Lainie." He sucked in a breath as if he were sobbing. He was outside, in the background she could hear wind buffeting the phone.

"What is it?"

"It's Evie, Evie, she's gone. Lainie, she's gone."

She's gone.

The phone went cold in her hand. "What do you mean?"

"Dead, Lainie, dead. I lost her yesterday."

Dead.

When that word registered, it was as if the world fell away from her feet. Lainie felt herself falling, with no bottom in sight.

CHAPTER 5

Ben sat in an interview room with Hank Bucshon. The little man wore federal prison duds: gray khakis and a gray shirt with gray slippers. Since he'd not yet been arraigned, he'd not yet been assigned a public defender.

"Thank you for talking to me, Mr. Bucshon."

He shrugged. "Thanks for getting me here. Much better than County."

"I need to make sure that you understand your rights. You signed a Miranda waiver in Long Beach. Do you understand what that means?"

"Yeah, I'll answer questions. As long as I can stay here, I'll tell you whatever you want to know."

"You work for Dallas Vine, correct?"

"Yeah, I do side gigs for him."

"We're interested in what you do for him at Sudsy Place, the car wash. Do you know it?"

"Yeah, I know it. I deliver messages, mostly to Raphael. He's Vine's main dude at the car wash."

"Do you ever interact with Efren Gomez?"

"The other detail guy?" He shook his head. "I seen him, but we don't talk."

"When was the last time you saw him?"

Bucshon scratched the two-day growth of beard on his chin. "The last time I picked up a message, last Wednesday."

That was two days before Efren missed his check-in. Ben changed tack a bit. "Do messages go back and forth every day?"

"Every other for me. Vine don't do computers. He don't even like phones. So one of his guys will give me a package, and I give the package to Raphael. I don't know what he does with the stuff."

"Do you ever interact with Crystal Benton?"

He gave a disgusted snort. "She'd be slumming to talk to me. But I see things."

"What do you see?"

"She's playing Vine dirty, I think."

"How so?" Ben asked.

"Her and Vine's main security guy, well, they're a little too close, if you get my drift."

"How is that playing Vine?"

"Crystal is supposed to be Vine's main squeeze. She's two-timing him. That kind of move don't ever end up good."

✦

In the end, the interview was good news/bad news for Ben. The information about Crystal cheating on Vine was something new, but he wasn't sure it deserved the weight Bucshon gave it. They had a file on Vine's security guy. He was a jamoke named Peter Ludwig Grant, but everyone called him Plug. He had a record, mostly assault and battery, and he was certainly involved in illegal activity, but he was not the Bureau's target. His boss was.

The little man also gave up the names of two hit men contracted to kill prominent Long Beach businessman Martin Straight, confirming something Efren had noted as a possibility in his last communication before he went missing. Vine ordered the hit. Straight had made several complaints to the California attorney general about Vine. This led to a couple of investigators from the AG's office visiting Vine. Ben and Efren guessed that had been what led to the hit.

The trouble was, even with Bucshon's knowledge, there was no proof. The AG and local cops had been working the case diligently. Nothing Bucshon said could be used to convict Vine in court without some corroboration. And the murder of Straight was not the task force's focus, though they would give all solid leads to LBPD.

All they knew now was that Bucshon was a low-level runner in Vine's organization, his information was mostly secondhand, which meant that what he gave them was thirdhand. They needed hard, connecting evidence.

Ben had the feeling Bucshon knew more than he was saying. He seriously didn't want to go to County, told them he would waive his right to a speedy trial and that he didn't mind being held at Terminal Island. If Ben and Mark could get him a spot in federal prison, maybe that would loosen his lips a little more.

When Ben had pressed him harder about Efren, he coughed up a little more.

"Yeah, I seen him around sometimes. If he's gone, maybe Vine sent him somewhere."

"Vine sent him somewhere? Like where?"

"Up in the mountains, maybe. Vine's got a summer place there. Maybe Efren is there to open it up, you know? Vine has a lot of cars. Some he keeps in the mountains. Maybe Efren went up there to clean up the cars for Vine."

While Efren had never mentioned being asked to go to Big Bear, they did know about the summer house. They'd asked San Bernadino sheriffs to check it out. A deputy drove up to the place and found it was still closed tight. In the end, they got nothing new from Bucshon.

Because of the missing agent, Ben's boss was able to work a deal with LBPD. They transferred Bucshon to LBPD for his arraignment, and after the judge ordered him held over for trial, they secured Bucshon in the federal pen on Terminal Island. It gave them a little breathing room.

After the interview, Ben got home late. Though he was assigned to the LA field office, he lived in North Long Beach. Efren lived in Lakewood, not far from Ben. There was a message on his home phone from Candy, Efren's wife.

"Ben, please give me a call, even if it's late. I need to hear something."

The cry in her voice broke Ben's heart. He hurt for himself because Efren was not only his partner for four years, but his best friend. Ben thought back to when they'd met.

"Hey, Legacy." Efren had used the nickname Ben had been given in the academy because his father and grandfather had been in federal service. To him it insinuated that he had nothing to offer, that he'd skated by on his forbear's accomplishments.

"Name's Ben, or Agent Isaacs."

Efren laughed. "You gonna be as stiff as your haircut, or are we gonna be the partners who get things done?"

At the spark of mischief in Efren's eyes and his confident manner, Ben relaxed. This guy was not a stiff "Bureau man." He wanted to be a working agent. So did Ben. They shook hands and over the years did good work together. The fear for Efren was a physical ache. Ben couldn't imagine how Candy dealt with it.

He picked up the phone, but first, he prayed. "Oh, Lord, please give me the words to comfort her, to give her some peace."

He made the call. She answered on the first ring. "Any news?"

"I'm sorry, Candy, there is no news."

"What do you think?"

Ben paused and bit his bottom lip. He couldn't verbalize his worst fear. "My thoughts are scattered, painful, but in the end, I trust God. And I will do everything in my power to find Efren."

"Thank you, Ben. I know you won't let him be forgotten."

No, Ben thought after he hung up. *I won't let him be forgotten.*

But by the weekend, the pressure of time weighed on Ben as if he were diving in deep, deep water. Every day Efren was missing made it more likely that he had been made and killed.

Ben continued to pray fervently for his partner and friend.

CHAPTER 6

Unable to even punch the button for her parents' number, Lainie raced to their house, praying that what she'd just heard wasn't true. Between sobs, Stan had told her an impossible story. He and Evie had been snorkeling in a beautiful bay. He'd thought he saw a shark but wasn't sure. They got separated. Evie loved to snorkel. She could spend all day in the water, and Hawaii was her happy place.

Stan claimed to have turned around, and suddenly Evie was gone. There was blood in the water, part of a snorkel, and a mask. No sign of Evie. As of the time he'd called, which had been 10:30 a.m. Hawaii time, Evie's body had not yet been recovered.

Lainie blinked back tears and pondered Stan's last few words. *"Evie's body hasn't been recovered."*

They stung like salty, cold water on an exposed nerve.

Lainie couldn't believe it.

She didn't want to believe it.

All the way to her mom and dad's house, she kept praying. Though she couldn't remember the last time she'd offered up heartfelt, fervent prayers and petitions, she kept at it. Asking that when she arrived, she'd be told that it was all a stupid mistake. Evie was fine. She'd just gotten taken along by a riptide and was okay farther down the beach.

Her father's expression when he opened the door told her there'd been no mistake. They hugged and Lainie fought desperately to keep her voice steady. "Dad, it's true? Is it true?"

"I'm afraid so. Stan called me early this morning." His voice wavered. "They started searching for Evie again, as soon as it got light; they're still searching. So far, no luck."

"We have to go there."

"I agree." He led her into the house.

"What about Archie? Where are Mom and the boys?"

Her parents were babysitting Evie's twin seven-year-old boys, Evan and Owen, while Evie and Stan were gone. Her mom had called last week, gushing that Stan and Evie were so happy about the anniversary that they had dropped the boys off a few days early so they'd be able to celebrate a bit longer.

"Mom and the boys are at the pool right now. We haven't said anything to them yet. I called Archie. He's in Texas at a conference."

Lainie fell onto the couch and held her head in her hands. "I can't believe this is happening. Not Evie."

Her father's phone rang. He answered right away on speaker. "Stan, any news?"

"No." He sounded somewhat better than the few minutes ago when Lainie had spoken to him.

"They had to call off the search early. The wind just kicked up, and the surf is up."

Lainie looked at the clock. It was now almost 2:00 p.m. here so it was two hours earlier in Hawaii. Evie disappeared *yesterday*.

"Still no sign of her?" Dad asked, and Lainie held her breath.

"N-n-n-no. I don't know what to do."

"Lainie and I are coming. We'll take the first flight we can. Hang in there, Stan. We'll be there soon."

Lainie said nothing as Stan and her father talked about the kids.

She got up and paced. Why hadn't she called Evie back immediately? What had her sister wanted and why hadn't she left a message?

Lainie's thoughts wandered back to the last time she'd seen her sister. Christmas, about five months ago. Christmas was Evie's favorite time of year, and she had hosted the whole family at her home. Archie had a girlfriend, but Lainie came alone. She didn't like to think about how long it had been since she'd had a steady guy—a steady guy she could introduce to her family. Glen was never that sort of guy.

Being single at any kind of gathering often made Lainie feel uncomfortable and just plain odd. Like *a third wheel* kind of described the feeling, but it wasn't nearly strong enough. The unspoken questions peppered her: *What's wrong with you? Why can't you find somebody?* They always echoed even if no one asked them.

She never felt like that with Evie. Her sister had welcomed her with a tight hug. "So good to see you. Why do I have to wait so long between your visits?"

Lainie relished the hug and took a minute to answer. "Ah, you know, work is crazy."

Evie pushed back and held Lainie's gaze. "We need to do a weekend or something, get back in touch."

"Good idea," Lainie had said, not really meaning it. She loved her sister, but Evie would frown on some of Lainie's recent life choices. She had just started flirting with Glen, a married colleague. She winced as she recalled the last conversation she'd had with the guy. Glen was a notorious philanderer, and she'd openly encouraged him.

That Christmas Day, Stan had been Stan. Lainie never knew what Evie saw in the man. He was boastful, opinionated, and a lot of the time offensive. The only positive thing she could see was that he was a good father. And she could grudgingly admit that he did try to be a good provider. The boys adored him. Still, Lainie prayed that they didn't grow up like him.

As usual, that day Evie did all the work while Stan sat in front of the TV watching football. Evie even set him up with a TV tray so he could eat while he watched. Everyone else sat at the table.

Evie was a saint. Why on earth was she gone and Stan still here?

Dad finished the phone call. His voice was thick with emotion when he faced Lainie. "It's not good."

"We need to book a flight."

Her father nodded, then reached out to wrap Lainie in a hug. "We need to pray."

Lainie said nothing, struggling inside. She'd prayed on the way over, but did it really do any good?

The look on her father's face pierced her. "Dad, I, ah, I just don't know if I believe in that anymore. It's . . ." She couldn't finish as emptiness was ready to swallow her.

"I do believe in it so I'm praying." He bowed his head and prayed that Evie would be found safe and sound. After he said amen, he pulled Lainie close. "No matter what, I love you, baby," her father whispered.

Lainie's voice thickened. "I love you too, Dad."

CHAPTER 7

With Archie on his way back from Texas to be with Mom and the boys, Lainie and her father caught a midnight flight to Hawaii to arrive early Sunday morning.

Saying goodbye to the boys was like taking twelve-gauge beanbag rounds at close range to the gut. When Owen gave her a hug, he said, "Aunt Lainie, remind Mom that she has to bring us back one of those tiny guitars they have in Hawaii."

"Tiny guitar?"

"He means ukelele," Dad said. "He and Evan want to learn how to play them."

Lainie gave him a tight hug. "I'll remind her."

Stan and Evie were vacationing on the Big Island of Hawaii, in a resort area called Waikoloa Beach. Lainie had been there before; the family made several trips to Hawaii over the years. The last time they went, they'd stayed in Kona, which was about an hour from Waikoloa. Lainie had good memories of the family times. They'd snorkeled in a place called Two Step. While Lainie had fun, Evie was a fish. She would have stayed in the water all day if their parents had allowed it.

At least she died doing what she loved.

Lainie squeezed her eyes shut as tears threatened. She leaned her head against the window.

I don't want it to be true.

After a while, the monotonous hum of the plane's engines played into her fatigue and Lainie fell into a fitful sleep. When she woke, they were making their approach to Kona Airport.

Her father patted her hand. "You ready for this?"

"As ready as I'll ever be."

The airport in Kona had no Jetway. Passengers deplaned by walking down stairs or a ramp. Warm, humid air hit as Lainie strode down the ramp. It wasn't unpleasant, but it was different than the hot, dry air in Long Beach.

Her father had arranged for an Uber. The guy was waiting at the curb outside baggage claim, and soon they were on their way to Waikoloa. Thankfully, the driver was not chatty. Lainie did not feel like talking. The two-lane highway from the airport to the resort was uncrowded, and they moved along at a good speed. They soon arrived at the Hilton resort where Stan and Evie were staying.

In past trips to this island, Lainie had always enjoyed the view of the ocean on the left and the wild volcanic scenery. Dawn was breaking and today, she barely saw anything. She did notice that it was very windy. Every so often their sedan was jostled by a strong gust. When they turned into the resort, palm trees were bent under the wind's force.

Stan met them in the lobby. It appeared as if he'd not gotten much sleep. Heavy stubble covered his chin, and dark circles shadowed his eyes. Still, he turned heads. Lainie could admit that Stan was a handsome man. A tad over six feet, he had a full head of sandy-brown hair and striking hazel eyes. He worked out and made use of tanning booths, so he was always an orangey-brown color.

To Lainie, he was a bright container. You were impressed by the outside, until you opened it up and saw that all it contained was grease and dust. Then you heard him speak, and it was like a corny infomercial, *"and there's more!"* He primped like a vain movie star. All show and no go.

As he walked toward them today, it looked as if he'd slept in the clothes he wore. Lainie tried to generate sympathy for him, but she couldn't. It was difficult not to blame him for losing Evie.

Why weren't you swimming right next to her? Why didn't you protect her?

While Stan connected with her father, Lainie let her gaze wander around the hotel lobby. The place was huge. It had a tram in the middle and a stream running through the massive ground floor. High-end boutiques rimmed the walkway.

This was their first real vacation in eight years of marriage. The job he held now was his first steady job in that time frame. He talked big but never lasted long anywhere. Used car salesman, real estate agent, day trader. He'd also tried his hand at YouTube channels. He talked about investing money on his last channel. Lainie couldn't wrap her mind around that. She'd never seen Stan make a sound financial decision or investment.

Now he managed a car wash. As she thought about it, he'd been there about a year, his longest gig yet. How long would it last? At Christmas, Evie had said that with the car wash, *"Stan has finally found his niche."*

If they had the money for this trip, maybe she was right.

Evie was the worship leader at church, and she was paid a small salary. The weeklong stay here must have cost big bucks. She tuned back into the conversation Stan and her father were having when she realized Stan was explaining why no one was searching today.

"The trades are up. It's too windy for boats or helicopters."

"When did they stop searching?" she asked.

"Yesterday afternoon, a few hours after I talked to you. That's when the wind picked up."

"I want you to show me the beach."

"Now?" Stan stared at Lainie.

"Yes. Now."

"Your bags?"

Lainie shot a glance at her father.

"I'll take them up." The sadness in his eyes cut Lainie.

"I need to see, Dad."

He nodded. "I know."

Lainie turned to Stan. "Let's go."

✦

The walk to the beach took about twenty minutes. They exited the hotel lobby, followed the long, serpentine hotel driveway to the sidewalk, and then walked along the road that wound through the resort area. Large condos stood on either side, and occasionally they passed tourists or hotel workers. The Hawaiian name for the beach was Anaeho'omalu. Lainie had a hard time pronouncing it. Stan simply called it A-Bay. It was down the coast from the Hilton and behind the Marriott Hotel, and they crossed through its lobby, past the pool—the space was eerily empty as wind buffeted the area—and out to the sandy beach.

They spoke barely at all. The strong wind made it difficult to hear, plus Lainie didn't really want to talk to Stan.

"Here we are," he said, when they reached the sand. "They reopened the beach this morning since there were no more shark sightings."

A few people strolled on the beach, a couple frolicked in the water, diehards, who probably had no other time to get to the water. Gusty wind swirled around them and every so often pelted Lainie with sand. Two catamarans were anchored in the bay, rolling with the swells and small whitecaps.

There was also a kiosk that rented kayaks and paddleboards, but it was closed. The boards and kayaks were securely tied down behind the kiosk.

Lainie started to walk down toward the water. "Where exactly?" she called out to Stan.

It seemed he was reluctant to follow her, and she didn't care.

He caught up and stood close to her, pointing to the right. "We were swimming over there. There's coral and it's shallow."

"Where did you lose sight of her?"

"She kept swimming to the right. I went toward the left because I saw a turtle. When I looked up to tell her, she was gone."

"What did you do?"

"I, uh, I searched, and I couldn't see her anywhere. I swam in, thinking maybe she got out of the water."

"Then what?"

He swallowed, his Adam's apple bobbing. If he were a suspect, Lainie would say that he took too long to answer. Was it grief? It was so hard to read him clearly.

"A woman on the beach screamed that she'd seen a shark. I walked along the sand, that way." He pointed to where the beach continued to curve around and then gave way to a trail along the water.

"I didn't see her. I thought I saw blood. Then I found the bit of snorkel and her mask . . ." His voice trailed off.

Lainie stared at him. Anger swelled up. She simply didn't believe his story. Was it just that she didn't like Stan, or were her instincts spot-on? Hands flexing and unflexing, she worked to control her anger.

"When did you call the police?"

"What?"

"How long before you called for help?"

"Uh, I'm not sure. I, uh, I wanted to be sure. I mean, Evie loves the water. She could have been anywhere."

"Why didn't you stay close to her?"

His face flushed. "You know your sister. She went her own way. What was I supposed to do, put a leash on her?"

Lainie lost it. She raised both hands and shoved him as hard as she could in the shoulders, pushing so hard he almost stumbled and landed on his backside. "You were supposed to take care of your wife. How dare you blame Evie."

Fury flashed in his eyes. Lainie saw a hardness there she'd never seen before. Where did the pain and grief go?

"You weren't here, were you? I did everything I could."

"I don't believe you. What was the name of the police officer who responded?"

He looked away. "I don't know the officer's name, but there was a Detective Yamada. He'll be back if the wind calms down. I have his card back at the hotel."

"I want it."

"Fine." He was petulant now.

With the wind whipping her hair, Lainie turned back and stared at the choppy water.

Evie, Evie, what happened?

A lump formed in her throat, and she swallowed hard. "All right, let's go back."

She turned on her heel and started back to the hotel, not caring if Stan followed her or not.

CHAPTER 8

Lainie retrieved the card from Stan and called Detective Yamada as soon as she got to her room. Yeah, it was Sunday, but Stan said that the detective would be back if the wind calmed down. He could still be on duty. In her experience, most detectives were available when they were needed. His voicemail answered, and she left a terse message.

Her father and Stan had ordered food from one of the restaurants downstairs and had gone to pick it up. Lainie was filled with nervous energy. If she could have, she would have rented a kayak and paddled out into the bay, wind and all.

She logged on to her computer. Messages were waiting from Mike, from Sara, and from her boss in violent crimes, Lieutenant Lopez. She'd only told the lieutenant what had happened and that she needed time off. He'd obviously told her friends. There was also a message from Glen. She passed it by without opening it. No part of her wanted to reconnect with him. She opened Mike's first.

Hey, partner, let me know what's going on. LT said you needed time off for a family emergency. I'll help if I can.

Sorry to hear about your sister, the lieutenant wrote. *You have time, take it.*

Hey, I'm praying for you and your family, my friend . . . Call when you can was Sara's message.

Lainie answered them all, except Glen's, with a brief thanks, writing that she'd explain more when she could. After the e-mails were sent, she realized that she needed to talk to another cop about Evie. Someone who would listen to her concerns, help clarify her thoughts, maybe help her digest everything surrounding Evie's disappearance. If she'd been able to, she would have called Beck. He'd been on her mind since the incident with Bucshon. Dredging up all her history with Vine brought to mind how helpful Beck had been during the most difficult time in her life—second now to what she was going through with Evie's disappearance.

He was a legend in the department. The old-school cop had gained hero status when he single-handedly thwarted a bank robbery and rescued a hostage—after suffering a gunshot wound to the shoulder. He neutralized two armed men and saw to it that the hostage was treated before having his own wound dealt with.

"Just doing my job" was his response to a reporter when asked about the incident.

She'd been his last trainee. He had thirty-five years in uniform as a patrol officer working only graveyard shift. After the stint as Lainie's TO, he was promoted to sergeant, and a year after that he retired. For the year that she had Beck as a resource, he was always her go-to person when things got tough, scary, or unexplainable on the job. Lainie tried hard to emulate Beck—to her he was the perfect cop. The right parts strength, wisdom, and compassion.

Beck had moved to a big ranch in Montana and was basically off-grid. Lainie punched in the last number she had for him, and it rang and rang. She hung up after a few minutes.

Next, she thought about Sara. Sara was friends with both her and Evie. Like she had with Evie, Lainie had distanced herself from Sara. Oh, she still backed Sara up at work when she could, but she hadn't hung out with her just to go to coffee in a while. Faith was the barrier.

Like my father, Sara will be all about prayer. Is that such a bad thing?

Sara went to the same church as Lainie's family and was way more dedicated than Lainie. When she had attended church regularly, Sara was always a good sounding board for life and they hung out often. *I've fallen so far away.* Pushing aside the shame that bubbled up, she called her friend, hoping she could keep her voice steady.

"Oh, Lainie, I'm so sorry. Such an unbelievable tragedy," Sara said after Lainie explained the situation. "How can I pray for you?" Tears filled in her friend's voice.

Throat tight, Lainie said, "I've been so far away from God lately. Oh, will he even hear prayers from me?"

"Of course he will; you know better than that."

"Maybe, but I don't feel it. Evie was the good daughter, the good Christian. How can she be gone?" Lainie was so close to losing it, her voice broke.

"Lainie, stop. I'll pray for you right now. Lord, I lift my friend Lainie to you. Please calm her heart, help her stand in the face of this great loss, and ease her mind—it was not her fault. We don't know the reason this horrible thing happened, but we do know and believe that you, Lord, are still in control."

Lainie took a deep breath.

Not her fault.

God is still in control.

Each word was like a slap. If God was in control, why was Evie gone?

"God seems so far away. I don't know if I can still believe."

"Lainie, God didn't move; you did. It's up to you to move back. Please don't give in to the evil selfish twins: condemnation and pity. None of that will help you or Evie."

"This is so hard." A tear slid down her cheek and she wiped it away.

"I can't imagine. Get out your Bible, pray. God has not left you. He never will."

After the call ended, Lainie mentally replayed the conversation. She'd heard the words before, knew they were true, but she couldn't *feel* them. Neither could she keep her thoughts away from the painful strangeness of all this.

Evie killed by a *shark*? It was a twisted reality.

Agitated, she perused local news sites and found a couple of articles about the attack.

In one newsclip, a reporter had gone to the beach while the search was in progress. A tourist filmed the chaos when a beachgoer began yelling "shark." The news station played a portion of her video. On the video, Lainie could see a truly frantic woman yelling "shark" and pointing to the ocean. The video was shaky, zooming in and out, and at one point showing only sand.

In another portion, Lainie made out Stan's profile briefly near the water's edge. All the phone video really showed was the back of people and the ocean with the tourist who took the video commenting, "I don't see anything." After the phone video clip, the tourist pointed for the cameraman, and she indicated the same area Stan had.

"I think that's where the missing woman had been swimming."

And then a uniformed officer was talking about all the resources they brought to bear in the search. They'd had helicopter and Jet Ski searches. A local surfer in the water at the time also tried to help.

"We have not located the missing woman."

The camera held the reporter's image with the ocean in the background. She began reciting a litany of other shark attacks at the same beach in the past couple of years.

Lainie closed her computer and put her head down on the desk. She heard the door open and knew her father and Stan were back with the food. Her stomach felt no hunger. All Lainie felt was pain and the overwhelming desire to wake up from this horrible nightmare.

CHAPTER 9

Late Sunday afternoon, Ben's phone buzzed with a text, interrupting his devotional time. It was from his boss, Mark Gentry. The clock said 4:00 p.m. Granted, he worked when duty called, but he hadn't expected a call today. Why would Mark be disturbing him now? Maybe with news of Efren?

The adrenaline disappeared as quickly as it had blossomed. Mark would have called if he had good news about Efren; he wouldn't just text. This was something else.

Ben sipped his Coke, waited a couple of minutes, then hit the text bubble and read the message.

Check out the news coming in from Hawaii.

He stared at the words, tapping his jawline with an index finger. Curiosity roused, he left the kitchen and sat down at his office desk. He didn't care to search on his phone; he preferred a larger computer screen. Once online, he checked for happenings in Hawaii. He saw *shark attack* and clicked on that one. Once he read the name Stanley Moffit, he knew he had the right story. When he realized the story was more about Evangeline Moffit, his heart nearly stopped.

He read the story twice, heart rate spiking at a horrible coincidence: The wife of a man whose name appears under the umbrella of their investigation suddenly went missing.

After he read everything available and checked out the posted newsclips, he picked up his phone and called Mark. "What do you think is going on?"

Mark sighed. Ben could visualize his boss striking a pensive expression, stroking his bushy salt-and-pepper mustache, and considering his response carefully. "I don't know. I've been researching this event since yesterday. It's very odd that this happened now. A coincidence."

"Neither one of us believes in that word, do we?"

"Accidents do happen." The tone of Mark's voice telegraphed his doubt.

Ben waited a few seconds before he responded. "How do you want to handle this?"

"Moffit becomes a priority. I want you to go to Hawaii, check this situation out. They haven't found a body, and since this involves Stan Moffit, we need to be certain the story he's telling is true."

"I won't argue about a trip to Hawaii. How much do I tell the locals?"

"As little as possible. I've done a lot of research since Moffit is already on our radar. An insurance policy is involved. Tell them you're curious because of the life insurance policy. Make it sound like a fact-finding mission."

"Is a big policy in play?"

"Moffit took out a four-million-dollar policy on Evangeline Moffit six months ago. I sent you some files."

Ben whistled.

"My understanding is that they have not found a body or body parts, and today the wind is too strong to resume the search."

Ben frowned. "I don't like how any of this sounds."

"That's why I want you there, to see firsthand what the locals know."

"I'm on my way to the island." Ben set the phone aside and pulled up his e-mail.

Mark's e-mail from work was in his inbox, and it had three attachments. The first was an article from *Hawaii News Now* about a woman who disappeared while snorkeling. She and her husband were celebrating their anniversary at the Hilton Waikoloa Village Resort on the Big Island of Hawaii. One document he hadn't yet seen was the life insurance policy.

"Hmm." Ben skimmed the policy.

The third document was a request filed by the beneficiary, Stan Moffit, for a payout. Ben's eyes went back to the news article. He noted the date and time. A mirthless chuckle escaped.

"You only waited eight hours after you told police your wife was missing to apply for a payout. That is not suspicious at all."

Another e-mail came in. Ben opened it. It was a ticket for a plane ride to Hawaii and a request for local cooperation in a federal investigation.

Ben downed his coffee and got up to pack. He had to hurry and catch a plane.

✦

The wind blew strong and hard all day Sunday. There could be no official search until the wind calmed down. The inaction made Lainie feel as if there were columns of ants marching all over her body, just under her skin. She couldn't stay inside.

She found a trail that ran along the shore, a crushed coral trail that took her back to A-Bay. In spite of the wind, she walked by herself to the beach. There were still tourists here and there. She didn't think the wind was as strong as the day before, and she hoped that meant it was decreasing.

All Lainie could do was walk along the beach. She did that until the wind really began to get to her, and she went back to the hotel. Her father and Stan were watching golf on TV. They'd gotten some food, and since she couldn't remember when she'd eaten last, she made herself a sandwich, then went out on the lanai to sit and eat. She barely tasted the food and only ate about half of what she'd made. The wind whistled around, but the lanai was protected.

When night fell, she went to bed early.

"I'd try to pray," she whispered in the dark. "But I still can't say that I believe it works. I did at one time—but right now I'm so rusty. And this is the most desperate prayer of my life. I don't want my sister to be gone. Please help us find her."

She was completely unconvinced that her prayer was heard. The only thing she was 100 percent sure of was that if they couldn't search the next day, she would lose her mind.

When dawn broke, the palm trees were calm, the slight breeze barely detectable.

Detective Yamada called Lainie back that morning. She was out by herself again, walking back toward the beach on the same shoreline trail. Her father had still been asleep when she left the room. She didn't know about Stan and didn't care.

"I'm Detective Jensen. Evie Moffit is my sister." She explained that she was a detective in Long Beach, California.

"Detective Jensen, how can I help you?"

At a loss for a second, Lainie mouthed a silent *O*. She wanted her sister back. Yamada couldn't help her there.

"I, uh, want to know where my sister is. How is it possible she disappeared completely?"

The line went silent for a moment. "I'm sorry, Detective Jensen. Sharks are mobile and quite destructive. I'm sorry, but remains can be difficult to recover. I assure you, we've searched the area completely for your sister. We did not find her."

"Are you sure my brother-in-law is telling the truth?"

Lainie blurted the question out without thinking. It was not something she would have asked if her father were standing next to her.

"There were at least two, maybe three, other people on the beach that day who thought they saw a shark. Several more helped your brother-in-law search. And we recovered a portion of your sister's mask and snorkel. Is there some reason we should doubt your brother-in-law's story?"

Lainie closed her eyes and tears leaked from the corners. "No, ah, no, I'm sorry. This is so hard to understand."

"I realize it's difficult. Many visitors underestimate the ocean and the dangers within. Detective Jensen, as a professional courtesy, I'll send you what we have on this case as soon as I am able. Can you give me your e-mail address?"

Lainie complied.

"I will be back at the beach in about an hour. We'll continue the search today."

"Okay, thank you. I'm at the beach now. I'd like to help in any way I can." Lainie disconnected and continued walking. The wind had calmed down to nothing, and Lainie planned to take a kayak out into the bay, to where Stan had said he'd last seen Evie.

She was early. The kiosk was not yet open. Frustrated, Lainie walked down to the water's edge. A few people were enjoying the now calm and gentle surf and even more were on the sand, chatting and laughing.

She wanted to scream. How could life go on so normally?

To ease her frustration, she walked along the water. A rock structure jutted out into the bay a bit, and she walked out on it as far as she could go. It was a warm morning, a gentle breeze waffling through her hair now and again, but nothing like the day before. Small swells lapped against the rocky shore. The two catamarans anchored in the bay were stable, only rolling gently.

Lainie studied the water, hating to think of her sister's remains being consumed by marine life. Tears fell and she wiped her face with her palms.

She stayed there until she began to feel too warm, then returned to the kiosk, which now showed signs of opening. An older Asian man strode along the water. He was not in uniform, but it had to be

Yamada. He looked like a cop. Someone once told her that cops tended to walk alike because of the weight of the gun belt on their hips, and the weight of the memories of tragic scenes in their hearts. Lainie could always tell a fellow officer by their situational awareness. The man strode with a purpose, he was taking everything in, he was not a tourist.

She changed direction and walked toward him. "Detective Yamada?"

He met her gaze, a neutral cop expression on his face. "Detective Jensen."

"Yes." She held out her hand and he took it.

"A pleasure to meet you. Sorry it is under such tough circumstances."

"What is the plan today? There's hardly any wind."

He nodded. "The helicopter is on the way. Also, two Jet Skis." He pointed and she and saw a couple of men farther down the beach dragging two Jet Skis down to the water.

He looked over her shoulder, and she turned to see her father and Stan coming toward them. "I'm going to go out in a kayak."

"You won't be able to go as far out as the Jet Skis as they follow the current, but please, paddle out if you wish."

Dad and Stan joined them. Stan reached out and grasped Yamada's hand with both of his. "Thanks for coming back out, Detective."

Lainie left them to talk and went to the kiosk to rent her kayak. While the attendant was unlocking a boat, her father caught up with her. When she turned to face him, she noticed that Yamada was now on the phone as Stan trudged off down the beach.

"Lainie, can I have a word?" Her father was not happy.

"About what?"

"Don't you think you're being a little too hard on Stan?"

"What do you mean?"

"Did you tell Detective Yamada you thought Stan was lying about the shark attack?"

Lainie stared at her dad. "I just asked if he was sure Stan was telling the truth."

Dad shook his head. "Evie is his wife. The mother of his children. He's devastated. You accused him of letting her die."

"I didn't—I . . . ah." Her heart pounded in her chest. Raw emotion erupted to the surface. "Dad, it's so suspicious. How could he swim off, get out of the water, and leave her to die?"

Dad leaned close. "We're all in shock. We're all hurting. There's nothing here that says it's Stan's fault. Lashing out at him won't bring Evie back. Please be a little more sensitive."

Lainie turned away, squeezing her eyes shut as tears threatened. "I hate this. All of it. Most of all I hate thinking of Evie in the past tense."

Her father pulled her into a tight hug. "Me too, baby, me too," he whispered, emotion clear in his voice. "All I'm asking is that you don't take it out on Stan. Try to be a little less police officer and a little more sister."

All Lainie could do was nod and swallow back tears as she stepped away.

"Renting a kayak?" he asked.

"Yeah, I need to do something."

"Want company?"

Lainie shook her head. "I need to do this on my own."

He threw his arm around her shoulders and squeezed. "Okay." He pressed his lips to the top of her head. "I'll hang out with Stan."

The kiosk operator explained the boundaries—basically Lainie was not to take the kayak beyond the bay. Lainie only half listened. She pushed the kayak into the water and hopped in.

CHAPTER 10

The longer someone was missing, the less chance that they would be found alive.

Despite wanting to leave and figure out what Moffit was up to, Ben felt a wrench in his gut when he buckled himself in on the plane. Glancing out the window, he felt as if he were abandoning Efren.

He'd exhausted all avenues.

Moffit was a new angle.

The plane took off and he prayed the trip would be worth it, that something would happen on the island that would further his investigation and help him find Efren.

Ben landed late Monday morning at the Kona Airport. Since Hawaii was a couple of hours behind, he gained time. He contacted the local police as soon as he arrived and was told that the detective in charge was at the beach where Evangeline Moffit had been attacked.

The officer at the desk was kind enough to give him the detective's cell number. Ben called it and Detective Yamada answered.

Ben explained who he was and why he was there. Yamada relayed the details of his investigation, and Ben's impression of the man was that he was thorough, careful, and methodical. Sometimes methodical men could miss the obvious.

"Is that story plausible to you?" Ben asked after learning what Stan had told the first arriving officers.

"I have no reason to doubt his story. Shark attacks happen."

"Is there any way Moffit could have killed his wife, then blamed it on a shark?"

"I have no evidence of such a thing." Ben could hear surprise in the man's voice and imagined raised eyebrows.

"But you have no evidence that Evangeline Moffit is dead, do you? Not by murder or shark."

It was a couple of seconds before Yamada answered. "A bit of snorkel and a mask. Not enough blood to test. Others at the beach think they saw the shark, but no one witnessed the actual attack."

"How did Moffit seem to you?"

"Distraught. He didn't do or say anything that made me doubt his story. However, I do know that anything is possible. If you know something I should know about the man, please tell me."

"No, I don't. My job is to be skeptical. I'm concerned about insurance fraud. The policy is large, around four million dollars. People have committed murder and fraud for less. We need to be certain. Thank you for your help. Do you know if Moffit is still on island?"

"Yes, he's here on the beach now."

"Still helpful?"

"There is not much he can help with; still, he appears very worried. I have a helicopter and two men on Jet Skis. Additionally, Moffit's sister-in-law is here. A detective from California, Elaine Jensen. She doesn't believe Mr. Moffit. Perhaps the two of you should talk. In any case, we will revisit everything if we find any indication of wrongdoing or subterfuge."

Elaine Jensen.

"She's there now?"

"Yes. She plans to kayak in the bay."

Ben thanked him, ended the call, then opened his iPad to pull up the file. There it was: Elaine Jensen was related to Stanley Moffit. Why hadn't he connected that earlier? He was preoccupied with Efren, that's why. He should have dug deeper into Moffit's background.

Moffit was not considered a major player. Even though he worked for Vine, his connection was tangential. The Bureau had cast a broad net, and Ben was familiar with all the pieces, but obviously not as familiar as he should have been with Moffit. Ben couldn't let Detective Jensen see him. Mark should have sent someone else.

But then would Ben have let anyone else come? Moffit was a connection to Vine, and no one wanted Vine stopped like Ben did—except Elaine Jensen.

How was Jensen doing now? She'd just lost her sister under what Ben considered suspicious circumstances. She was a good cop. If he found any discrepancies, she probably would as well.

Ben wasn't certain of his next move. He prayed for Detective Jensen and found himself hoping that whatever happened to Evangeline Moffit was simply a tragic accident, not anything more sinister.

✦

Ben had booked a room at the Hilton, where Moffit was staying. The closer his rental car got to the hotel, Ben knew that he wouldn't approach Moffit. He couldn't approach Elaine, so his plan was simply to study the report and to observe everyone. This was a flyover after all. He was getting a feel for the situation, not conducting a full-blown investigation into the attack or the fraud. That was not his job.

Ben knew that the insurance company would eventually send their own investigators, and they would tell Moffit that he would not receive an insurance payout until his wife was officially declared dead. That bit of information was likely to provoke a reaction. Of course,

Ben had no idea if Moffit killed his wife. Yet there were notes in the file from one of the original task force agents. *"Subject lies easily—no objective evidence he's involved in illegality, but he bears watching."*

Ben remembered talking to Efren about Moffit. Efren was on the fence about the man. He had taken pains to befriend Moffit. He'd been over to the man's house for dinner, met Evangeline and their two boys.

"He's not really complicated. A con man for sure. Loves money and pretty women, but I'm not certain he has the nerve or the smarts to be in very deep."

Knowing Vine, the way Ben knew Vine, he couldn't imagine anyone working for him being a straight arrow. For all he knew, Moffit was simply being used by Vine, kind of a useful-idiot scenario.

Ben gazed out at the ocean as he drove, wishing for a moment that he were here on vacation, maybe with a female friend, and with Efren and his wife. Ben loved the water and wished he could get in at some point. But that wasn't possible. Right now, all he could do was pray for the entire family of Evangeline Moffit.

CHAPTER 11

Lainie paddled along the curve of the bay. It was very shallow in spots, and she could see the coral. She was careful not to hit it with her paddle or the kayak. It was also murky in spots. It didn't seem like a good place to snorkel. However, as she got farther out, the water cleared up some and she understood why this was a snorkel spot.

Above her, the sound of a helicopter droned. Off to her left zoomed a Jet Ski. Lainie concentrated on her paddling. Toward the center of the bay, the water was much deeper. She saw some bright-yellow tang and other colorful fish she couldn't identify. She paddled to Evie's last-known location. Lainie could see the coastline, and the trail paved with crushed white coral she'd walked on yesterday. It ran along the coast down in the direction where the Hilton hotel stood.

She stopped paddling when she felt she had reached the right spot. The pain she felt at that moment was like a sharp knife rammed into her insides and twisted. She and Evie were born only eighteen months apart, and they were close. At least they had been close, up until the last few years. They'd drifted. Or rather Lainie had moved away. Evie had stayed the same sweet, steady person she'd always been.

Sara had told Lainie that it was not God who had moved.

But how do I move back?

Her failing faith started with that traffic stop fifteen years ago. When Dallas Vine got off with a slap on the wrist, Lainie knew with every fiber of her soul that he'd murdered the woman in the back seat of his car, so she'd focused her anger on God.

How could he let this murderer just walk out of jail and continue his life?

Her early years consisted of an easy, uncluttered life. Lainie became a cop with a lot of naivete to overcome. Beck's voice came back to her loud and clear.

"You're not in Sunday school anymore, Jensen. Take off those rose-colored glasses and get skeptical. Everyone lies to the police. Everyone. If you can't accept that and work with it, find another job because you won't be any good at this one, and you might get yourself or someone else killed."

Lainie clenched her fists as memories surfaced. When she had been new to the uniform, she was on fire for the Lord, an involved church member, and very close to Evie.

Seeing gross injustice firsthand, she felt as though God had let her down. She could see that clearly now.

God betrayed me so I walked away.

A lot of Christians on the force attended a weekly Bible study called Iron Sharpens Iron. Lainie hadn't attended in a long while. The officers who did go were good people, accountability partners, steadfast—like Lainie used to be. Beck had often led those meetings. As long as he was on the job, she went. But then he left, and Vine happened, and in her mind's eye, Lainie could see her faith crashing and burning.

Then she'd met Glen. He was another excuse to stay away from church and God. It didn't matter that he was married. It wasn't Glen who had changed her; she'd been drifting before they started flirting. While the relationship never crossed any physical boundaries, it crossed emotional ones. She flirted and considered more. Because she'd drifted, nothing anchored her anymore.

When Evie met Stan, Lainie never saw the attraction. She never believed he was a Christian. Evie, someone who always had such a level head, was totally taken in by the guy.

"You can't judge his heart, Lainie. He's good to me."

Did Lainie stop going to church completely because of Stan and seeing what a jerk he had been to Evie? Lainie's heart had left the church long before her physical body stopped going.

Evie was the good girl, she never missed church, she was involved in everything good, yet she married a man who was not a good husband. He was selfish and prideful from what Lainie had seen. He claimed to be a Christian but often acted any way but Christian.

Her dislike of Stan was no excuse. Vine's plea deal was no excuse. She couldn't blame anything or anyone but herself.

Tears began to fill her eyes as the weight of all the lost time settled on her soul. She could have spent precious moments with Evie; they could have been so much closer. The loss hit her like a knee strike to the chin.

Floating in the bay, paddle resting across her knees, Lainie let the tears fall. "Evie, Evie, I'm so sorry."

At one point the Jet Ski slowed at a location off to the right. It was outside the boundary she'd been given by the kiosk worker, but she paddled that way.

Her father's request echoed in her mind. *"Be less cop and more sister."* She couldn't be angry with her dad for asking, but neither could she shut off the instincts screaming inside her that something wasn't right.

She paddled the kayak around so she could see the shore. After a minute, she made out Detective Yamada speaking with her father. Stan was off to the left a little bit, on the phone. Lainie hoped he was talking to the boys or her mom.

Realizing how much anger swelled inside as she thought about Stan, Lainie knew she had a problem. She sighed, then prayed for help and vowed to be more objective when it came to her brother-in-law.

Lainie paddled back around as the helicopter completed another sweep. The Jet Skis had also continued their survey. Her hour was almost up, and with intense pain and sadness, Lainie conceded that her sister wasn't here and the ocean was not going to tell her where she was.

Never in her life had she felt so empty and lost.

CHAPTER 12

Ben arrived at the Hilton hotel deep in thought. He left the rental car with the attendant, grabbed his bag, and entered the lobby. A surprise hit him square in the chest when he approached the reception desk.

Crystal Benton.

He almost stopped in shock but forced himself to keep walking, face blank. She was a pretty woman, tall and athletic, yet something was different about her. He couldn't put his finger on it, but the hairstyle and color were different. This was the woman Hank Bucshon had called Vine's main squeeze.

There was no reason Benton should know him. He knew her because her name was prominent on the investigation board, IB.

"She's higher on the food chain and someone who could give us hard evidence, but she's no snitch. And she'd likely be incriminating herself as well," Efren had said.

The contrast being that Stan Moffit was lower on Vine's organizational chart with virtually no power. That Benton was here, now, was beyond coincidence. Did Moffit know she was here, or was she here because Moffit was? Could Moffit have called her for support? Though that might be a possibility, Ben couldn't see it. This could move his involvement with her from marginal to full-on. Benton was at the reception desk in front of him, and he moved as close as he dared to eavesdrop on the conversation.

"I need a rental car for a couple of days," she explained to the receptionist.

"We've been busy with rental cars lately, and unfortunately you might have to Uber to the airport to pick up the car."

"Are you serious? That will take me over an hour to get back here with the car."

"It's possible they may have a car for you here. I just don't have that information. You need to speak to the concierge." The receptionist spoke calmly, aloha in her voice, smiled, and gestured across the lobby.

"Fine." Benton's tone cut like fingernails on blackboard. Without thanking the receptionist, she stormed away, stomping to the other desk.

Ben watched her go. Being supportive probably was not one of her life skills. Her arrival made what happened to Evangeline Moffit more suspicious. Benton and Moffit had come up in conversation together once, and Ben worked to remember exactly all that Efren had said about her.

"She's pretty, but a hardness pervades her core. Benton is not sentimental at all, but she is very loyal. Everything about her is mysterious and ambiguous. Gossip on one hand says she's involved with Vine, but whispers on the other hand say she's involved with someone else. Whatever the case, it's all very hush-hush. She's at the car wash a lot. Drives a Bentley and wants it cleaned all the time. She is always with Vine's bodyguard, a guy they call Plug."

Ben raised an eyebrow. "Plug, as in fireplug?"

"Pretty much."

"Could she be involved with Moffit?"

Efren laughed. "I don't see that. Benton is all about wanting money and prestige. Moffit may run the car wash, but he is not the boss. He drives a Kia."

Was Efren wrong? Improbable as the relationship would be, if it were so, did Benton fit into Evangeline's disappearance somehow?

Guilt and fear swelled inside. He believed less and less that Evangeline's fate was simply a tragic accident. He stepped forward to check in, his thoughts drifting again to Elaine Jensen.

Maybe he should talk to her, join forces, let her know he was here investigating this situation.

No.

Ben knew he might be responsible for her sister's death. He wouldn't put Lainie at risk as well. Besides, he'd need to get permission to read her into everything. The higher-ups would not approve.

✦

After he'd settled his luggage in his room, Ben logged into his laptop. He brought up the case files for the Dallas Vine investigation. He needed to dig into Benton a little deeper.

He read over everything in the file they knew about her. She had an accounting degree from California State University in Long Beach. She'd also completed law school and worked for a time as an attorney. Her occupation with Vine's LLC was listed as an office manager, but she was more than that. Efren had used the outdated term *girl Friday*, meaning she completed whatever administrative task Vine requested.

Vine owned and ran several different businesses. Confidential informants believed Vine used his multiple business interests to launder money for a large-scale interstate human-trafficking organization. The car wash Moffit managed was a piece of the puzzle because it was one of Vine's more lucrative endeavors.

Efren's task had been to find evidence connecting Vine and his businesses to money laundering. He landed a job at the car wash because Vine appeared to be more involved there than even at his classy cigar club, Smokey Dreams, in downtown Long Beach. Efren had had his own business detailing cars when he was a kid. He quickly caught Vine's eye because of his work ethic and his attention to detail. Though a young man named Raphael Diaz was the main detailer at the car wash, Efren handled all business vehicles and referrals from Vine. When it came to his personal vehicle, Vine always requested Efren.

Soon, Efren became responsible for maintaining Vine's fleet of vehicles. Vine was rumored to conceal money and the location of trafficked individuals in his vehicles. Efren had found evidence that different parts of the cars, such as armrests, door panels, and seats had been removed and replaced shoddily, but he'd never found any money or instructions. He had used a drug-detection test that told him drug residue remained in one or two vehicles. When there was damage to a vehicle's interior, Efren was told to simply fix it and not ask questions.

Originally the task force thought it would be easy to find evidence against Vine. He eschewed technology, believed in paper records. Some thought a paper trail would be easier to uncover than a digital trail, but that had not proven to be true. Vine had perfected codes and subversion; nothing incriminating had as yet been uncovered.

Moffit had been hired a little over a year ago. The man who had held the job before had been targeted for investigation, but he died of a massive heart attack before any criminal filings. There was no indication that Moffit continued any illegal practices. Efren didn't think Stan was that bright.

"He's kind of like the high school nerd who really wants to fit in with the cool kids but just can't. At times I think he's completely harmless. But the love of money can change anyone's personality."

The task force's overarching investigation had been in progress for over a year and involved countless man-hours. Everything had hit a snag when Efren disappeared.

Requesting the assignment had been Ben's idea.

"It's another trafficking case," he told Efren.

"But we won't get in on that part of it; they need a team on the money side."

"The money side is just as important. Dry up the money, we dry up the crime."

"Okay, I trust your judgment, partner. Let's follow the money."

The memory pierced Ben. "You trusted me, partner, and look what it got you."

He shook away the pain because now was no time to sink into destructive, fatalistic thinking. The fact that Efren had dropped off the face of the earth made Ben do something unconventional and out of policy, something in retrospect maybe he should not have done.

The day before he took Bucshon from Lainie, he'd contacted Evangeline Moffit and explained as much as he dared about the investigation into Vine. They met at a local coffee shop in Long Beach: Grounds Bakery & Cafe. He tried hard not to alarm her and explained that Vine was under investigation, not her husband, but he could not guarantee that Stan might not be entangled. To her credit, she took the news stoically. Things had been off with her husband until recently.

"I don't know what to do with what you're telling me. For a few months now, I've feared that Stan is having an affair. But a couple of weeks ago, he came to me excited because he got a bonus at work and he was taking me to Hawaii for a honeymoon we never had."

Ben didn't know what to do with that information. Vine was not known as a generous boss. Before he could respond, Evangeline continued.

"Is my husband into something illegal? Are my children in jeopardy?"

"I don't believe so as far as your children are concerned."

"Okay, okay, then how can I help you?"

"Have you ever heard the name Efren Gomez?"

"Yes, I know Efren. He works for Stan, but he's a good friend. I saw him at the car wash the other day."

"What day?" Ben perked up. She might be the last person to have seen Efren—he hated to use the word *alive* because it meant that the opposite was a real possibility.

"On Friday morning. I wanted to get my car washed before I got too busy getting ready for vacation. He is the best detailer Stan employs." Distressed, she paused, and then asked, "Don't tell me, is he a bad guy as well?"

"No. But right now, he's missing. Has your husband mentioned him at all? Maybe wondering where he is?"

She shook her head. "Do you want me to ask?"

"No. Don't mention my visit or Efren to your husband at all. All I'm asking is that if you hear anything about Efren, or see him, that you give me a call." Ben slid a business card across the table. "If that makes you uncomfortable, then forget I asked. I don't want you to feel any pressure."

"I'll need to think about this request. You're asking me to go behind my husband's back. And to keep secrets from him." She twisted a napkin with both hands.

"Yes, I am. If this request bothers you, say no."

"It's not that." She paused and sipped her coffee. Ben could see by her expression that she was fighting a battle within.

"We've been such strangers lately. The second honeymoon is an answer to prayer. It feels like I have my husband back after a long separation. He insists that we're fine, we're just comfortable marrieds, and that the trip to Hawaii will bring back the romance. I'm not likely to see or hear anything about Efren until we get back."

"I understand. I pray that you have a great time and that Efren will show up and you can forget I ever contacted you."

Thinking about that conversation, two big questions bounced around in his mind: Did Moffit kill his wife? If so, was it because Ben had spoken to Evangeline? Was he responsible for the woman's death? Ben prayed the answer to both questions was no.

Mind swirling with curiosity about this shark attack, he changed into shorts and flip-flops and headed out of the hotel for the beach. It was time to view the scene and talk to people. Was it a crime scene or simply the scene of a tragic accident?

CHAPTER 13

Lainie paddled back in and returned the kayak. Her father and Stan were talking with Yamada. Not feeling up to interacting with Stan yet, Lainie took a seat on a retaining wall and watched the chopper work. After checking her watch, she knew from working with police helicopters that they would have to finish soon and head in for fuel.

It was a beautiful day but hot. The sun was a mocker as far as Lainie was concerned. Shining so bright on a day when Evie's light had been snuffed out. The day should be cloudy and overcast, as gloomy and bereft of hope as she felt. When the chopper turned inland, Lainie realized the search was ending.

Her father saw her and joined her at the wall. "Yamada is calling off the search. They need resources farther down the coast with a missing paddleboarder."

"I saw the helicopter leave." She swallowed, not trusting herself to say more.

"Stan and I are going back to the hotel. He wants to talk to the boys. What are your plans?"

"I'm going to hang out here for a while."

"Okay." He gave her a hug and then walked to where Stan stood waiting.

Lainie wanted to scream. Emotionally, she didn't want the search to end. The police officer part of her knew that after all this time—it was Monday and Evie disappeared the previous Friday—there was no hope. Even if she was not mauled by a shark, she would not have survived in the ocean all this time. Where had she been for three days?

Lounge chairs were stacked on the far side of the beach. She walked over, grabbed one, and dragged it closer to the water, then sat and stared out over the ocean. How on earth could she go on?

At about two in the afternoon, Lainie realized she couldn't sit and stare at the water anymore. It felt as if she was developing a sunburn on the part in her hair and on her legs. Everything else was pretty much covered. She could return to the hotel walking along the water, but she'd been staring so hard at the water that she decided enough was enough. She would walk out to the street. She was also tired and thirsty. There was a grocery store in the Queens' Marketplace, where she could buy a bottle of water, so she headed that way.

She felt it was time to go but hesitated, ignoring the activity around her. The pain of loss was like a throbbing, dull ache that vibrated through her entire body. Truly believing Evie was gone was hard. Lainie's mind couldn't grasp the thought that a shark so consumed the dynamic person that was her sister that there was no trace left.

A swimmer yelled out, "Turtle! Turtle!"

Lainie turned that way as a crowd of snorkelers hurried toward the location. As several of them dove underwater to chase the turtle, a question popped into her head.

Would I feel better if I'd found a portion of her body?

Lainie didn't know. All she did know was that she could barely stand the pain she felt. Nothing would make it better.

✦

Ben arrived at the beach sometime after two o'clock. Yamada had called him when the search ended.

"I have an emergency in South Kona. I can't allocate any more resources here."

"How will you classify Evangeline Moffit?"

"Missing, presumed victim of a fatal shark encounter."

Ben wasn't surprised by the classification. He considered the case as he walked along the beach. The sand was crowded with happy, laughing vacationers. He tried to imagine what was going on in Elaine Jensen's mind and couldn't. Ben himself had one older sibling, a sister. She was a pediatrician in Florida. He couldn't imagine losing her, especially in a way that was so completely bizarre and unexplainable. His elderly parents also lived in Florida. Stacey checked up on them, helped them out all the time. He doubted they would survive if something happened to her.

Just thinking about it made him want to call and check up on them all. He ignored the desire. He needed to concentrate on the here and now.

Where was Moffit?

Then he saw Elaine Jensen off by herself on a lounge chair. He'd almost walked right in front of her. Subtly backtracking, he made his way behind her. She appeared to be deep in thought. His heart went out to her, right now a sad, hurting figure in the middle of a beautiful beach. He said a silent prayer that the Lord would heal her heart and give her peace, then moved across the sand to find a place he could occupy unobtrusively and not be seen by her.

It was a stunning day at the beach. Ben could never be a cop in paradise. A place like this should be far removed from any type of violence and tragedy. Unfortunately, he knew that wasn't the case.

✦

Lainie made her way off the beach, crossing past the large outrigger canoes stored on the sand. A concrete path took her out to the parking lot. On the way she saw a colony of feral cats. A blonde woman, bright red from the sun, sat on the lava rocks feeding the cats. Making her way through slow-walking, toasted tourists smelling of suntan lotion, Lainie continued up the asphalt road that ran through the parking lot.

There was no sidewalk after the parking lot. The road leading to and from the beach was a narrow two-lane road, banked on either side by vacant, rocky dirt lots. Lainie followed the road, walking on the dirt edge. She could see the grocery store in the distance across a lava field. Cars came and went down the road, but Lainie was in her own world, paying only basic attention to what was going on around her. Some kids were ahead of her, on the other side of the street, walking toward the beach. Their screams broke into her thoughts.

"Watch out, Auntie, watch out!"

Jolted into the here and now, Lainie turned just in time to see a Jeep bearing down on her. She leapt to her right, into the rocky, dusty unpaved lot. The Jeep veered toward her.

That driver wants to hit me.

Barely escaping a direct strike from the vehicle, Lainie avoided the front fender only to be struck by the back end as the jeep swerved and fishtailed back toward the road.

Her hip took the brunt of the impact, and Lainie was sent sprawling into the dirt. Her right hand broke her fall, lessening the impact on her shoulder but not preventing her landing in the lot of sharp lava rocks and gritty dust.

Pain blossomed across her right side, and she tasted blood in her mouth when her chin hit the ground.

That driver just tried to kill me.

CHAPTER 14

Ben had seen Elaine leave the beach. He'd waited to make his exit until after she was out of sight. He didn't want to run into her in the parking lot. When he made his way off the beach, he could hear shouting in the distance. What was that all about? Paying attention as he walked toward the lot, he saw a cloud of dirt and then a Jeep zigzagging through the dirt lot that bordered the roadway, heading away from the beach. The Jeep hit the pavement and burned rubber out of the lot. In its wake, three or four people ran toward the big cloud of dust the Jeep had kicked up.

He kept an eye on the dust cloud, wondering what caused it, as he climbed into his rental. He pulled out of the lot and headed in the direction of the commotion. A Waikoloa security vehicle crossed in front of him and pulled up to the group. Slowly Ben cruised by as the crowd of people helped someone off the ground. He slammed on his brakes when he recognized the victim.

Elaine Jensen.

He fought the urge to hop out of his car and run over to find out what happened. The security officer got out of his car and took over. A few people from the group who had helped Jensen up turned away from her and walked toward him. The security officer handed Elaine a towel and began talking to her. Ben rolled down his window.

"Hey, what happened over there?" he asked the group.

One of the kids walked over to his car. "It was crazy. Some lady in a Jeep tried to run Auntie over."

"You're kidding." Ben knew that locals often referred to older people as Auntie and Uncle, even when there was no relation. It seemed a sign of respect for age.

"No, we saw it all." The boy pointed. "Almost ran her right over."

"It wasn't an accident?"

He gave a head shake. "She drove right at her. Then she just took off that way. Crazy tourist."

"It was a tourist?"

"Yeah, a white Jeep. Common rental car, you know?"

Ben nodded toward Elaine. "That lady okay?"

"A little bloody but yeah, she's okay."

"Thanks." Ben let the kids go and continued on his way slowly. He watched Jensen as surreptitiously as he could. She was talking and holding the towel to her lip. He drove past, and when he reached the stop sign to the main road, a police car passed him traveling the other way. Myriad thoughts swirled in his mind.

Drunk driver?

Inattention?

Foul play?

When that last thought popped into his head, it was hard not to think of Crystal Benton. Why his mind went there immediately, he wasn't certain. But something wasn't right. If someone had accidentally run into Jensen, it wouldn't be unreasonable to think that a tourist would stop for the police, but that vehicle peeled out of the lot. Although it was a little early for a drunk driver, that could also be an explanation.

What kind of vehicle had Crystal Benton rented? But then, what reason would she have to run Jensen over?

A honk behind him made Ben realize that he'd been sitting at the stop sign for a while. He waved an "I'm sorry" hand and pushed the accelerator, turned left, and headed back to the hotel.

There was too much weird here, that was for sure.

✦

"Are you okay?" Dad grabbed Lainie's shoulders and peered at her face when she returned to the room.

"Yeah, Dad, I am. It's just a couple of scrapes." She told him what had happened, leaving out the thought that it had all been intentional. That had sounded crazy to the security guard, and it now sounded crazy to her.

Who would want to kill her in Hawaii, where she knew no one? She certainly hadn't arrested anyone here.

She'd decided after talking to the police that it had been an unfortunate accident. The tourist was likely to come forward any minute and apologize.

"The road is narrow," the officer who had come by said. *"There is no sidewalk, just dirt close to the asphalt. Often people are not paying attention."*

To Lainie that sounded plausible.

"The car hit you?" her father asked.

"Sort of. I moved, she grazed me, and I fell into some rocks. Give me some time to change and clean up."

She went to the bathroom to check out the damage herself. She'd scraped her right arm and chin, just enough to draw blood but nothing serious. Little bits of lava rock were stuck in her arm. She washed it out. Thankfully the bleeding had stopped. But she would have some angry red marks on her for a while, and her hip was sore. Lainie was glad the kids had alerted her to the Jeep's presence. It would have been bad if the vehicle hit her full-on. Once she cleaned up and changed her clothes, she went back to where her father was.

Stan was now in the room, his bags packed.

"You're leaving?"

"I am. There is nothing else I can do here. The boys need me."

Lainie stared at him, angry but not sure why. There *was* nothing else Stan could do here. Nothing at all.

"We Facetimed the boys," Dad said. His eyes were red, and that broke Lainie's heart.

"They took the news hard. Stan wants to get back and so do I."

Lainie stared at her father. "You've given up."

He stepped toward her. "Lainie, we have to face facts." He reached his hand out and she batted it away.

"I'm staying. I'm not giving up on her. I can't." She pushed past her father and left the room, fighting the threatening tears. Blindly she found her way to the elevator and down to the lobby. Running, she made her way back out to the shoreline and the crushed-coral walkway.

She was alone there, and she couldn't stop the sobs.

CHAPTER 15

By the time her father texted her that he and Stan were waiting for an Uber to take them to the airport, the sun prepared to set and Lainie had come to her senses. Everything still hurt, emotionally and physically as the scrapes on her arm and face throbbed, and everything was still raw, but she was back in control of her emotions, and she met him in the hotel lobby.

"Sorry I wigged out on you, Dad. I'm not really sure how to handle all of this."

He smiled. "I get it, baby, I get it." He gave her a hug. "I don't know that either."

She looked around her father. "Where's Stan?"

"Bathroom. The car will be here in a few minutes."

"You don't mind if I stay here and keep searching, do you?"

Before he could speak, Stan walked up. "What do you think you can accomplish? You're not a cop here." His tone was sharp and a little snarky.

Lainie waited for a beat before she responded. "I'm going to talk to the witnesses, get my own read on what happened."

"You can do that?"

"Yamada said he'd send me the report."

"Why don't you just leave it alone?" he snapped. "She's gone. You can't bring her back."

"I can't let it go."

For a second, they glared at one another. Lainie knew that everyone handled grief differently. As Stan's anger incensed her, she realized she had her own anger problem. She had no pity or compassion for him at that moment. He was showing a side she'd never seen, and she didn't like it any more than any of the other sides she'd already seen. All she could think was, what did Evie ever see in him?

"Okay, okay." Dad stepped between them. "Everyone is on edge right now. And I think our car is here."

Stan turned away first, his gaze following her dad's hand as he waved toward the Uber.

"Call me when you get home, Dad." She gave him a kiss good-bye, then stepped back as they loaded their things into the car. Once they were gone, Lainie went back up to the room, hoping Yamada had sent the file he'd promised to send.

✦

The detective came through: The report was waiting for her when Lainie opened her e-mail. He'd included contact information for the witnesses. She read through the statements. The woman who'd screamed and alerted everyone to the shark was identified as Gail Boyce. She claimed she'd seen the shark and blood in the water, was certain she also heard a woman scream. Boyce listed a local residence address and a workplace address in the Queens' Marketplace. Lainie guessed this was the woman featured on the tourist's cell phone video. Lainie made a mental note of the shop and planned to head over there when she rented a car.

According to the report, one of the men who had said he saw a shark fin was a tourist from Washington state. Lainie wrote down his phone number. The other local who said he saw the shark gave an address up the road in Waikoloa Village.

Briefly she considered the photo of what evidence had been located—a bit of snorkel and a mask.

A second newer e-mail arrived from Yamada where he explained about how Evie was now classified. Evangeline Moffit—*missing, presumed victim of a shark encounter.*

Swallowing tears, Lainie went back to the crime report. Nothing more was there than what she'd seen on the news. Lainie wanted to hear the story firsthand from the witnesses.

Oh, Lord, won't you tell me why this happened?

Tears threatened anew. After getting up from her computer, she went to the bathroom and washed her face again, wincing at the sore red spot on her chin. The emotional tenor of the day had drained Lainie of all energy. She did not feel like leaving the room again for any reason, and her mind was too scattered to interview people.

She walked back to the report on her screen and saw that the witness from Washington state, Jerry Fontaine, should be home by now. After checking the time in his home state, she punched in his number. This was one interview she felt she could conduct. He answered after two rings.

"Mr. Fontaine?"

"Speaking."

"My name in Lainie Jensen, Detective Lainie Jensen. I wondered if you had a couple minutes to talk to me about the incident in Hawaii?"

"The shark attack, ah, sure. But I told the police everything that day. I'm not sure I can add anything. They haven't found her yet?"

Lainie cleared her throat. "No, they haven't. Sometimes memories get clearer the further away one is from the trauma. Did you actually see the shark?"

"Ah, I think so. There was this woman on the beach screaming, 'shark.' She pointed, I looked to where she pointed. I think I saw a fin. I didn't see the woman—you know, the missing one."

"The woman yelling was certain she saw the shark?"

"She was making such a racket, everyone got out of the water because of her screams."

He couldn't tell her much else. She ended the call and then lay down on the bed. First thing in the morning she would find out about renting a car. She'd visit the shop where Gail Boyce worked and then find the local witness, Kimo Alonzo, to talk to him. Would that help anything? She didn't know. All she knew was that she had to try.

✦

Ben returned to his room, still thinking about Elaine Jensen being hit by a car. The only way he could find out exactly what had happened to her was to ask her, and he didn't want to do that. It might be possible to find out what kind of vehicle Crystal Benton had rented, but his hunch was so flimsy. Did Benton even know Detective Jensen?

Was it possible to be too suspicious of someone?

No, not someone like Benton.

Fatigue hit Ben at that moment, and he shut down his computer and left his room to get something to eat at one of the many restaurants in the resort. He needed to wind down, stop his mind from churning, and get some rest. Once back in his room, sleep came quickly.

The next morning Ben woke up feeling somewhat rested. As early as he could he went downstairs to take a swim in the huge Hilton pool before it filled with families and kids. Then he grabbed a coffee and a breakfast sandwich to take back to the room and eat while he reviewed everything anew.

The incident with Jensen and the car still weighed heavily on him. He tried to put it out of his mind and return to the original problem:

the shark attack. He read over the police report he'd received from Yamada. Specifically, the witnesses listed. He wanted to reinterview everyone he could. A total of three people were listed as witnesses, one resided in Washington and another two were local. He decided to visit the local witnesses first and then call the out-of-town witness later.

He called Mark to update him and got his voicemail. After that, he finished his breakfast, then showered and changed for the day.

When he left the hotel, he drove to the Queens' shops first. There, according to the report, a woman by the name of Gail Boyce worked. She was the main police witness the day of the attack. Queens' Marketplace was an open shopping area with a large market, several restaurants, and many specialty shops. Boyce had told police that she was employed at a small shop that sold locally made items. He found the shop easily enough and was told that Gail's shift started later in the afternoon.

He continued to the residence of the second local witness, in Waikoloa Village, about six miles away. Kimo Alonzo lived in a cluster of condos near a golf course. Ben knocked on the door, hoping Alonzo was home and not at work.

The door opened and a man, face scrunched with suspicion, peered out. "Yeah?"

"Mr. Alonzo?"

"Who's asking?"

"I'm an FBI agent"—Ben held up his ID—"investigating the incident the other day, the shark attack. I just wanted to go over Mr. Alonzo's statement. It concerns an insurance claim."

The man relaxed visibly, opened the door wider, and leaned against the door frame. "I'm Kimo. What do you want to know?"

"Did you see the shark?"

He shrugged. "Maybe. I heard the lady scream. I looked out into the water. I saw something. I was there with my cousins. I was more interested in getting them out of the water."

"Did you see the woman who disappeared?"

He shook his head. "The woman who saw the shark, she was hysterical. I was afraid she'd have a heart attack. She got most of my attention. So much noise she made. I kept an eye on her. I'm training to be an EMT. I tried to calm her down."

"Did you see the man who said his wife was gone?"

Kimo nodded. "I called 911 for him. He didn't seem to know what to do."

Ben hadn't seen that tidbit mentioned. He'd assumed Moffit called the police.

"Did you see blood or anything?"

"Nah."

"Is there anything you can tell me that maybe you remembered after you spoke to the police?"

Alonzo thought for a moment. "Something weird, but it was later, after the police came."

"What happened?"

"The lady who screamed, and the guy, the husband, it almost seemed like they knew each other. They stood close for a minute and then separated to talk to the cops."

It was Ben's turn to pause. "After the police came? Before the search?"

"Yeah, I was leaving with the kids. They didn't want to leave; they wanted to see everything. I made them go. I saw those two, and they were going to hug."

"Maybe one stranger comforting another stranger?"

He shrugged and rolled his eyes.

"Can you describe the woman?"

"A tourist. Pale skin, dark reddish-brown hair to her shoulders, tall but not quite as tall as me. I'm six feet. She wasn't really dressed for the beach. She had white shorts on and a flowery blouse."

"Anything else?"

Kimo thought for a minute, then shook his head.

"Thanks for your help."

"FBI? Was the attack a scam?"

"I don't know. I'm just asking questions. If you remember anything else, tell the police, okay?"

"Yeah."

Ben pondered what Kimo had told him. He stopped at his car, stunned, when a realization hit. Kimo had described Crystal Benton. Though her hair was not reddish, it was brown. Ben realized what was off about Benton when he saw her in the hotel. There had been a reddish tint to her normally dark hair. And the cut was shorter than normal.

Evangeline Moffit had reddish-brown hair. Heart rate spiking, Ben hurried back to the hotel. He needed to pull up some photos and make some comparisons.

CHAPTER 16

At the last minute, Ben decided to stop back at Gail Boyce's place of employment. He needed to talk to her. Was it possible she could pass for Crystal Benton? The more he thought about Evangeline and Benton, he could see that there was a fleeting resemblance, though Evangeline struck him as soft and feminine while Benton had an aura of hardness about her. He drove back down to the Queens' shops, hoping that Boyce was at work now. He was in luck.

"She's in the back helping those people." The clerk pointed to an elderly tourist couple.

Ben walked down the aisle stuffed full of artwork and knick-knacks. Three people were in the back, but Ben frowned and stopped before he reached them.

The person helping the tourist couple did not resemble the person Kimo Alonzo had described. The couple found what they wanted, and the woman he guessed was Gail Boyce turned to face him.

"Can I help you?"

Ben stared, the woman before him was short and round with multicolored hair, lines of pink and blue and orange. "I was looking for Gail Boyce."

"That's me. How can I help you?"

"Were you down at the beach last Friday, when the shark attack happened?"

She frowned. "No, I don't do the beach. Skin cancer, you know. Why would you ask me that question?"

"Someone used your name on the police report written about the missing person, saying you were the first person who saw the shark."

The woman's eyes narrowed, clearly upset at this information. "Why would someone do that?"

"Good question."

✦

Disturbed by this incongruity, Ben left the shop to return to his hotel. His phone buzzed. Mark calling. Ben answered and filled him in on the investigation so far. When he finished, Mark was quiet for a moment.

"The witness gave a fake name, and you think she really was Crystal Benton?"

"I do. I know Benton is here. I saw her. Can you check flight logs for me, find out when she got here and if she is still on the island? And there's something else." He explained to Mark about Elaine Jensen being hit by a car.

"How does that tie into anything? I'm not making the connection."

Ben was at a loss; he couldn't make a factual connection either. "I'm just throwing it out there."

"Back to Benton and Moffit. Are you thinking they murdered his wife?"

"I haven't gotten there yet, but I fear that is where the path leads. You must admit, it all appears suspicious. According to the police report, the Moffits arrived on island on Wednesday, and Friday morning Evangeline Moffit disappears, presumably eaten by a shark. It might have been Crystal Benton who got everyone on the beach thinking shark."

"Still no sign of the body?"

"No. The search is over."

"Hmm. I'll check the flight logs and get back to you as soon as I can."

"Do you want me to tell the police here what I've found?"

"I think we're obligated. But wait until I can confirm the flight logs."

Ben ended the call and continued to his hotel room.

✦

Lainie forced herself to eat something downstairs at a coffee bar. She really had no appetite but knew she'd eventually feel the calorie deficit. The coffee was good, and she downed one large as she picked at a bagel sandwich and then ordered a refill to drink while she went to pick up a rental car.

Lainie had an Uber take her to the airport to get the car. Driving back to the resort, she stopped at the Queens' shops to talk to one of the witnesses of the attack. Gail Boyce had seen the shark. Maybe she was the last person to see Evie alive. The thought gave Lainie pause. The loss of Evie drained Lainie. She still could not accept that her sister was gone. Taking a deep breath, she exited her car and walked toward the store.

A woman with multicolored hair stood behind the cash register.

"Excuse me, I'm looking for Gail Boyce."

The woman frowned. "You're not here about that shark attack, are you?"

"Ah, yeah. Is Ms. Boyce here?"

"I'm Gail Boyce and I was not on the beach that day. Who are you anyway?" The woman's hostility took Lainie by surprise.

"Detective Lainie Jensen." She showed the woman her ID. Why was she so upset?

"That's not a Hawaii ID."

"No, it's not. But the missing woman is my sister, so the detectives here gave me some leeway."

The woman's demeanor softened. "Oh, I'm sorry. But some guy was just here asking me if I was at the beach when the shark attack happened. I don't go to the beach."

"Some guy? A police officer?"

She shook her head, clearly frustrated. "I don't know, it caught me off balance, I didn't ask. And now here you are. Am I in danger?"

"I don't believe so. Someone, claiming to be you, was on the beach yelling shark that day. I got your information from the police report."

"Someone with the same name? It wasn't me."

Lainie showed her what she'd put in the notes app on her phone. "Is this your information?"

Profound confusion settled on the woman's face as her brow creased. "Well, it's the phone number and address here. And my home address." Her face scrunched into an irritated frown. "I don't go to the beach. Why is someone impersonating me?"

Lainie was at a loss. Why indeed? "I'm not sure. You might know the woman. I'll pull up the newsclip where I believe she's the one pointing to where the shark was."

Lainie took a few minutes to find the newsclip on her phone, then she showed it to Boyce.

The woman squinted as she watched. "She doesn't look at the camera. I just can't place the voice."

"Maybe you know her?"

"I'm not sure about that. Why would she give the police my name and address?"

Lainie's shoulders tightened with stress. What was going on?

"I'd like to know the answer to that as well. I'll let Detective Yamada know that someone was lying that day and pretending to be you. Sorry to have bothered you."

"And I'm sorry about your sister."

✦

Was Kimo Alonzo fake as well? Lainie thought back to her time in uniform, taking down witness information. Generally, you trusted witnesses. They weren't suspects—usually. And if they were describing a shark attack, there was no crime involved. An officer would have no reason on the face of it to doubt a person who was ostensibly trying to be a helpful witness.

The woman was at the beach—Lainie could see the scenario in her mind's eye. *"I'm sorry, Officer. I don't have my ID. But I can give you my information."*

He'd write it all down, and it would be up to the detectives to recontact if needed.

The officer trusted that the woman was not lying. After all, it was a local address: easy enough to check. If she intentionally misidentified herself, it was a good bet she was long gone. She'd have to be in case there was any follow-up, like Lainie was doing.

Hopefully, Alonzo was the real deal. His residence was about six or seven miles up the hill from the resort where Lainie was staying. It was late afternoon, and no one answered her knock.

She stepped back and studied the area. Alonzo lived in a large, spread-out condo complex. She heard kids playing behind the condo unit. As she walked toward the back, she saw a golf course there and kids kicking a soccer ball around on the fairway.

There was a hole in the hedges between the condo and the course, and she stepped through it. Lainie guessed golf was done for the day. There was one adult who was coaching the kids. A tall guy she recognized from the newsclip.

Walking toward him, she called out, "Kimo Alonzo?"

He'd just caught the soccer ball. He turned toward her, bouncing the ball in his hands. "Who's asking?"

"My name is Lainie Jensen. You were at the beach the other day when the woman went missing."

He rolled his eyes, tossed the ball into the air, then kicked it across the course, causing the kids to scream and all run after it.

"What do you want to know about it? I already told that other guy everything."

"What other guy?"

"There was a guy here earlier, asking about what I saw."

"A police officer?"

"No. His ID said he was FBI. He was investigating an insurance claim."

"Insurance?" That stopped Lainie cold. The implications were dark.

"You don't work with him?"

She shook her head. "The missing woman is my sister."

"Oh." He nodded once. "I'm sorry."

"What was this guy's name?"

"Ah, I don't remember. I only saw his ID for a moment. I asked if the whole thing was fraud, and he said he was just asking questions."

"Do you think it was a fraud?"

"Ma'am, I don't know. That day I thought maybe there had been a shark, but in hindsight, maybe I just saw what the woman wanted me to see."

"What woman?"

"The woman screaming shark. She was so loud she had everyone staring out at the ocean. That's what I told the FBI guy. It seemed like she knew the guy, ah, you know. I guess your brother-in-law. Well, I got the impression that they knew each other well."

The kids were back with the soccer ball, and Lainie found herself with a lot of questions, yet at a loss for words.

FBI?

Insurance?

Stan knew the woman yelling shark?

"Were they friends?"

"Ah." He gave a tilt of his head. "They seemed to be a whole lot more than friends."

CHAPTER 17

Deeply disturbed by what she'd heard from the two witnesses, Lainie called Detective Yamada as soon as she returned to her car. She shared with him what she'd learned.

"I'll speak to the officers who recorded the witness information."

"Did Stan say anything to you about a life insurance policy? Was that in the scope of your investigation?"

"No. As I told the agent when I spoke to him initially, we had no reason to doubt Mr. Moffit's version of events. Now, I'm not so sure."

"Agent? Have you spoken to one?"

"Yes. One arrived on the island yesterday."

"What's his name? Where is he? I'd like to talk to him."

"I have his name here somewhere. Benjamin Isaacs. If he's still here, I believe he's staying at the same hotel you are."

Lainie nearly dropped the phone. "I'll find him." Anger flared and she felt as if she'd just been hit by a Taser. What was he doing here, of all places?

She disconnected, her heart rate pounding. What did a shark attack have to do with the FBI and Ben Isaacs? Why was he here investigating her sister's disappearance? What did any of this have to do with Dallas Vine?

She checked the time and then called her boss.

"Lainie, I'm so sorry about your sister. Is there any good news from the search?"

"No, ah, they stopped searching."

"Oh, wow, um, no hurry to get back. Take as much time as you need. What can I do for you?"

"I have a couple of questions. Remember that Fed who came and took Hank Bucshon away from us?"

"I do."

"His name was Ben Isaacs, correct?"

"I believe so. What does this have to do with your sister?"

"That's what I'm trying to figure out. There's an agent here poking into my sister's disappearance. His name is Ben Isaacs."

"Hmm, that is odd. As far as I know, shark attacks are not federal crimes. Do you want me to investigate?"

"Please. I'll try to find this guy and ask what's going on."

✦

Back at his computer, Ben revisited everything he had on Crystal Benton and Evangeline Moffit. He thought back to when he'd met with Stan's wife. She was tall, athletic, not unlike her sister. Her deep-red hair was long enough to be tied back. Benton was the same height and general build, her light-brown hair was shoulder length, a bit wavy, and parted in the middle. She wasn't as athletic or as toned as Moffit.

He put the headshots of both women side by side on his screen. There was a facial resemblance, though not a strong cheekbone match. But when he pulled up copies of their driver's licenses, it got stronger.

If he imagined Benton with reddish hair, styled like Moffit's, the resemblance was closer. If Benton did pretend to be Moffit, he doubted the TSA agent at security would have questioned her ID.

His phone buzzed. It was Mark. "What did you find?"

"There is no record of Crystal Benton flying to Hawaii. We checked from two weeks back through today. I also checked the last couple of days to see if she showed up on a return trip to the mainland. I didn't find her name."

"She must be using an assumed name. The trouble is, we don't have any known aliases listed in the file, do we?"

"No. What have you found?"

"Despite what you just told me, I think Benton flew here with Moffit. I don't think Evangeline was ever here."

"There is a record of Evangeline and Stan Moffit flying to the island. Do you think something happened to Evangeline on the mainland and the shark attack is a cover-up?"

"I think Benton impersonated Evangeline on the flight, and then they hatched an insurance scam. For some reason they thought a shark attack was a plausible way to cover up murder."

There, he said it. Ben believed that Evangeline Moffit was dead.

As the thought worked its way through his psyche, Ben felt some guilt ease. This had nothing to do with Vine or the fact that Ben had talked to Evangeline. This was much baser—it was all about adultery and greed.

"You're sure that Evangeline Moffit is dead?"

Ben remembered the sweet, calm person who had met him for coffee. "I can't imagine her being part of a scam like this."

"I agree. But for Benton to pull this off, she'd have to defeat facial recognition. That is not easy."

"I'd bet my pension that she found a way."

Mark sighed and said nothing for a minute. "Logs indicate Moffit caught a flight back to the mainland. He should be back in Long Beach anytime now," Mark said finally. "Is Crystal Benton still there?"

"I haven't seen her lately. I doubt she's staying under her name, but I'll check. Are you going to pick Moffit up?"

"Not sure we have enough yet. We need to find Benton and we need a body. I'll talk to LBPD."

"I'll look for Benton here. We'll talk later." Ben put down his cell phone and picked up the hotel phone. He asked to be put through to Crystal Benton's room.

"I'm sorry. No one here by that name."

She had been here; he knew that. Probably registered with Moffit. But would she still be staying in that room since they started the shark attack story?

Just to be sure, he called back and asked for Stan's Moffit's room.

"Mr. Moffit has checked out."

Ben realized that for Benton, all it would take was her return to the room for people to have questions. No, they must have had two rooms from the beginning.

He remembered Yamada telling him that Detective Jensen doubted the story Stan Moffit gave to police. So she was suspicious. If Benton was involved with Moffit, and Moffit told her that his sister-in-law didn't believe his story, then it was not a stretch to think Benton saw Jensen's being here as something of a threat. There were a lot of ifs, but this case was exploding right now, and his gut told him that his hunch was spot-on.

Knowing that Benton was here and concealing her identity gave his theory that she had tried to run over Jensen some credence.

Ben hung up and stood to pace the room. Benton could still be here registered under an assumed name. Mark was right: They needed more evidence. And this wasn't his case. It needed to go to Long Beach because that was most likely where whatever happened to Evangeline occurred.

What a mess. Efren was missing still, and now an innocent woman was likely dead. And they were no closer to arresting their initial target—Vine.

The hotel phone rang. Ben picked it up. "Hello?"

"Agent Ben Isaacs?"

"Speaking."

"What on earth does my sister being missing have to do with you?"

CHAPTER 18

"When the story hit about your sister, my boss asked me to come here and verify what happened."

"Why?"

"It's complicated. Why don't you come to my room? I'll explain what I can."

She didn't say anything for a few seconds. "What's your room number?"

Ben told her.

"I'm on my way."

He opened the door a few minutes later to an angry and frustrated Elaine Jensen. Her jaw was tight, and an angry red scrape blazed across it. He guessed that was from the car incident. She also looked as if she hadn't slept in a while, and her hazel-green eyes were on fire.

"Please, Detective Jensen, come in."

She walked past him and stopped. He stepped around her and pointed to the armchair he'd pulled up next to the desk. "Have a seat."

She sat, arms folded tightly around her chest.

Ben took his own seat at the hotel desk and turned his laptop to face her. "I'll start from the beginning. I'm sharing this information with you with the understanding you will not share anything with anyone else, not even your partner."

He paused and Jensen nodded.

"Your brother-in-law has been in the background of a larger multistate investigation. One of our targets is Dallas Vine."

She eyes widened. "What on earth could Stan have to do with Dallas Vine?"

"Vine owns the car wash he manages. Every business associate or employee of Vine is on the periphery of our investigation."

Her jaw dropped. There was no hiding the surprise on her face. "Stan works for Vine? How did I not know that?"

Ben nodded. "Vine's ownership is hidden under layers of dummy corporations. Most of his more lucrative endeavors are held under the banner of Quartz Enterprises. Stan was not being investigated for any specific reason, but when his name came up in the news and we saw the life insurance policy, the situation needed to be checked out."

"What kind of life insurance policy?"

"Four million. Moffit filed to receive the proceeds about eight hours after your sister supposedly went missing."

He watched as a cascade of emotions crossed her face—surprise, disbelief, anger. She stood and paced.

"I knew something was off here." She took a breath and seemed to be gathering herself. "It's painful to go there, to think about what might have happened. I've studied so many cold cases like this . . ." She faced him, hands on her hips. "What are you saying did happen?"

"I have a theory but no evidence." He brought up the picture of Crystal Benton on his laptop. "Do you know this woman?"

Jensen stepped forward and peered down at the screen. "No, should I?"

"Not really. Her name is Crystal Benton. She's Vine's right-hand person. I saw her in the hotel lobby yesterday. And she fits the description of the woman who yelled shark when your sister allegedly went missing. I also think she might have been driving the Jeep that hit you yesterday."

Surprise again flashed across her face. "How did you know about that?"

He hiked up a shoulder. "I drove by right after. Security was talking to you. I saw that you were scraped up a bit. I would have stopped if I thought you needed help, but I hadn't put everything together yet."

She nodded. "The kids said the car headed straight toward me. I've done my best to convince myself it was simply an accident. Is Benton involved with Stan?"

"I'm leaning that way."

Jensen leaned forward and peered closer at the picture. "She could be that woman from the newsclip, yes. I didn't have a good view of the Jeep's driver."

"Benton is at the car wash often. When I saw her in the lobby, she'd added red highlights to her hair." He pulled up the two driver's license comparisons.

Jensen studied them. "She almost looks like my sister."

"I think she took advantage of that and flew here to masquerade as your sister."

CHAPTER 19

Evie was never in Hawaii.

Lainie got back to her room, but she wasn't sure how. Her mind reeled as if she were on the deck of a ship pitching in stormy seas. Her body vibrated with shock as she tried to process everything Isaacs had told her.

Stan and this Benton woman had likely killed Evie in California, then come here to stage the shark hoax.

To say that Ben's theory stunned her was an understatement. She felt flattened, as flat as Wile E. Coyote when the large anvil crashed down on him. She didn't know what to do with the information.

How could she tell her parents?

What had happened to Evie and where was her body now?

It was late. She wanted to call her boss but thought it was better to wait until the morning. In reality, she'd lost her voice. She didn't know how to articulate what she'd heard to someone else yet. Maybe by morning she'd know what to tell her family. Her nephews had lost their mother. Would they understand when it was explained to them that in all probability their father did it?

"What a nightmare," Lainie muttered.

The hotel phone rang, startling her. Everyone she knew would call her on her cell. This could only be Isaacs. More bad news?

After taking a second to gather her thoughts, Lainie answered. "Yeah?"

"It's Ben. How are you holding up? You were quite shell-shocked when you left."

Lainie sat on the bed, waiting a beat before answering. "I feel like I fell into an alternate universe. What is real and what is fake? Since you're here and you've discovered this fraud, what will the Bureau do about it?"

"First and foremost, try to find Crystal Benton. I don't think she's still here. I'm flying to California in the morning. I'll know more when I'm back in the office and I'm briefed on the latest updates."

"Is Benton likely to give you any answers?"

"I doubt it. Only if we have some leverage. It would be nice if . . ." He stopped and it took Lainie a second to realize why.

"You were going to say, *'if we had a body.'*"

"I was, I'm sorry. But I could also be speaking about my partner. I have no idea where Efren is or what happened to him."

Lainie pinched the bridge of her nose. "I want to know where Evie is as well. I never liked Stan, but I always thought he was harmless, kind of a doofus. I never imagined he would be so evil and cold."

"Hmm, how long will you be staying in Hawaii?"

"I guess I should go back tomorrow as well. There is nothing left for me to do here."

"Would you like to meet early for coffee? Maybe share a ride to the airport?"

Lainie thought for a moment. Right now she was exhausted, all played out. All she wanted to do was sleep. She hoped she'd feel better in the morning, and she did want to know more about the FBI investigation into Vine as well as the search for Benton. But her heart was so very heavy. "What time is your flight?"

"I have to be to the airport at ten."

She'd have to get up early and think about the day. "I'm too tired to think about the morning. And I don't have a flight yet. Maybe I'll touch base with you in Long Beach."

"I understand. Take care, Detective Jensen. I'm very sorry for your loss."

Lainie placed the phone back in its cradle and sat on the bed. She opened the drawer by the bedside, hoping there was a Bible inside. She knew hotels were moving away from keeping Bibles in the rooms, but she hoped one had survived here. Her hope was rewarded.

Lainie took the book out and opened it to the Psalms. She rubbed her forehead with her fingertips and tried to remember the verses that used to provide her the most comfort. Psalm 23 came to mind, and she turned there.

I need to move back to God. I want to feel the peace that I once did.

"'The Lord is my shepherd; I shall not want . . .'" The words rolled over her, not providing the comfort she needed. Snatches of a verse about God being with you in fire and water came to mind, but for the life of her she couldn't remember where in Psalms it was, or if it was even a psalm.

Frowning and squinting tired eyes, she searched the back of the book for words related to what she remembered. After thumbing through several references to *fire* and *water*, she found the verse. It was in Isaiah.

"'When you pass through the waters, I will be with you; and through the rivers, they shall not overwhelm you; when you walk through fire you shall not be burned, and the flame shall not consume you. For I am the Lord your God.'"

Lainie read the verse over and over as tears filled her eyes again.

"Oh, Lord," she prayed. "The river is overflowing me, and the fire is scorching my heels. Please forgive my backsliding, my lack of faith. I have no strength of my own to get through this. I am broken and weak, please keep this from overwhelming me."

She lay back on the bed, tears rolling down her cheeks. The Bible fell from her hands, and she drifted off to sleep.

CHAPTER 20

When Lainie woke up, she felt a tad better. At least she could think about booking a flight home. Online, the earliest flight she could find didn't leave until three thirty in the afternoon. She had to check out by eleven. Halfway through her shower, she made the decision to head to the airport and see if there were any earlier flights she could maybe get on as a standby passenger.

She called her parents to tell them she was on the way home but said nothing about the new developments in the case. She couldn't tell them everything. Dread still shredded her soul when she thought about telling them what she could; intuition said it was better to do that in person.

"How are the boys doing?" Lainie asked her mom.

"They hurt, and they don't understand. Stan's doing the best he can. He's been trying to sort through insurance and trying to find someone to manage his business while he deals with everything. The boys are staying with us for the time being."

Lainie was glad to hear that. "He's not there now?"

"He had to go to work."

"What did he tell them?"

"What *could* he tell them? He explained about the shark." Mom's voice broke. "I'm glad you're coming home."

Lainie heard the pain in her mother's voice and almost lost it.

She bit her tongue to keep from saying something she shouldn't. Her mom and dad would be traumatized all over again when they found out what Stan had really done. How on earth could she break it to them? Certainly not over the phone.

"Right now, my plane doesn't take off until three thirty. I'll text you if I get an earlier flight."

"Okay. Love you, Lainie."

"Love you too, Mom."

Lainie packed quickly. She hadn't brought much and checked out. She still felt out of sorts but could sense some normalcy returning to her thinking. She called Lieutenant Lopez from the car on her way to Kona Airport and told her what she knew so far.

"The Feds contacted the chief earlier," LT told her. "The case is going to Bobby Shea and Hugh Collins. They will conference with cops in Hawaii later today."

"Wow, the ball is already rolling."

"Of course it is. If we're discussing a possible murder, the sooner we get the suspect in custody, the better. So sorry this has happened to your family, Lainie. I remember hearing your sister sing at the big beach baptism last summer. She had a beautiful voice."

Lainie caught her breath. She remembered that as well. It was the last big Christian event she'd attended. She'd only stayed for the music, then left when the baptisms started.

She swallowed hard. "Yeah, she did."

"No rush to come back to work, Lainie. You do what you need to do."

Lainie thanked her as she pulled into the rental car drop-off.

Once in the terminal, Lainie read the list of planes heading to Southern California. Three flights were leaving before her scheduled flight. She asked the gate attendant if there was any possibility of getting on an earlier flight.

"Possibly, the next departure is eleven forty-five. Boarding just began." She took Lainie's name and information and said she would be paged after boarding was complete if there was a spot on the flight for her. On the monitor Lainie saw that three other people were ahead of her on standby. She was not optimistic, but it was what it was.

Since she hadn't eaten breakfast yet, Lainie went to the small airport snack shop to get something to eat while she waited.

She'd eaten half of a ham-and-cheese sandwich when she heard her name being paged. Rushing out of the little shop, Lainie hurried to the gate. Lainie was happy to know that she didn't have to hang out at the airport until three thirty.

With her one carry-on bag, Lainie was the last person to board. Hers was a middle seat, but beggars couldn't be choosers. Lainie watched the numbers for seat 19E. When she found it, the man in the aisle seat stood, and she was face-to-face with Ben Isaacs.

"Detective Jensen, we meet again."

"Ah, yeah." She pulled her Kindle from her bag, found a place to shove her carry-on above her seat, then slid into her spot. After fastening her seat belt, she quickly typed out a text to her mother with her new ETA, then set her phone on airplane mode.

Isaacs took his seat and strapped in.

Because all it did was remind her that her sister had been murdered, Lainie did not relish spending five hours with the FBI agent, but she had absolutely no choice in the matter.

CHAPTER 21

Ben couldn't believe his good fortune when Detective Jensen appeared on the plane. He'd prayed for her the night before, and after saying amen, he had not been able to get her off his mind. Her tenacity in the face of the crushing loss of her sister touched him to his core. She had not fallen apart. She was engaged and thinking like a cop. Her strength and composure attracted him. On the whole, the woman intrigued him on many levels.

After the flight crew announcements and the emergency procedure demonstration, he turned to Jensen. "How are you doing today?" After the question was out of his mouth, he winced inside. *Wow, that was as smooth as sandpaper!* Thankfully, she didn't seem put off.

"I'm glad to be heading home. I think I got the last seat on this flight. Any luck finding Crystal Benton?"

"Not on the island. We're guessing she's back in Long Beach by now. Just like your brother-in-law."

At first, Ben felt like Jensen wanted to stay quiet. Her stiff posture and the way she played with her Kindle made him think she was struggling with an inner demon. Or maybe she simply wanted to read. He would not be the one to bug her. If she wanted to engage in conversation, he would.

She fidgeted for a few moments. "How long has the Bureau been investigating Dallas Vine?"

"The larger aspect of the investigation, in other states, has been ongoing for over a year. My partner and I were assigned to the Long Beach part about six months ago. Vine has proved himself slippery."

"I think that I know that better than anyone. I'm certain he murdered Daphne Sparks fifteen years ago, but no one could prove it then. Are you guys poking into that case at all?"

Ben sighed. "No. The scope of the multistate investigation concerns federal crimes, not local ones. The Sparks case is cold and up to LBPD to solve. I'm sorry it's not a priority for us."

"I hate to hear that. I still think about that poor woman."

Was there a catch in her voice?

"She was only twenty-three years old, well-liked, and trying to make a life for herself when she was murdered. She should never be forgotten."

"She's not forgotten . . ." Ben felt her pain.

"But not a priority." She turned to face him, her voice vibrating with hurt. "Her mother broke down at the first press conference, when detectives asked for the public's help in solving the case. She had to be hospitalized, and she never recovered. She died shortly thereafter. It broke my heart then, and it continues . . ." Jensen paused, turned away, and swallowed. "They both deserve justice."

"I confess I don't know as much about that case as I should. What can you tell me?"

She leaned back in her seat and closed her eyes. "It's a stone-cold case, but it still twists my gut in knots. Daphne had just moved to Long Beach for work. She was hired down at the harbor as an office manager. Back then, Vine was heavily involved with the longshoremen's union and active in the harbor. That's where I think he met her."

"I don't recall any connection between the two of them noted in the reports."

"No one admitted to a connection. But there was evidence that Vine often visited the building where Daphne worked. He was involved in an import-export business at the time. For him to say that he never saw or interacted with Daphne in the time she worked there defies logic."

"Sounds like you have a theory."

Her whole countenance perked up. Ben bet that thinking about something other than her sister was therapeutic.

"There used to be a bar on the west side of Long Beach, the Barn. A lot of people from the port and the harbor offices frequented the bar. We discovered that that was where Vine was drinking the night I arrested him. He'd been kicked out at closing time, or so they said."

"You don't think so?"

She shook her head. "Closing time was two a.m. I stopped him around six thirty a.m. If they kicked him out at two, where was he between then and six thirty? He was drunk when I stopped him. Blood alcohol was .20."

"Was that time ever accounted for?"

"No. In court paperwork he claimed to be driving home from the Barn when I stopped him. He never had to explain further. He had no record at the time, hired good lawyers, and got a sweet plea deal. You know he killed another man about five years before Daphne?"

"I do. He was acquitted; the jury saw it as self-defense."

"They got it wrong," she said through clenched teeth.

"Maybe, but that case never would have been mentioned, even if Sparks's case had gone to trial."

"I know you're right. It still cements the idea in my mind that he is a killer."

"So, back to the night Sparks was killed. Either the bar let him stay there and drink, long after it was legal, or Vine was doing something else."

"I think he killed Daphne and was on the way to dump her body. She'd been deceased a couple of hours at least when I stopped him, and most of her blood volume was gone—she bled and died somewhere else, not in the back of that car. I think . . ."

"Sounds like a solid take," Ben said.

"My theory got panned by the homicide detectives."

"Then I want to hear it."

Jensen took a deep breath. "Vine was in the middle of remodeling a property he owned very near to where I stopped him. The place had been taken down to the studs, and they were getting ready to pour the foundation for an addition. I think he was going to encase her body in the concrete foundation at that property. The detectives at the time thought that I watched too many TV crime shows."

Ben sat back as he considered her theory. "I know enough about Vine that I would not dismiss that idea out of hand. Did anyone put Sparks with him at the Barn that night?"

"Not that night, but she often went to the bar—never by herself—always with others from her office. She was not interested in dating; she liked to socialize in a group. I think she was killed in the alley behind the Barn. Her clothing had grime consistent with substances there."

"Was her blood found there?"

"No. By the time investigators checked it out, it had been power washed."

Ben raised an eyebrow. "No one saw anything fishy in that?"

"Yeah, but there was no way to prove he'd done it to destroy evidence. It was two days after her body was recovered before detectives went to the bar. The owner said complaints about rats prompted the cleanup."

"Were there any other suspects besides Vine?"

"Two men she worked with were questioned, but they both had solid alibis."

"So why do you believe that Vine and Sparks knew each other somehow?" He tried not to sound skeptical but feared it came out that way.

"She kept the books for various entities that operated in the harbor, several that Vine interacted with. She was visible, very pretty, and it was only logical that she interacted with him at some point."

"So, if they knew each other, was it a case of him not handling rejection?"

"I think she caught on to something illegal he was involved in. Remember, Vine was just starting out in his career of crime. Numerous rumors flew around down there about illegal shipments, payoffs, and grafts. After Daphne's murder, two harbor managers were arrested and convicted of falsifying records and embezzling money. It wasn't long after that Vine divested himself of every business he had in the harbor."

"Did any of the rumors pertain to Vine?"

"No. The only thing we found out about him was that he couldn't handle his liquor. He cultivated a lot of influence in the harbor, spreading money around. It's not a stretch to think he paid people off to tell police the story he wanted told," Jensen said. "The detectives who handled the case were good, but they never found any actionable leads."

The smartest crooks knew how to keep their mouths shut. Ben heard the defeat in her voice, and it broke his heart.

"I'd like to tell you that we can swoop in to arrest him any moment, but losing Efren really set us back."

"Do you think your partner was made?"

The question pierced Ben. "I pray not. Though the longer we don't hear from him, the more that possibility looms."

CHAPTER 22

Lainie found while she talked to Isaacs about Vine, she felt her balance returning. Anything to take her mind off of explaining to her parents what she now believed Stan had done to Evie. Chatting with the agent made the time in the air zoom by. By the time the pilot made the announcement that they were preparing to land, Lainie almost felt like her old self—almost.

"Take care, Detective Jensen," Isaacs said when the plane arrived in Long Beach and stopped at the gate, and he stood to pull his carry-on and then Lainie's down from the overhead bin. "I have to hurry. Got a text my ride is already here."

"Thanks, and it's Lainie." She unbuckled her seat belt but stayed seated for a minute. "I hope the next time we speak it will be about positive developments."

"Count on it, Lainie, and I'm Ben." He turned and headed for the exit.

She stood and let the person in the window seat out before she entered the aisle to disembark the plane. By the time she exited the terminal at baggage claim, she'd lost sight of Isaacs.

Outside baggage claim, she quickly caught sight of her dad's car and waved her arm. He pushed through the traffic, and Lainie hopped in the passenger seat.

"How was the flight?" her father asked as he pulled away from the curb.

"All right, as far as flights go. I'm wiped out emotionally." Lainie took a deep breath. She'd tell her father first about Stan's betrayal. Then they could both break it to the rest of the family.

"We all are glad you're back." He patted her knee.

Lainie gripped his hand. "I have something to tell you, Dad."

Lainie told him everything she knew about the supposed shark attack on her sister. The words flowed out like a waterfall, and he didn't interrupt.

When they reached residential Long Beach, her father pulled over to the curb before they arrived home, then turned to face her. "Do you know what you're saying?" His face was pale, and a muscle in his jaw twitched with tension.

"I do, Dad. And before you say it's just because I don't like Stan, the FBI is all over it. They've already contacted the LBPD. Stan most certainly will be taken in for questioning."

He took several deep breaths. "I can't . . . I can't. This is just too much." Tears pooled in his eyes. "What will we tell the boys? That their father is a monster?"

"The boys are still with you, aren't they? That's what Mom said."

"They are. Stan is planning for a memorial . . ." His voice broke.

"There's another person involved—this woman, Crystal Benton. He's obviously been having an affair with her." Lainie stopped when her father closed his eyes and rested his head on the steering wheel.

"I can hardly take this. It will kill your mother."

Lainie's throat tightened. She agreed and dreaded telling her mother. This nightmare just kept getting worse.

✦

As it turned out, Lainie didn't have to tell her mother. Detective Robert Shea and his partner Hugh Collins pulled up at the same time she and her father arrived at the house. Both men were great investigators. They were an odd couple for sure. Shea resembled the quintessential rumpled detective. Even his freshly pressed suit looked slept in. Collins, on the other hand, was all spit and polish. His nickname was *GQ*. Still, they worked well together and had the highest case-closure rate in homicide. Lainie guessed that they had something to say about Stan.

"Lainie," Shea and Collins approached, and Shea greeted her. "You're back."

"Just got in. What brings you here?"

"We're searching for your brother-in-law. He wasn't at his house or at the car wash."

"I think he went downtown to plan a memorial." Lainie cast a glance at her father, whose face was creased in consternation.

Dad nodded. "He wants to have a memorial for Evie on the *Queen Mary*."

"We planned to pick him up and bring him in for questioning and hopefully get his consent to search. If he refuses, we'll get a judge to sign a warrant to search his home and place of business."

Lainie nodded. This was what she expected. They had enough circumstantial evidence to justify a warrant.

Just then the front door opened, and her mother stepped out. "Jim, Lainie? Why are you standing out here, and who are they?"

"They're detectives, Mom." Lainie swallowed. "Bobby, can you fill my mom in on the latest developments?"

She felt like a coward deferring to him, but this situation was too close. The news about Stan would destroy her mom, and Lainie couldn't be the one to do that.

CHAPTER 23

Watching Archie and her mother try to comprehend what everyone believed Stan had done was painful. Lainie sat in the living room with them while Bobby Shea explained the status of Evie's investigation.

She heard some information she didn't know. Gail Boyce had been reinterviewed by the detectives in Hawaii, and they found a connection to Benton. Boyce was shown a picture of Crystal Benton, and it jogged her memory. The woman had been in the store, had chatted with Boyce, been extra friendly, and taken a business card. In fact, during the questioning, Boyce also found her checkbook missing. She rarely wrote checks, so she hadn't noticed when it went missing, but she thought maybe Benton had taken it and that's where she'd gotten her home address.

Lainie thought about that. If it were true, it showed quite a bit of premeditation. However, it probably couldn't be proven unless Benton was caught with the checkbook in her possession.

The best lie was one with a shade of truth in it. When Benton gave the name, it was a real name, a real address, making her story more believable at first blush. She didn't know the lie would be uncovered so quickly.

While Shea laid out the intricacies of the investigation, Lainie's father stayed out in the backyard with the boys. After Bobby finished, Mom turned to her.

"Lainie, I can't believe what I'm hearing. I just can't believe it. You think Stan murdered your sister?"

"Mom, where is she? She didn't die in a shark attack. I don't believe that for a second. I don't know what happened to her. I want to find out."

"Stan has been in this family for seven years. Can you really be certain Evie married such a . . . ?" Her voice trailed off, and tears ran down her face.

Lainie could barely speak. "I'm considering the whole picture. At the very least, Stan has some explaining to do."

Archie stood and ran both hands over his face. "If you find Stan, will you arrest him?" he asked Shea.

"We'll have warrants to search his home and place of business soon, and we want to talk to him."

"Is it possible this woman you mentioned, this Benton, coerced him in some way?"

Lainie held her breath, not surprised her brother would ask such a question. Archie had a soft heart; he always saw the best in people.

"Right now, anything is possible. Our goal is to talk to both Stan and Crystal and find out what exactly happened," Hugh Collins explained.

"Do you know where she is yet?" Lainie asked.

Shea shook his head. "The Feds are trying to track her down." He and Collins left after a few more minutes and asked to be notified if Stan came to the house before they found him.

With moist eyes, Archie touched Lainie's arm. "I don't want to believe Stan could hurt Evie."

"But where is Evie?" Her voice threatened to break—she hated the fact that this was the foremost question. "Why did he lie about the shark attack?"

"This breaks my heart, Lainie. Everything points to a horrible truth." Her mother sniffled and blew her nose. "What are we going to tell the boys?"

Lainie didn't have an answer.

She left shortly after Shea and Collins, feeling as wrung out as a microfiber towel just squeezed tight in a vise. It was late by the time Lainie got home. Tired and emotionally drained, she took a quick shower and then tried to go to sleep.

Her phone rang, and it was Mike. "Hey, partner."

"Are you back in LB?"

"I am. I keep praying I'll wake up and find that the last couple of days were simply a bad dream. Yet the nightmare continues."

"Anything I can do for you?"

"Pray we find out the truth."

"Got it," Mike said. "I talked to Bobby Shea. He's sharp. He'll get to the bottom of things."

"I trust him. I just can't believe this whole situation."

"It's crazy, no doubt."

"Sorry about leaving you with the whole workload," Lainie said.

"Not a problem. Take as much time off as you need. If I can help with anything, let me know."

"Actually, there was one thing. Can you find out what happened to Bucshon?"

"The little wife beater?"

"Yeah, I met the FBI agent who took him away from us. The agent was in Hawaii. He said he didn't get anything they could use from the guy. If you can talk to him—just to find out exactly how close he was to Vine and if he knew Crystal Benton, I'd appreciate it."

"I'll see what I can do."

"Thanks, Mike, I owe you."

"Naw, you'd do the same for me."

Lainie ended the call, thankful for Mike. He'd do a good job if he were able to talk with Bucshon. Thinking about the warrant service that would happen soon, she wanted to be there for it, but that was not appropriate.

Sleep was elusive. She tossed and turned until 6:00 a.m., then got up and went for a run. Lainie lived near California State University, Long Beach, and her course took her around the campus. It was early, not much was going on. Sometimes the route gave her energy because of the bustling campus. Not today. The run was hard, and Lainie felt as if all her energy was sapped.

As she neared home and slowed her pace to cool down, she saw that someone was on her porch. Slowing to a walk, she stood on her tiptoes and breathed a sigh of relief. Sara.

Breathing steady and calm now, Lainie hurried to greet her friend. "What a great surprise."

Sara jumped up for a hug.

"I'm all sweaty," Lainie protested weakly, and accepted the hug because she was so glad to see Sara.

"I don't care. I had to come see how you are doing."

Lainie closed her eyes and relished the embrace from her friend.

After a minute, they sat on the porch.

"I forgot that you were off today," Lainie said.

"I'm working an overtime shift, but it's an afternoon shift so I don't go in until two. You have a lot on your mind. Tell me what's going on."

Lainie shared what was happening with her sister's disappearance.

"Wow. I remember Stan and Evie together. He never seemed like the type to stray. He wasn't as involved with church as Evie, but he was always there, he always supported her."

"Is that what you saw?"

"Yeah. Church was the only place where I interacted with Stan. He seemed proud of her. Evie had a beautiful voice. I heard Stan compliment her more than once."

The comment set Lainie back on her heels. "I always thought Stan was a jerk. I don't think I've ever heard him compliment Evie."

"To me, they were a nice couple. I certainly never saw strife. Did Evie tell you there were problems in her marriage?" Sara asked.

"No. Evie always defended Stan if I made any comments. She didn't nag him or complain. She wasn't that way; she wasn't a complainer. The only time she would ask for help was for something she didn't think she could handle or something that needed prayer. I guess I got to a place where Evie didn't come to me to ask for prayer."

"You never had an inkling?"

Lainie shrugged. "I didn't like Stan when they were dating. He just struck me as fake, not dangerous. By the time they got married, I wasn't going to church regularly." Frustration built and Lainie tightened her fists and hit them together.

"I can't believe I moved so far away. Evie and I used to be so close. I think I only saw her a couple of times a year after the twins were born. She called me, you know." Lainie stopped as a lump formed in her throat.

"I told you, don't beat yourself up. When did she call?"

Lainie nodded and cleared her throat. "A few days before I got the call from Stan about the shark hoax. She didn't leave a message. Oh, how I wish I had called her back right away. Maybe she would have told me something important—"

"Lainie, you can't let the past drag you down. It can't be changed. You know that. You need to move forward. I want to help. What can I do?"

"I'm not sure. I guess it depends on what happens when they find Stan. When we find out what really happened to Evie. You can pray."

"Count on it."

CHAPTER 24

"Efren's car has been located." Mark met Ben the minute he walked through the FBI field office door the day after returning from Hawaii. The night before, he'd heard there were no new developments. He'd fallen asleep wondering what the new day would bring. Now he knew. Things had obviously changed overnight.

Coffee in hand, Ben's heart nearly stopped at the expression on Mark's face.

"Where?"

"Smashed up in a desolate part of Joshua Tree. On BLM land. It's remote, and it has likely been there a few days."

Ben mentally repeated the information, trying to process what it could mean.

"There was no sign of Efren. In fact, the car was completely stripped. The agent who went out there to recover the car is not optimistic any evidence survived."

Ben looked from Mark to the investigation board. Pasted there was a photo of Efren's car and the information regarding who had found it and when. This was bad. Their relationship flashed through his thoughts. Efren was a partner and a friend. Efren's wife, Candy, hadn't wanted him to go undercover. Ben had helped to talk her into it.

"He'll be okay. He's smart, and we'll all be backing him up."

All of that rang hollow now. "Have you told Candy?"

"I thought I'd leave that to you since you're closer to her than I am."

Ben nodded and said nothing. Mark was right. But it would be difficult to rip the heart right out of his partner's wife.

Mark continued. "The assistant special agent in charge will be here. He wants us to brief him on our investigation while he briefs us on what's happening in other parts of the investigation."

"Will he shut us down?"

"I don't know, Ben. We've messed up. Not only have we lost an agent, but we also barely have anything actionable on our target."

"We were getting there." Ben set his coffee down. Frustration building, he'd been tempted to squeeze the paper cup flat.

"On another front, Long Beach will pick up Stan Moffit. They conferenced with the PD in Hawaii, and both concluded the shark attack was fake."

"Did they get an arrest warrant?"

"Not that they've said. They're planning to bring him in for questioning first. I've asked to talk to him when they do. Maybe he can tell us something about Efren. Everything is moving fast right now. I doubt you'll have a chance to unwind from Hawaii time."

Ben shrugged. "I'd like to see the car."

"There's nothing to see."

"Humor me. If Efren was in trouble, I know he'd try to find a way to get a message to me."

"It should be in the Long Beach impound yard later today. Right now, let's go over everything we have and get ready to brief the ASAC."

✦

After Sara left, Lainie went inside and started coffee. She itched to call Shea and find out the status of the search, but she restrained herself.

She was halfway through her first cup when her phone rang. "What's up, Shea?"

"A lot. We completed a search of your brother-in-law's residence earlier this morning and waited there quite a while in case he returned home. He did not. After a short break, we served a warrant at his place of business. We still have not located Stan, but we do have a development. We found a body at the car wash—a female."

Lainie went numb. Speech fled.

After a minute of silence, Shea spoke up. "Lainie, you still with me?"

She cleared her throat. "Ah, yeah, any ID on the body?"

"No. No ID. Her purse is gone, Lainie. Do you want to come down here and check her out? The coroner is delayed. There was a multiple-person fatality on the freeway, so we'll be here for a while."

"I'll be right down. I really need to know."

CHAPTER 25

All during the twenty-minute ride to the car wash, Lainie dreaded the moment she would get there. Her thoughts returned to the time she'd spent in the kayak in A-Bay.

I wondered what I would do if I found Evie's body.

Am I facing that scenario now? What if Evie is dead in the car wash?

Before she left home, she'd called Ben. She wanted support, but she didn't want to put her brother or her parents in the position to have to see Evie in death—if this woman was Evie. Though the more Lainie thought about it, it wouldn't make sense that it was Evie. But the mere possibility was enough to rattle her.

Ben answered quickly. "Detec— Lainie, what a surprise. What's on your mind?"

"They found a body at Stan's car wash."

"What?"

"You hadn't heard?"

"No. We haven't been keeping tabs on LBPD's investigation. Do they have an ID?"

"I'm heading there right now. No ID on the body. It's female."

She thought that she heard a sigh of relief.

"Do you mind if I join you there?"

"Not at all."

Lainie wasn't sure how far away Ben was. When she reached Sudsy Place, it took her a minute to get out of the car. Shea had closed the business, so the big roller brushes were immobile, and the normally bustling business was quiet. About half a dozen employees loitered around—some sitting on the small wall that encircled the wash. Some walking around, talking on their phones. They must have arrived thinking the wash would be open for business. Now they were at loose ends.

Suddenly the fear was real that it would be Evie, and that thought made Lainie sick to her stomach. She'd only ingested coffee, and it came dangerously close to coming up again. As she swallowed and took deep breaths, her stomach settled down and she got out on shaky legs.

"Oh, Lord," she breathed a quick prayer, "please keep me standing if this is Evie, please."

She joined Shea, who stood just under the awning before the entrance to the place with lab tech Bryce Parker.

"Glad you could make it," he said. "Here's the deal, Lainie. The wash had been running, the workers you see hanging around said that it was unlocked, so they proceeded with business as usual. None of them went back to the office because they didn't need to. We shut everything down, went inside, and found the body. Coroner is not here yet. No one in your family has heard from Stan?"

"Not that I know of. You think he's on the run now?"

"He might have seen us searching his house, or someone might have told him about the warrants."

"If Stan contacted my folks, they would tell him to talk to you. And they'd tell you. Right now, their big concern is for the boys. Stan has proven himself to be dangerous in their eyes. I would be the last person he'd contact."

Shea nodded. He paused to run a finger between his collar and his neck. "One way or another, he got tipped off. As for the scene in there, it appears as if the woman got here, opened things up, and walked in on someone because the office was trashed. Cameras are placed everywhere, but they were all disabled."

"How long ago?"

"Within the last twelve hours."

Lainie frowned as her nerves mellowed and her shoulders relaxed. "That doesn't make sense, not if it's Evie. Stan was just in Hawaii telling everyone that she was killed by a shark four days ago. If she were here and alive the whole time, surely she would have tried to contact someone."

Bryce shrugged. "I can't give an exact TOD, coroner will have to, but whoever she is, she hasn't been dead long." He handed her a pair of booties and gloves.

Another car pulled up.

"Who is this?" Shea asked.

"FBI Agent Isaacs. I called him. He's the one who noticed everything was off in Hawaii. I just thought he should be here."

"Good," Shea said. "The Feds have been helpful. They briefed us on their investigation."

While Lainie put on the booties and gloves, Shea explained to Ben what was going on.

Ben put on gloves and booties as well, and together they followed Bryce into the car wash office.

"We found her in a back-office closet," Shea said as they walked through the business. While it was bright with sunshine outside, inside the business the light was low. In the darkness, they walked past a gloomy, silent wash area. A closed car wash was certainly a creepy place to be in, Lainie thought.

"From the drag marks, she was shot in the doorway and then pulled back to the office. Her purse is missing, maybe so we would think theft or burglary."

"There was blood leaking under the door," Bryce told them as they reached the office.

He pointed to an open door. Shea went in first, Lainie followed him, and Ben brought up the rear. Bryce hung back; it was a tight space.

The office was dimly lit, and it was a mess. Drawers were opened; papers were strewn everywhere. The closet was shaded. Shea stopped short of the blood puddle and shone a flashlight into the space. The light illuminated the body. Lainie saw a hand first, fingernails painted green. Red hair spilled out like tendrils from a mop. She stepped closer and bent down.

Relief swept over her. "That's not Evie." She straightened up and stepped back.

Ben leaned in. "It's Moffit's payroll person, Taylor Abbott. She was only hired a month ago. Most likely she was here early to open the place up."

"She must have had something on Moffit," Shea said. "He certainly shut her up."

Lainie shot Shea a side glance, not sure that what she was seeing indicated Stan was the perpetrator. She stepped back and surveyed the office. It had been torn apart, as if someone was searching for something. She remembered a conversation with Stan from years ago. "There's gotta be a floor safe somewhere."

"How do you know?" Ben asked.

"I'm guessing. Years ago, when Stan tried to get a YouTube channel off the ground, he found a sponsor who sold floor safes. He wanted to install one in his house, but it's on a concrete slab so he couldn't. He settled on a wall safe, but I remember him often saying that he thought floor safes were the most secure."

Ben stomped on the floor, and it sounded hollow. "He could definitely put one somewhere in here."

Lainie and Ben moved back to the doorway while Shea and Bryce began inspecting the floor. It wasn't long before Shea found the safe.

"Unfortunately, whoever tore up the office found it first."

The safe had been under a carpet. When he exposed the opening, it was obvious the lock had been broken. Removing the lid exposed an empty container.

CHAPTER 26

"You're thinking Stan was here to remove things from his office, Ms. Abbott walked in on him, and he killed her?" The whole thing was odd to Lainie.

"That's what I'm seeing," Shea said, but he didn't sound convinced.

"Stan wouldn't have to destroy the safe; he'd know the combination," Lainie said.

Shea folded his arms. "He should know it, I agree. But I believe that we're dealing with a desperate man. He's on the run and he needs money. He tried the scam in Hawaii to get money and it failed. He somehow knew we searched his home; he came here looking for something, and Abbott surprised him. If he doesn't have a motive to clean out his office, then who?"

"Benton," Ben said, and Lainie and Shea turned to him. "She didn't work here; she came here often to collect paperwork and money for Vine. Maybe she entrusted Moffit with important items and wanted them back before you found them or him. Right now, Benton and Vine would be the only ones who'd be concerned about you searching this business, especially if they knew Moffit was about to be arrested."

Lainie considered this for a minute before asking Ben a question. "You see Benton as the killer? Not Vine? Not Stan?"

"Vine never does his own dirty work. And I'm not convinced Moffit is a killer."

"I've got nothing on Vine," Shea said. "But I can put out a BOLO for Benton." He punched in a number and put the phone to his ear.

"As much as I dislike Stan, him murdering someone in his own business seems too obvious. Did you figure out when Benton came back from Hawaii?" Lainie asked Ben.

He shook his head. "We don't know what alias she would have used."

Just then, Bryce yelled out from the bathroom, "I found another one."

Lainie and Ben let Shea precede them into the room. It was a large space, handicap accessible. She looked over his shoulder when he bent down to see what the tech had found. A square of the flooring had been removed in the corner to reveal another floor safe. Lainie saw that the trash bucket had been over the patch.

"Well, I'll be," Shea said. "How did you find this?"

Bryce fairly beamed. "The linoleum square was off a tad. Searching every corner of the space paid off."

"Can you open it?"

"I've got a crowbar coming."

In a few minutes another tech brought in a crowbar and some other tools. They got to work.

"I think you're right," Ben said to Lainie. They stood close together in the doorway while the sounds of banging and prying emanated from the bathroom.

"About what?"

"If Stan had been the one here cleaning out his office, he would not have missed this safe."

"Besides that, he would have to be an absolute moron to kill a woman in his own office."

Ben leaned against the wall, a thoughtful expression on his face. "It's all staged. Someone ransacked the office and killed Abbott to make it appear as if Stan had done it. She had no ID, and her purse is gone, leading me to believe that whoever killed her took it." He nodded to the floor safe. "Maybe some of the answers we want will be in there."

It took about ten minutes, but the techs got the safe open. Shea pulled out three manila envelopes: two were rather thick, one was thin. He took them into the office and set them on the desk.

The first one he opened was filled with cash, bundles of hundred dollar bills.

"Wow." Lainie whistled.

The next one was filled with passports and IDs.

Shea opened one. "Picture is of Stan Moffit, under the name Clinton White." He opened another. "This one is a Canadian passport, Stan with another name. And here we have a woman." He handed the passport to Ben.

"This is Crystal Benton with the name Martha White."

Shea pulled out all the IDs. After he finished opening all of them, six were for Stan, six were for Benton, different names, various nationalities.

Ben studied the one in his hand. "These are professionally done. It would fool me. I now have a list of Benton's aliases to check with the flight logs. She probably used one of these names to return from Hawaii."

"What's in the last envelope?" Lainie asked.

Shea opened it and leafed through the papers. "Bank records, a lot of money in a foreign bank. Moffit and Benton set themselves up with offshore accounts." He looked up from the papers. "I'm not an accountant, but if I'm reading this right, Benton and Moffit were stealing from the big boss. All of this might lead straight to Vine."

Lainie felt lightheaded. It was so surreal. It didn't line up with the selfish, self-absorbed person she hated seeing across the dinner table. How was Evie so fooled?

"We need to work together on this," Ben said. "I'm calling my supervisor. We'll get a team down here as well." He stepped aside and made the phone call.

Shea jutted his chin. "Moffit's our guy. Maybe he didn't kill that woman in there, but I'll bet he knows who did. I'm putting out a BOLO for him as well. We'll find them both and sort all of this out."

Ben finished his call. "Team is on the way. We have a couple of forensic accountants. They can figure out all that paperwork. If Moffit and Benton were trying to pull something over on the boss, they should wish that we find them first. Vine won't wait for explanations."

"No turf war? My arrest?" Shea asked.

"I just want the man in jail."

Shea nodded. "Okay, I'll call my boss." He walked off and Ben turned to Lainie.

The expression on his face troubled her. Despite what he'd said, she feared a turf war when things got going. She'd seen egos at work when there were jurisdictional battles. "What's the matter? You don't think Shea will cooperate?"

"It's not that. We're missing something," Ben said. "Things have moved along too quickly."

"I don't agree. Things are not moving fast enough. I'm no closer to finding Evie than I was on the beach in Hawaii."

There was such tender understanding in Ben's eyes it took her breath away.

"This has to be a lot for you to take in." He touched her elbow. "I can't imagine; you haven't even buried her yet."

Emotion bubbled up and Lainie felt sad, tired, and angry all in a swirl. She turned away. "I don't have a body to bury."

Ben cleared his throat. "I'm seeing things in this office that make Stan appear like a real bad actor. Efren never hinted that there was this kind of activity going on here. Fake IDs, offshore accounts. Efren had no inkling. He made friends with Stan. Is the man capable of all this?"

"A week ago, I would have said no. Now, I don't know what to make of everything." Thankful for the change of subject, Lainie felt her control return, and she turned back to Ben. "Everything here says he was involved with Crystal Benton. Did Efren see that?"

Ben shook his head. "Efren believed that the relationship between Benton and Stan was purely professional. She had a good head for numbers and was as ruthless as Vine. He didn't think Stan was her type."

"Her type being?"

"Powerful mover, the boss of things, lots of money. Efren saw Stan as a family man. He talked about his boys a lot. Whatever your brother-in-law did, whatever he is, he loved his kids. It made an impression on Efren."

Lainie considered his words. "If there was one positive comment I can make about Stan, it would be that he does love the boys. It's hard for me to be charitable about anything else. Have you heard any more about Efren?"

Lainie didn't miss the pain that flashed across Ben's face. "I hit a nerve."

"It's not you." He clenched and unclenched his fists, then relaxed. "We found his car. Stripped and dumped in the desert."

"I'm so sorry, Ben. Just the car?"

"Yeah. I'm heading to the impound lot to check it out. Hoping that Efren left some kind of clue in the car—" He stopped. "Crazy, huh?"

She shook her head. "You guys are friends, partners. I'd try to leave a clue, if I could. Do you mind if I tag along?"

Ben raised his eyebrows. "Why?"

"I got nothing else to do. At least until Stan and Benton turn up. And I believe Efren and Evie's disappearance are linked in some manner. I won't get in the way."

"I'm not worried about that. Follow me over?"

"Lead the way."

CHAPTER 27

Lainie could hear the pain and fear in Ben's voice when he had told her about the discovery of his partner's vehicle. It was a clear sign that Efren was dead. He didn't want to say it or think it, she bet, any more than she wanted to admit that Evie was gone. The knowledge made Lainie feel connected to Ben. In reality, they were both in the same place, both grieving a loss they couldn't prove.

Pain would hit them both like a freight train when proof arrived, and Lainie dreaded that day.

"Why did they bring the car to Long Beach?" Lainie asked when they exited the car wash.

"It's temporary, until it can be moved to our lab to be processed, though I doubt that will happen."

"Why?"

"From the picture I saw, it was picked clean, like a body decimated by vultures. Maybe it was left in the desert to make sure any evidence was destroyed."

She followed Ben to the impound lot. The tow yard was north of downtown, on the border with Signal Hill, on Willow Street. Years ago, when Lainie was a rookie, she'd worked many overtime shifts at the yard when there were lien sales. She knew the lot well.

Lainie considered the mystery of Efren's disappearance as she drove. There were too many mysteries in her life at the moment. The biggest one she couldn't solve blared in her mind ever since she'd learned who her brother-in-law worked for.

Why did everything in her life circle back to Dallas Vine?

In so many ways that traffic stop fifteen years ago had defined her career. It destroyed her faith in the system, and in part her faith in God. It shredded her idealism. It made her more cautious. The fact that now, so many years later, Vine could touch her life so destructively defied logic.

She hadn't had a chance to process the loss of her sister when his evil name burst into the drama. Everything here had to be connected—Ben's partner's disappearance, Evie's disappearance, and the murder of Taylor Abbott. For the life of her, Lainie couldn't see how Stan fit in with all this. She considered herself a good judge of character. She missed the boat where Stan was concerned. He was annoying, prideful, and always boasting about himself. She never saw him as dangerous. It still rattled her brain that he worked for Vine.

Vine.

She would never stop wishing that they'd been able to convict him all those years ago. After he sued her for harassment, Lainie had been ordered to stay away from him, and she followed orders. She'd been forced to admit to herself that she had been obsessed and the obsession was not affecting him; it was only affecting her, and in a negative way. So she backed off, but she never stopped paying attention to what he was doing. Every time he came under the scrutiny of law enforcement, she prayed that he'd finally receive the justice he deserved.

He always evaded a conviction, and she hated to admit it, but he did appear to be bulletproof.

At one point she wondered if he would get so cocky that he'd slip up. But he never did. As far as Lainie was concerned, Vine figured into everything evil in the city of Long Beach. Lainie couldn't separate

Vine from Stan now even if it only came down to Stan having an affair and killing Evie to be free for his girlfriend. Vine had to be mixed up in it somewhere.

Lainie parked next to Ben and climbed out of her car. The loud whine of a motorcycle caught her attention, and she watched a bike zip by on Willow Street. Never a cop around when you needed one, she thought.

Together she and Ben approached the gate.

The yard had always been gated, but now it was a fortress. Black metal slats had been woven into the chain-link fence, and a person had to be buzzed into the lot after speaking into an intercom at the entrance. The gate that opened to let vehicles in was several inches thick and topped with razor wire. Cameras were also set up all over the place. All the security had been installed because of the rise in catalytic converter thefts. One night before all the precautions were in place, someone had climbed the fence and stolen six converters.

Lainie pushed the intercom button. "Hey, anyone in there awake? Or are you all snoring?"

It took a second for anyone to respond. "Only one copper thinks she's funny with a line like that. Come on in, Detective Jensen."

The buzzer sounded as the lock disengaged. Mel, the impound lot supervisor, met them once they stepped inside the yard.

Mel held out his hand. "Long time no see."

Lainie gripped his hand. "Unfortunately, I don't have time for overtime shifts anymore." She indicated Ben. "This is FBI Agent Ben Isaacs. You have a car the Feds brought in."

"If you want to call it a car. The mess you want is off to the right, in the back in section A-8. Can't miss it. Almost looks as if it was cut apart by the fire department." He pointed.

"Thank you, Mel."

She and Ben walked in the direction Mel had pointed.

"Sounds like whoever had the car was searching for something," Lainie said as she and Ben made their way through the lot. "Just like in Stan's office."

He nodded. "It might have something to do with Efren's job. He oversaw Vine's fleet of cars. Please keep this to yourself, but he found evidence that Vine secrets things into cars: money, instructions, et cetera, all designed to further his criminal endeavors. The only thing Efren didn't find was solid evidence, but he kept after it. My fear is Vine found out Efren was asking questions, and that blew his cover."

"What kind of evidence?"

"Loose armrests and door panels. And some coded notes. Vine uses a complicated code for money drops and trafficking exchange arrangements. We can't figure it out. Efren had found a note hidden in the headliner of one of Vine's SUVs. It makes no sense to us. We need more information to break the code. We were hoping he could find more."

They made it to the wreckage of Efren's SUV, at least Lainie thought it was an SUV. It was hard to tell.

Ben stared at the wreck, hands on his hips. "Wow, it does look as if they used the Jaws of Life on this thing. The only way the local cops knew it was Efren's was by the VIN."

"What kind of car was it?"

"Chevy Blazer." He walked around it. It was encircled by crime scene tape.

"I can see why FBI technicians would be reluctant to take this wreck," Lainie said.

"Yeah. The agent in Joshua Tree didn't think they'd find anything. Besides being destroyed, it was exposed to the elements for a couple of days."

The chassis had been stripped, then cut almost completely in half. Tires were gone. The interior had been removed, even the steering wheel. All that was left was the bare steering column. To Lainie it seemed as if someone had even peeled back small pieces of metal or aluminum, as if searching to see if something was underneath.

"Where would Efren leave you a message if he had a chance to do so?"

Ben bent down near the driver's side window, about where the windshield VIN number would be. His brows creased. "There's something else going on here."

"What do you mean?"

"On the surface it appears as if someone was searching for something, but it's just overkill."

"Trying to send a message?"

"Maybe. But if it is, I'm too obtuse to understand all of it. If Efren is dead, where is he?"

"I ask that same question about Evie."

He turned to face her, the frown eased and understanding filled his eyes. "I know you do. This certainly can't help you any more than it helps me."

"It keeps my mind occupied." She turned away and her foot caught on part of the metal frame, causing her to stumble. As she did, something whistled by her ear, slamming into the frame with a solid thunk.

Two more zinged by as it registered—someone was shooting at her.

"Get down!" Ben yelled and lurched toward her.

Lainie didn't need further encouragement. The shots came from her right. She rolled left and scooted behind a derelict pickup truck, rolling against Ben as she did so. There were more pings as more shots hit the truck and puffs of dust where bullets hit the dirt.

Ben made his way toward her, gun drawn. "Can you tell where the shooter is?"

"North corner of the yard, in the alley."

The impound yard was an uneven, triangular-shaped lot. On the long side it abutted a dead-end alley. Lainie whipped her fanny pack around to the front as she searched for a muzzle flash, but it was broad daylight. She doubted she'd be able to detect it. More puffs of dirt bloomed as bullets hit very close to her.

Unzipping her pack, she drew her own gun and then scooted forward.

"There." Ben raised up behind her. He now had a better vantage point than she did. He fired a burst of four shots.

The yard was quiet. If she had a target, she would take a shot. "Do you think you hit him?"

"It would be pure luck if I did. I see a motorcycle helmet peeking over the fence. He must be standing on something on the other side. What's over there?"

"Just the alley."

"Whoever is out there knows we are not unarmed." He inched his head up, gaze directed toward where Lainie believed the shooter was.

Shouts came from the direction of the tow yard office. Then Lainie's phone rang.

It was Mel. "Who is out there shooting?"

"Someone at the north end of the lot, in the alley. Call 911 and stay inside the office."

"We called 911. Are you okay?"

She was about to tell Mel to advise police to approach on Redondo Avenue. The alley opened onto that street; it would be the shooter's only escape route.

Two more shots pinged the car frame. One came so close to Lainie that she dropped her phone. She drew herself back when Ben grunted in pain. He dropped his gun and fell backward.

CHAPTER 28

Fearing Ben was dead but still facing a threat, Lainie ignored her phone on the ground and brought her gun up, firing in the direction Ben indicated, though she had not seen what he saw. She moved in front of the fallen agent and then forward, firing as she went, not rapidly to conserve her ammo but consistently, trying to keep the shooter down. She wanted to sight in the helmet, if the shooter was still here.

Need to stop the threat.

She halted behind a tow truck to calm her breathing. As she peered through the towing apparatus, she could not see what was on the other side of the fence that encircled the yard. Just as she brought her gun up on target, she caught a glimpse of the helmet. She lined up the shot and fired. Direct hit. Bits of plastic flew up and the helmet dropped out of view. Lainie thought she heard a groan.

Keeping her gun up, she cautiously moved toward the fence. She could barely make out movement—the black slats in the chain-link fence did not block her view completely. As she got closer, she heard the rider kick-start the bike with a roar and speed away, east toward Redondo.

She broke into a sprint, but it was no use—she couldn't see over the fence. She jumped up and scanned left, glimpsing a motorcycle taillight turn right on Redondo before she dropped below the fence line.

Now she wished that she'd picked up her phone. She could hear sirens approaching and she regretted the absence of a radio. If she had one, she could give direction of travel. There was no way to see the fleeing cycle's plate.

She lowered her gun to her side and sprinted back to Ben. He was moving, his face a bloody mess.

"Ben, can you hear me?" She set a hand on his shoulder.

He opened his eyes and wiped blood off his face with the back of his hand. He'd been grazed by a bullet above his left eyebrow.

"Yeah, I can hear you. I'm fine. Just feel like a horse kicked me in the head."

She helped him to his feet. Mel came running toward them.

"Oh my goodness. I'll get you some towels." He skidded to a stop, then turned back around for the office.

"Are you dizzy or disoriented?" Lainie asked as Ben pressed his palm to the wound.

"Not really, but I've got blood in my eye." He squinted.

Mel sprinted back toward them along with a uniformed officer. Sara. She'd probably just started her afternoon shift.

"Lainie, what happened?"

"Someone started shooting at us." She pointed to the fence. "The shooter was over there, in the alley. We both fired in that direction. I think I hit his helmet. Whoever it was took off toward Redondo on a motorcycle. Sorry, I don't have any more."

Sara keyed her mike and relayed that information to dispatch and asked for a paramedic for Ben.

"Hey, I'm fine. It's just a scratch."

Mel gave Ben some paper towels.

"Thanks." He wiped his face and turned to Lainie. "It feels like it's minor."

She assessed the injury to his forehead. "It is, but it's a pretty deep scratch. And it's bleeding a lot. You might need stitches."

"Perfect." He sucked in a breath and held the towels to the wound.

"Why would someone be shooting at you guys?" Sara asked.

"Good question," Lainie and Ben spoke in unison.

✦

Ben let the medics take care of his wound. They also suggested he see a doctor for stitches. He said he would after they dressed the wound. What stung more than the gash was the fact that he hadn't seen the ambush coming. And he couldn't figure out who would be shooting. Moffit? Benton? Vine?

He called Mark and explained the situation.

"I'm glad you're okay. I certainly didn't see this coming," Mark said. "I'll meet you at the ER."

Ben resisted Jensen's offer to drive him to the hospital.

"Other than a monstrous headache," he told her, "I'm fine."

"I still can't let you drive yourself. You lost consciousness. I can bring the medics back and ask them to transport you."

"You're making more of this than it is."

"No, she's not." The uniformed officer jumped into the argument. "If you have a concussion, you should be medically evaluated before you drive anymore. It's a duty injury in any event. If you were PD, seeing the doctor would be mandatory."

"Wow, is this a tag-team gang up?"

"It is," Lainie said.

"All right, all right, I'm outnumbered. I'll go with the medics."

"I'll go get them." The uniformed officer left Ben staring at Lainie.

Her posture remained stiff, and Ben felt like she had more to say. "What? You got your way. What now?"

She held his gaze. "I was willing to sit in the back seat until now and let everyone else investigate. Someone just shot at me. I take that personally. I'm not going to sit back and watch anymore."

"I get it. I'll do what I can to help keep you involved."

The medics returned and walked Ben to their rig.

"I hope it's not too many stitches," Lainie said to him as he walked off.

The exertion made Ben realize that it was the right move. He probably shouldn't be driving right at this moment. As he walked to the medic truck, he heard police radio traffic explain that one of the responding units had found a motorcycle and a broken helmet abandoned near the airport. It had been reported stolen the night before.

Ben settled into the ambulance and tried to relax. Being brought in by medics got him into an exam room immediately. He was still waiting to be seen by a doctor when Mark showed up.

"I can't figure out why anyone would be shooting at me or Jensen," Ben said, trying to ignore the throbbing pain in his forehead. "We don't have enough evidence to arrest anyone right now."

"Not exactly true. I've been thinking about this ever since you called. You were able to expose the shark attack as a hoax. Moffit and Benton have good reason to want you dead."

Ben considered this for a moment. "Still, it makes no sense for me to be targeted. Killing me won't put the genie back in the bottle. Other cops will take up the cause. LBPD has the investigation. Killing us won't stop that."

"Maybe you weren't the target."

"You think Jensen was the target?"

Mark hiked up a shoulder. "It's her brother-in-law who is on the run. Family ties are often the most volatile. All the evidence now points to him killing his own wife. What's to stop him from killing Jensen?"

Just then the doctor stepped into the room. As the doctor examined him and cleaned out the wound, Ben considered Mark's words. The boss was right; Moffit and Benton could have a strong motive to kill Elaine Jensen, even if it was simply revenge. He was very much cornered right now.

He winced when the doctor began to stitch him up. He hoped the man would hurry. Detective Jensen was in danger and suddenly Ben felt protective.

CHAPTER 29

In addition to finding a stolen motorcycle two miles from where the shooting occurred, Sara and assisting units found a rifle dumped in the alley just outside the tow yard fence. The gun was a beat-up Remington, and the rounds were .223. Basically, a hunting rifle. It was probably stolen like the bike.

Lainie was still inside the yard while Sara collected the evidence in the alley. A homicide team had also arrived; they handled officer-involved shootings. Technically, Lainie was not on duty, and as far as they knew, her bullets had not injured anyone, so she was interviewed but her gun was not confiscated. After they spoke to her, they left to see how Ben was doing at the hospital.

She stood on a stepladder to see over the fence and could see pockmarks in the brick wall of the building abutting the alley from where Ben's and her bullets had hit. There were also scattered bits of hard plastic from the helmet.

"Good shooting, Lainie," Sara said. "It always amazes me how good you are under pressure."

"I skimmed the top of the helmet. I hope camera footage has a clear image of this guy. He must have had his visor up to shoot."

Sara pointed up at the camera. "There's no good angle on this specific spot. He figured that out. And that is likely why he wore the helmet." She nodded to everything she had collected. "He left the rifle, the brass. Obviously he's not concerned about leaving prints." Sara looked up. "Did Stan own a rifle?"

"Not that I know of. I don't even recall him knowing anything about guns. But at this point, I think there is a lot I don't know about Stan." Lainie climbed down from the ladder and walked to the office. She waited there until Sara and the others finished gathering evidence.

She wondered how Ben was doing and planned to drive to the hospital if he was still there.

"You sure brought a lot of excitement to the yard, there, Detective," Mel commented.

"You guys always need a wake-up call," Lainie told him.

"Not this kind." He shook his head.

Her phone rang and she answered. "Are you calling with good news, Bobby?"

"I think so. Got a call from a hospital in San Bernardino. They have Crystal Benton."

"What?"

"They've had her for three days. She's in a coma—car accident, tire blew out, rollover on Route 330."

"Three days?"

"Yeah, they have her ID, purse, and stuff. They've had no luck finding next of kin. When the BOLO I put out on her came across the desk at the sheriff's office, they put two and two together."

Lainie was speechless.

"You still there?"

"Three days ago, Crystal Benton should have been in Hawaii."

"I don't know what to tell you, Lainie. They have her ID, credit cards. And some other weird details."

"This whole case is weird. What else?"

"Two men in the car were both killed in the crash. Neither of them wore seat belts, so they were ejected. Benton was strapped in. Her hands and feet were also bound with duct tape. Being so immobilized saved her life."

"What?" Her pulse pounded; her face grew hot.

"Yep. The driver was a known MS-13 gang member, wanted in several counties for a lot of violent crimes. The other guy was not wanted, but he was one of Stan's car wash employees. What do you make of that?"

"I don't know what to make of it. Give me a minute." She set the phone down at her side, trying to process everything she'd just been told. After a minute, she found her voice. "It removes Benton as the suspect in the murder of Taylor Abbott, doesn't it? No way she could have done that if she's been in the hospital for three days."

"I realize that."

"Are you going to San Bernardino?"

"Yes," Shea said. "I suppose you want to come?"

"I do."

"Well, before you hop in a car, the docs aren't certain when she'll wake up. Head trauma. The coma was induced because of swelling on her brain. They've been trying to find the next of kin for three days. She's breathing on her own, and they are guardedly optimistic. They wanted family apprised in the event she crashes."

"I still need to go, Bobby. This woman was involved with my brother-in-law. I need to see her."

"St. Bernardine. We're heading out in about an hour. It'll be a late night."

Lainie ended the call and tapped her palm with the phone. Sara walked into the office.

"Who was that?" Sara asked, and Lainie told her.

"Maybe Isaacs was wrong. Maybe Benton wasn't in Hawaii," Sara said when Lainie finished.

Lainie shrugged. "If he was wrong, does that mean there was a shark attack?" She shook her head and answered her own question. "I feel with every fiber of my soul that there was no shark attack. Crystal Benton had to have been in Hawaii. What Ben postulated is the only thing that makes sense. Especially with what we found in the car wash. Do you think he is finished in the ER yet?"

"Depends on how many were ahead of him."

"I think I'll go check on him, at least call and make sure he's okay."

"And I've got a long report to file." Sara patted Lainie on the shoulder. "You'll have to file something about your weapon discharge."

"I'll get to it."

"All right, be careful."

They left the office together. Sara headed for her black-and-white and Lainie to her car. She called Ben as she started her car, but he probably wouldn't answer. She was prepared to leave a message.

He answered, sounding tired and worn out.

"How many stitches?"

"Eight and a painful tetanus shot."

"You okay?"

"Other than a headache, I'm okay. Just got home; Mark brought me. I'm getting ready to lie down. I hope they'll let my car stay at the impound lot all night."

"Not a problem. Mel knows that it's your car." She explained about the call from Shea regarding Benton.

His voice took on new energy. "That's not possible. I know she was in Hawaii."

"That's what I told Sara. Up for a drive out to San Bernardino?"

"I just took some pain pills. I can't drive. Besides the fact I don't have my car."

"If you want to go, I'll pick you up. I need your address."

He gave it to her. "I might fall asleep on the way there."

The way he said it made her smile. After a minute, she realized it was the first time she'd smiled in what seemed like a very long time.

CHAPTER 30

Ben was bruised and pale when she picked him up, and Lainie felt guilty about asking him to come along.

"You look awful. Maybe I should let you rest," Lainie said as he settled into the passenger seat.

"My wound is not life threatening. Doctor said no concussion. But who likes to have a needle and thread pulled though their skin? The pain pills are making me loopy."

"All right, Loopy, I'll let you rest."

"Humph."

A few minutes later a side glance told her he'd closed his eyes. She concentrated on the road, though she longed to talk to the guy next to her. After she had called Ben and asked if he wanted to come along, she realized that she truly had no idea what she would or could do at the hospital. But if this woman really had impersonated her sister, then she was a part of whatever happened to Evie—most likely a big part.

I'd like to confront her, Lainie thought. *Shake the truth out of her.* Why did she help Stan with his hoax and what else did she help Stan with?

But right now, Benton couldn't talk. Still, she was the last link to Stan. Lainie was glad she didn't have to do this alone.

The drive to St. Bernardine took forty minutes, and Ben slept most of the way. He woke up when she exited the freeway. He yawned. "I hope I didn't snore."

"No snore, just a little drool."

"What?" He wiped his face, and she laughed. She was giddy because she was tired.

"Ha, ha." He stretched. "Seriously, what are we going to do here? She's in a coma."

"You're just asking that now?"

"I'm on pain pills. What's your excuse?"

The giddiness faded. "I need to find out what happened to Evie. The reason we were certain Evie didn't die in Hawaii was because of Benton being there. And if Benton is here in this hospital, how could she have been in Hawaii? She also couldn't have shot anyone at the car wash."

"The more I thought about it, the more I realized that she could still have been in Hawaii." Ben rubbed his eyes. "I need to see the collision report and check the times, but she still could have been here. She would have had to leave right after she tried to run you over."

"And then she got snatched up by Vine?"

"That's the direction I'm going."

"I'm not sure that works for me, but I have nothing better. I want to see her and confirm that she's really seriously injured. If so, then Stan is the only one left to find."

He nodded and grimaced in pain. "I've been praying that we get some answers. Maybe they will all be here."

"You're a believer?" Lainie asked, surprising herself with the question. She hadn't been bold enough to ask such a question in a long time.

"Yes, I am. You?"

She nodded. "I'm kind of a failure at it. But I'm trying."

"We're all failures at some level. That's why we need a Savior."

"I've heard that before."

"Because it's true."

Lainie didn't have a comeback for that.

She parked the car and respected Ben a little more knowing where he stood spiritually. *I am moving back to where I belong,* she thought.

They met Shea and Collins in the hospital lobby. They stood with a third man. Shea introduced him as Detective Gardner, San Bernardino County Sheriff's Department, accident investigation. Next to Gardner on a small table was a banker's box, the kind officers used to store belongings and/or evidence.

"Any change in her condition?" Lainie asked.

"Actually, maybe she's a little bit better. They've begun the process of weaning her off the coma drugs. She hasn't declined in the last several hours, and the swelling in her brain has decreased.

"We've hit dead ends on her next of kin," Gardner continued. "We were able to contact next of kin for the two men who died in the car. But none of those we've interviewed can shed any light on what was going on, why Benton was bound, where the trio had been, and where they were going."

"Have you been able to contact anyone who knows Benton, say from her work?" Lainie asked.

"No. We've left messages. But the address for her place of business is in Long Beach. I haven't driven out there yet. I'm hoping you guys will be able to take care of that." Gardner gestured to the box. "Here are all the personal belongings collected from the crash, both for Benton and the phones taken from the two deceased individuals. They're damaged, but maybe they'll prove useful to you. Also, the folder on top is the completed accident report."

"Thank you," Shea said.

Collins picked up the box. "Thanks for your help with this, and thanks for the report."

"No problem. If you need anything, don't hesitate to call."

Gardner left, and the four of them headed for the elevator. It was late, past visiting hours. The ride to the Critical Care floor was quiet. They exited the elevator to the waiting room. The Critical Care Unit itself was behind two locked double doors. To access this floor, a visitor would need to be with a doctor or nurse who could open the doors with a magnetic card, or there was an intercom through which a visitor could speak to a nurse on the floor and ask to be buzzed in.

"Her doctor said he'd come talk to us about her condition." Collins handed Lainie the box. "Maybe you and Ben could rummage through this, check out the report and the nature of the belongings."

Lainie took the box and set it on a small table in the waiting room.

Collins removed some disposable gloves from his pocket. "I think there are two pairs here. I always like to be prepared."

Ben took the gloves. "Thanks." He separated two pairs and handed one to Lainie. She was about to open the box when a doctor stepped off the elevator.

"I'm Dr. Hardin. Which one of you is Detective Shea?"

Shea stepped forward. "That would be me."

"All of you can't go in to see her. In fact, I don't know if anyone should. We've been unable to locate next of kin."

"Detective Gardner indicated that she might be getting better."

"I'm guardedly optimistic. She's not getting worse. The swelling in her brain is easing. It's possible we can try and wake her up tomorrow, but I can't say for certain. Is it necessary to see her?"

"She's a suspect we need to speak to regarding an ongoing investigation. I need to document her condition and her status."

"Okay, I understand. I'll take you back, Detective Shea, but only you."

Lainie felt discouragement bite. However, she'd get no satisfaction just seeing a comatose woman lying in a hospital bed. She felt the need to pray for the woman, that she did heal and that she would face justice if she did, in fact, have something to do with Evie's disappearance.

"Sorry, Lainie."

"That's all right, I get it."

The doctor slid his card and opened the magnetic lock. The two men entered the double doors, and they closed behind them with a whoosh.

"We have the box to go through," Collins said, donning his own gloves.

The three took seats around the box, Ben next to Lainie, as she removed the lid.

"Let's start with the accident report." They began to sift through the file.

Lainie noted that the primary collision factor for the crash was listed as "tire failure," followed by "excessive speed." Route 330 went up from the valley floor to the ski areas in the San Bernardino Mountains. It was steep and winding, and an over-the-edge rollover accident was more likely than not to be fatal. Especially if the vehicle was traveling too fast.

They passed around the photos, which were graphic. The vehicle was a Chevy Suburban, and it was flattened. It was a miracle anyone survived. The driver and front passenger didn't.

An old booking photo of the gang member who'd been driving was included in the folder. Hector Rollins was his name.

Lainie studied it. His tats gave him away, but he was not anyone she'd ever seen before. The only photo of the car wash employee, Raphael Diaz, was of his body. She couldn't say she recognized him either. But then she didn't ever get her car washed at Stan's place.

"Here." Ben pointed to a paragraph near the narrative's end. Lainie had been concentrating on the pictures. "They recovered three handguns, duct tape, handcuffs, and several knives from the wreckage."

Lainie looked up at Collins. "What's up with all the weapons?"

"Rollins was a known gangbanger. Not sure about Diaz. The inventory sheet states that the guns were legal, registered to Diaz, as was the car." He shook his head.

"My read on this situation is that since Benton was bound, maybe Vine found out she and your brother-in-law were embezzling from him so he ordered her be taken care of," Ben said. "That's only speculation. What was going on in that car, we just don't know."

Collins nodded. "With the speed the vehicle was traveling, it would not have taken much to make the driver lose control. He obviously could not react correctly when the tire blew. The Suburban is a top-heavy vehicle. The gang member driving didn't have a valid license."

"It's a miracle anyone survived this," Ben said, as he flipped through more photos. Lainie had to agree.

She continued reading through the accident report. There was not a lot in the narrative because no one in the vehicle could tell them where they had been or what they had been doing. And there were no witnesses to the crash. A motorist some distance behind the vehicle saw the broken guardrail and called the police. Since there was still a cloud of dust from the crash, he told the officers he thought maybe the crash had just happened. Toxicology was pending for the two deceased individuals.

"What else is in the box?" Ben asked, reaching for it. "Is there anything in there belonging to Benton?"

"There's a purse with a wallet and ID according to the inventory sheet," Lainie said. "Do you think you'll find something in her belongings?"

"It's been my experience that women tend to keep a lot of stuff in that bag they call a purse," he said, and Collins snickered.

"Humph," Lainie said. "I'd smack you for that, but I happen to agree with you. What specifically do you expect to find?"

"Maybe a clue as to where she's been. A receipt, something. I do know from our investigation that she does not have any family locally. She hails from Chicago."

"We'll figure out next of kin," Collins said.

Lainie looked up when Shea rejoined them.

"How is she?" Lainie asked.

"There was not a lot that I could see. Benton can't move, her head is wrapped in bandages, her face is puffy and bruised."

"She's a lot better than when she arrived here," Dr. Hardin said. "She is improving. I will contact you if we proceed with reversing the coma tomorrow."

"Thank you." Shea shook the doctor's hand. "We also want to be notified if anyone tries to visit her."

"We've tried several internet searches to locate family and have had no luck. So unless a family member suddenly appears, I doubt there will be visitors. Maybe you'll have better luck finding a contact person." The doctor rang for the elevator and left them in the waiting room.

They all went back to the report and the property. Collins handed the purse to Ben. Lainie noted that it was an expensive and pretty white Coach bag, now stained with dirt and blood.

Ben opened it and Lainie turned her attention to him. He took out the wallet and handed Lainie the purse. As he flipped through the wallet, Lainie opened up the purse. There was expensive makeup, a checkbook, a few pens, and a baggie labeled *jewelry*. Curious, Lainie set down the purse and opened the baggie. A watch, two rings, and a cross necklace fell into her hand.

Lainie's heart stopped. This was Evie's jewelry. She'd given the cross to her sister years ago. And she recognized the wedding ring.

Ben held out a business card. "This card is for Vine's cigar club in Long Beach . . ." He stopped. "What's wrong?"

Lainie's pulse pounded. "This is Evie's jewelry."

Ben turned toward her. "Serious?"

"Yes. I recognize all of it."

"Now we know for certain that she had something to do with your sister's disappearance," Shea said. "How else would Benton have this? We'll put it into evidence. And we'll get a warrant to search her home."

Shock rocked Lainie like an 8.0 earthquake. She held in her hand almost certain proof that Evie was dead. She would never have parted with these items willingly.

What was Benton doing with her sister's jewelry?

Every answer Lainie came up with disturbed her to the core.

CHAPTER 31

Lainie dropped Ben off after midnight.

"Be careful when you go home. There's a gunman out there hunting for you," he said as he opened his car door. "Stay on your toes."

"He might have been shooting at you. You be careful as well."

Their eyes met, and it was hard for Lainie to deny the connection she felt with Ben. They'd only known each other for a week—the worst week of her life—yet she felt as if she'd known him and depended on him a lot longer. Then, with a smile and a nod, he was gone.

As light as she tried to keep her thoughts, Lainie was on edge as she drove home. She thought about Crystal Benton in the hospital bed.

She'd been bound.

There were guns, duct tape, and handcuffs in the car.

The car's driver was a hardcore gang member.

It was obvious that something nefarious had been planned for the woman. How long had she been held captive? Where had she been, and where was she going? If it was Vine reacting because Benton was stealing from him, it surprised Lainie that he would do that to someone he knew—but then again, Benton did betray him.

As tired as Lainie was, she couldn't deny that being shot at had amped her up a bit. She double-checked all the locks, windows, and doors, then placed her loaded gun on the nightstand before she lay down to sleep.

✦

Ben was stiff and sore when he woke up. He took a shower though the doctor had advised him not to get his stitches wet. It was a guilty pleasure to stand under the hot water, get rid of the grime, and the smell. He was certain he smelled like a dirty gym bag. At some point he needed to Uber over to the lot and pick up his vehicle.

Carefully, he tilted his head to wash his hair. He enjoyed the hot water for as long as he could.

When he moved the wrong way and tweaked his injury, he thought about Efren. Efren would have been first in line to give him grief about getting shot.

"Don't you know how to duck, Isaacs? I thought I trained you better than that."

The memory of his buddy made his heart hurt. Worse than the pain of the stitches in his head. For a few minutes Ben let the water run down his face to soothe his psyche and wash away the tears.

When he finished showering, he knew he had to call Efren's wife and tell her about the car.

She answered on the first ring. "Ben."

"Candy, I wish I had good news, but I don't."

"Just tell me, Ben. Don't beat around the bush."

He broke the news as gently as he could. "There is no evidence on the car to tell us anything about Efren." He could hear her breathing, but she didn't say anything for about a minute.

"Thanks for staying on this."

"I would never let it go. I will find him, Candy. He's my partner—I will never turn my back on him."

Grief or no grief, there would be no lazing around today. He dressed to head to the office and ordered an Uber. Today was the meeting with the assistant special agent in charge, and Ben wasn't certain what was to become of the investigation. All he was certain about was that chances were slimmer and slimmer that Efren would come home safe.

Ben dreaded the meeting with the ASAC. Gunther Packard was known by the rank and file to be by the book. Ben had violated policy when he went to talk to Evangeline Moffit, and he was ready to accept the consequences. It was possible he'd be pulled from the case. He got to the office about 9:00, and he and Mark stepped into the conference room to wait for Packard. They completely reviewed all the information their six-month-long investigation had amassed. The boss was due at ten, but at five minutes till, they were told that he would be delayed.

Packard did not arrive until noon. When he did, he was surprisingly upbeat.

"Gentlemen, I recognize this meeting is difficult for you both." He looked at Ben. "You can take time off if you need it, Agent Isaacs."

"It's really just a scratch, sir."

Packard nodded. "I'm glad you're okay. I've authorized two agents to assist LBPD in the investigation. On the other front, I'm very concerned about Agent Gomez."

"As are we," Mark said. "He is now more than a week overdue. One reason why we'd like to find Stan Moffit is the hope that he may know what happened to Efren."

"I'm glad you brought that up. I do have some good news."

Ben and Mark exchanged glances.

What good news? Ben wondered.

"I was on a conference call with Chief Mackall at Long Beach PD before I arrived here. They have apprehended Stan Moffit."

"What?" Ben sat up in his chair.

"He was notified of the apprehension while I was speaking to him. I asked if I could relay the news to you. I was prepared to chastise you today, explain that I always thought concentrating on the car wash was the wrong play. However, evidence recovered in

Moffit's vehicle appears to indicate that he was the right person to focus on after all."

"Sir?" Mark asked, looking as perplexed as Ben felt.

"Moffit was the SoCal guy helping in the human-smuggling operation with multistate contacts. Vine was a smoke screen. Your instincts were correct in wanting to speak to Moffit. He might be the one responsible for Agent Gomez's disappearance."

✦

Lainie woke up to the sound of her phone vibrating on the nightstand next to her bed. She picked it up as it stopped. Squinting at the screen, she saw that she'd missed a call from her father.

She sat up and stretched. It was 9:00 a.m., and after all the tension of the day before, she was surprised that she had slept so long. Lainie stood, dragging her hands through her hair, trying to clear her head and wake up enough to call her father back.

After a few minutes, she redialed. "Dad, what's up?"

"I was going to ask you the same thing. You've been a stranger. Do you have any news?"

Her family should know about Evie's jewelry and Benton being in the hospital, though it didn't answer any old questions. It just raised new ones.

"I do have some news. I'll take a shower and come over. How are the boys?"

"They're still asking about their father and mother. It's getting a little harder to distract them. Archie has been a big help. How are you holding up?"

It took a second for Lainie to respond. How was she holding up? She felt as if she'd been running a marathon at a sprint. "I'm not sure. I haven't had much time to think." Ben's comment that she hadn't even had time to bury Evie replayed in her mind. Lainie wasn't ready to say that Evie needed to be buried. Where were her parents on that score? She hated to think about the conversation they would have to have.

"I understand that. Come on over and take a break for a bit."

"I'll be over in about half an hour."

She set about making coffee and then hopped into the shower, trying to think only about the next thing and not about the difficult decisions that would need to be made in the future.

When Lainie arrived at her folks' house, Owen and Evan bounded out the front door to greet her.

"Aunt Lainie! We're going to the movies. Do you want to come?" Owen said. He reached her first, and she grabbed him in a tight hug. She didn't know exactly what the boys had been told, but she was glad they were amenable to distraction.

Archie followed them out of the house. "We're going to see a Marvel movie. You want to join us?"

Lainie released Owen and hugged Evan. "I'd love to, but I have a lot of things to do. You guys have a good time."

"Missing out on good popcorn." The expression on Archie's face told her he was doing his best to keep the boys' spirits up.

"Tempting." She gave Archie a hug, so very glad he was there to help. "You know that popcorn is my favorite."

"You might wish to change your mind." He nodded toward the house. "Long article in the paper this morning."

"Oh no."

Archie winked and then shepherded the boys to his car.

"I don't think they're ready to go back to school yet." Mom greeted Lainie at the front door. She handed Lainie the *Press-Telegram*, the expression on her face disapproving. "Stan made the front page."

Callen West had written the story about Stan and the warrant service at the car wash. He detailed the murder of Taylor Abbott in Stan's office and noted that police were trying to locate Stan as a possible witness, not a suspect.

Lainie was certain Shea had told West that so whatever was written did not spook Stan. There was nothing in the piece about Crystal Benton in San Bernardino or about the shooting at the tow yard.

Lainie saw no point in telling her parents about the shooting. It would just give them something else to worry about. The only new information she had to impart was about the jewelry found in Benton's property.

"Do you have Evie's jewelry with you?" Mom asked.

"No, it's in evidence. We won't get it back until everything is adjudicated."

Mom rubbed her face with both hands and then sat at the table. "This entire situation is so unbelievable. When I think of how many times I sat next to Stan at church. How did I not see that he was a monster?"

"Evie lived with him and didn't see it," Dad said.

"Evie always saw the best in people." Speaking of her in the past tense made Lainie suck in a breath as if she'd been punched. Was she on the road to acceptance? Before she could answer herself, her phone rang. It was Shea.

Lainie answered.

"We found Stan."

CHAPTER 32

Lainie hung up from the call, not sure if she should feel satisfied, bewildered, or both. Slowly she explained to her parents what she knew about Stan's arrest.

"A Ventura County sheriff arrested him at a beach parking lot in Ventura. He was sleeping in his car. Shea and Collins are on their way up there to get him and bring him back."

"He said a lot more, Lainie," her dad said.

"I know that he did. I'm trying to process everything. Apparently, there was evidence discovered in his car about human trafficking, the disappearance of an FBI agent, and even the murder of Mr. Straight, remember him? He was killed a couple of months ago."

"Stan was responsible for that?"

"All the evidence they found in his car has to be sorted through carefully," she said. "From what they've found so far, it's possible Stan was involved." Though she barely believed it.

Back at home later that day, Lainie got a text from Collins saying that Dr. Hardin would continue to lower Benton's coma drugs. Hopefully she would wake up in the next couple of days.

They now had Stan. Did they even need Benton?

✦

The next day, Lainie checked the calendar and reflected on the number of days it had been since she took Stan's phone call and was told that Evie was gone. A week later and she still had no idea what had happened to her sister.

She poured her first cup of coffee and did something that had at one time been a habit but she had not done in years.

She sat in a chair with a Bible to do a daily devotional. The reading was from the book of Esther, and the theme was the providence of God. The words tore at Lainie's heart. God's hand could be seen in *every* life situation. Nothing, not the sad, the bad, or the wonderful was outside of his control.

It was a truth she'd heard often. Now it scorched her soul.

Why Evie?

She knew she'd never understand. She also knew that the only way to peace was to trust the Lord—his plans were always the best because he knew the end from the beginning. She used to believe that with all her heart, and it gave her peace.

In Acceptance Lies Peace was the devotional's title.

Leaning back, she closed her eyes. *Oh, Lord, please help me get to the point of acceptance, because where I'm at right now hurts too much.*

She held her hands out, palms up, trying to let go of the fear and self-recrimination she felt. None of that would help anything get better. After a few minutes, she closed her Bible and devotional.

Do the next thing echoed in her mind, and she had to decide what the most important next thing was.

Was it time to go back to work?

She still had plenty of time to take off, but what could she do off duty?

Everything was so unresolved.

They found Stan, but where was Evie? Would he tell them? Did he know?

The last point was the one that tied her in knots. She'd loved cold-case stories, and just about every one that she'd ever seen started with the crime and relatives of the victims asking two important questions: who and why? Then years went by before they got any answers. Sometimes they never got answers. Lainie didn't think she could take *never* knowing, *never* finding her sister.

The day before, she and her parents had danced around planning some sort of memorial for Evie. While she'd been at their house, several people from church stopped by to bring food and to extend their support and pray.

Before Evie had disappeared, Lainie would have run from that idea and left the house as soon as possible. But yesterday she sat, head bowed, completely moved by the sincere prayers offered by people who loved Evie. It left Lainie so very sad that she had stayed away from her church family for so long.

The prayers stayed on her heart as she paced her home, still wondering if it was time to go back to work. The one thing they had that many of the cold-case stories she remembered didn't have was a suspect in custody. This case was fortunate enough to have two. Benton and Stan.

At least Stan was awake and alert and in jail. Hopefully, he would answer questions and tell the truth about what happened to Evie. Right now, no one knew where to search for her or had any real inkling of where she might be.

Lainie's phone rang and she saw that it was Mike. Maybe that was a sign that she should return to work. "Hey, partner, what's up?"

"Couple of things are cooking. I was checking in. Everyone is talking about your brother-in-law. I hope that settles some things for you."

"Yes and no. I will never make sense out of this situation."

"I guess you're right. And I wanted to tell you that I finally got approval to talk to Hank Bucshon. I'll be heading out to Terminal Island later today."

"So the Feds have him. I kind of lost track."

"Yeah, the Feds agreed that he might be in danger in county jail. He was arraigned in Long Beach for spousal abuse, but not yet given a court date. I'm not sure if he'll go to trial or take a plea. I'm leaning toward plea because we caught him red-handed, but you never know. His public defender said it was okay for me to talk to him."

"Maybe I'll go with. I was thinking that it's time to return to work."

"You think you're ready?"

"I don't know, Mike. Honestly, my whole world is off-balance now. But there isn't a lot for me to do around the house, and if I don't have something to occupy my mind, I will lose it."

His response was interrupted by her phone telling her she had another call coming through. "Can I call you back? Shea is on the other line."

"Sure."

Lainie switched to Shea's call. "Bobby, you have news?"

"I have news. I don't know if you'll consider it good or bad."

"Stan lawyer up?"

"No, but he won't talk to us. He wants to talk to you and only you."

"You're serious?"

"As a heart attack. We're waiting for you."

CHAPTER 33

The request knocked Lainie back on her heels. For a second, she thought her answer should be no—she didn't want to look at Stan much less talk to him. But the overwhelming need to find out what had happened to Evie prompted her to say yes. Lainie prepared herself to talk to Stan like she would for any criminal she arrested.

Shea met her in the homicide office. Ben Isaacs's presence with him took her by surprise.

"Our agencies are working together on this," he said.

"I hope that means more resources."

"We have carte blanche right now. At the heart of our investigation is the need to find Efren. You need to find your sister—our interests have merged. I hope you can get Stan to come clean on both subjects."

"I'll do my best. How is your head?" His bandage ran from his left eyebrow back toward his ear.

"It's healing."

Shea handed her a thumb drive and an inventory list of all the evidence they found in Stan's car, diverting her attention from Ben.

"Here's what you need to review before talking to Moffit. The trunk of his car was filled with—" Shea paused, rubbed his chin. "Well, you'll see. You know how to interview a bad guy, Lainie. I know you're good at it. But this is a relative. Are you sure you're up to this?"

"I want to know what he has to say. Do I wish he was talking to you or the Feds? Yeah. But since he won't, I'll do my best."

He nodded and then he and Ben left her alone to read the arrest report and review the evidence recovered from Stan's vehicle. She sat in front of a computer, inserted the thumb drive, and pulled up the file. There was also a report from the forensic accountant who had reviewed the paperwork found in the safe at the car wash.

She remembered thinking while she was at the car wash that it was a setup, that Stan could not be that stupid. Now, she began to rethink that assessment. Stan could simply be a consummate actor. Maybe trying to be more sister and less cop interfered with Lainie's instincts. In Stan's car they found a 9mm handgun that had been recently fired. It was the same caliber that likely killed Abbott. They'd found more financial paperwork, and the coup de grâce was that they'd also found a gun, wallet, and badge belonging to Efren Gomez.

Still, it was hard to fathom that this man who had been part of her family for over eight years was a cold-blooded killer as well as a stone-cold criminal.

Then it hit her like a bolt of lightning. Stan was always an opportunist, a follower, never the leader. Was that dynamic working here?

We'll see. She rolled her shoulders to release some tension and fought the headache that threatened. She also prayed for wisdom and clarity. Way more was going on here than what she was reading.

The more she read, the more she wondered what she'd hear from Stan. He'd never had her as conned as he had the rest of her family. In Hawaii she almost came right out and accused him of hurting Evie.

In truth, she just wanted to get this over with. *I pray that this isn't just a game or a stall tactic.* Lainie turned when the door opened.

Mike walked in. Lainie stood and gave him a hug.

"They got a lot of stuff on him." He nodded to the file she had opened. "I talked to Bryce. He's got the 9mm in the lab for ballistics testing."

"Still, it's baffling. Stan as a crime boss was not a square I would have picked on my bingo card."

Mike shrugged. "Are you ready to talk to him?"

"As ready as I'll ever be."

Mike patted her shoulder. "You'll do fine."

She grabbed her notebook, and together they walked downstairs. Stan was in the same booking interview room she'd sat in with Bucshon not too many days ago. It seemed like a lifetime ago, and Lainie felt ten years older with all that had happened in the intervening days. But she was fundamentally the same person, the same driven investigator who wanted to work in homicide one day. She owed it to Evie and to Efren to do her best.

Shea, Collins, Chief Mackall, and Ben were all watching through the one-way mirror. The interview would be recorded, and the camera was on and blinking. Stan sat at the interview table, hunched over like an old man. He hadn't shaved or combed his hair. Lainie could not remember ever seeing him so unkempt. In Hawaii he'd appeared tired and stressed, but now he looked like he'd been living on the streets for a month.

Putting her notebook under her arm, Lainie opened the door and went into the room to hear what Stan had to say.

CHAPTER 34

Stan's head was down on the table when Lainie stepped into the room. He raised his head as she closed the door behind her, and she thought she saw light come into his eyes.

"Lainie, thank God. How are the boys?"

That question surprised and disarmed her a bit. She swallowed. "They're fine, with Mom and Dad."

Stan seemed visibly relieved. "Please tell them I didn't do what I'm being accused of."

"How can I tell them that, Stan?" She stood at the table.

His eyes widened. "What do you mean? You know me. I'm not a killer."

"Do I know you?" She pulled the chair out and sat. "Where's Evie?"

He leaned back in his chair and stared at her saying nothing.

"Detective Shea advised you of your rights, didn't he? Do you understand them?"

"Yeah, I understand. I don't want a lawyer. I'll talk to you. You have to believe that I am innocent."

"Why didn't you answer my question about Evie?"

"I didn't hurt Evie."

"That's not what I asked. Where is she?"

He put his head down on the table again. "I thought you of all people would believe me."

"What's to believe?" She fought to keep emotion out of her voice. "You haven't answered any of my questions. You told Detective Shea you wanted to talk to me. I'm leaving if all you want to do is lie to me."

"He'll kill me." He spoke so low she barely heard him.

"Who?"

"You know who."

"Say it."

He raised his head. "Vine took her."

Lainie lost her voice for a moment. Her heartbeat pounded in her ears, and her mouth went dry.

When she could speak, she lowered her voice. "What do you mean?"

"I know I haven't been—" His voice broke, and he took a couple of minutes to compose himself. "I know I wasn't the best husband. I cheated, okay? I admit it. I was conned."

"What does that have to do with Evie? Did Vine con you?"

"Crystal. She made it sound so easy."

"You're talking in circles, not completing thoughts. Just tell me what happened to Evie."

"I don't know where to start."

Lainie fought frustration and had to clench her teeth. "How about from the beginning."

He rubbed his forehead. "It started with the car wash job. I found out that a lot more was going on there than just washing cars. A lot of money came through the place. I wasn't supposed to ask questions. Crystal is Vine's accountant. When I told her I thought something illegal was going on, she seduced me."

Lainie worked hard not to let the admission of infidelity anger her more than he always had. An overtly angry interview was rarely a good one.

"What was happening that worried you?"

"Money I couldn't account for, but Crystal made everything jibe. And there were messages—cars would come in that were directed to Raphael, my detail guy. One time I saw him remove a door panel and remove money and paperwork. When I asked him about it, he told me to talk to Crystal."

"Raphael Diaz?"

"Yeah."

Raphael had been the front passenger in Benton's vehicle. He was dead, no way to talk to him.

"You were the boss. Why didn't you make him tell you?"

"I wasn't really the boss. I had to run everything by Crystal. Like I said, for a while lust blinded me." His face scrunched in pain. "It sounds awful, doesn't it?"

Lainie said nothing and waited for Stan to continue.

"I didn't know it at the time, but I think she did it to keep me quiet about the money. I admit it, I was weak. I fell. I thought . . ." His voice trailed off as if he was trying to collect his thoughts.

Lainie worked hard to keep her features blank. Stan was disgusting.

"Then she explained to me how easy it would be to take a little bit of that cash. So easy that Vine would never know it was gone. There was so much money. It was right there for the taking, so we took it. We were skimming off the top. Padding an offshore bank account. At first it was a game and so exhilarating. For the first time in my life, I had money, lots of it. She played me—I, ah . . ."

"You were having an affair and stealing. Is that supposed to help me believe that you aren't also a killer?" Without giving him a chance to respond, she went for the throat.

"You took out a four-million-dollar life insurance policy on Evie."

He sat back as if slapped. He opened his mouth, but nothing came out. He licked his lips. "That was Crystal's idea," he said in a whisper.

Lainie blinked, realizing that all he was going to do was deflect.

She backtracked. "You haven't gotten to Evie yet. How does she fit into this mess?"

"Crystal made all these promises. It just sounded easy, so different. We were only taking money from a criminal. That's how I justified it."

"Why did Vine take Evie?"

"I'm getting there."

"You knew the entire time you worked with him that Vine was a criminal, didn't you?"

"I didn't. Not at first. Crystal hired me. I've never met Vine. I had questions. Crystal walked me through the money trail and his name came up. She talked me into believing that he deserved to be stolen from, and we'd never be caught. I admit that it was wrong, all of it. I strayed, cheated on Evie. Crystal kept stringing me along."

He leaned forward as far as the table would allow. His voice took on a pleading tone. "I was ready to break it off. I realized at some level she was only using me. That's why I planned the trip to Hawaii. I was going to come clean with Evie and ask her to forgive me. I did not hurt Evie. I did not hurt anyone."

He paused, looking lost and dejected to Lainie. Like a child who'd just been embarrassed in a room full of peers.

"If Crystal knew how to access Vine's money, why did she need you?"

"I didn't think about that until I was arrested. It was part of the con. In retrospect, we were a team at first. She stole from Vine but used me as a cover. She made it sound as if she needed me and that Vine would never miss the money. When he found out about the missing money, he only blamed me. Crystal was able to keep herself out of it. Because he thought I was the thief, he took Evie. He told me if I gave the money back, he'd give me Evie back."

"I don't get it. How would faking a shark attack, making everyone believe that Evie was dead, get her back?"

He tried to talk with his hands, and all that did was make the cuffs clink on the desk.

"With Evie gone, I was desperate, grasping at straws. The only person I could go to was Crystal."

"You could have come to me or gone to the police."

"Hindsight is twenty-twenty. Crystal said we could stall Vine, promise him his money plus interest. She swore that it was only money he wanted; he wouldn't hurt Evie." Stan began to cry.

"Crystal came up with the life insurance scam? It still makes no sense. How would that play out if you got the money pretending Evie was dead and Evie suddenly appeared alive and well?"

He avoided her gaze, tears streaming down his face. "Don't you understand? Like I said, I was desperate. All I wanted was Evie back. When she was back and safe, I planned to cross those bridges when I got to them."

The explanation didn't make sense to Lainie. Was Stan really that naive?

"When exactly did Vine take Evie?" It was hard to keep the fury out of her voice. Lainie fought the urge to stand and bang the table. Beneath the table her hands were tight fists.

Stan took several deep breaths. "He took her on the Tuesday before we were to leave for Hawaii. That's why I took the boys to Mom and Pops' house early. I was a mess. Crystal kept me from losing it completely."

"Why didn't you call the police if that monster took your wife?" Jaw tight, she barely kept her cool. The thought of an evil man like Vine having anything to do with Evie came close to making Lainie grab Stan by the neck.

"Because he said he'd kill her. And I stole money—they would have arrested me!"

Lainie nearly launched herself at Stan. She prayed for restraint. This was why detectives didn't investigate crimes concerning their families. It's too close—they couldn't be objective and get the answers they needed. Lainie needed answers. She took a deep breath. "Did Crystal go with you to Hawaii, pretending to be Evie?"

Stan gave a slight nod. "None of this was my idea. I've been played and manipulated. The trip was planned and paid for. Crystal said we could use it to our advantage. Extra money so we didn't have to give back what we stole. She said we could have it both ways. I could get Evie back and we could still fool Vine."

Lainie worked to control her breathing, and her anger percolated anew. She'd known that this interview would be hard—she had no idea it would be this hard.

"If it was her idea, you certainly worked hard to sell it. Your phone call to me, to my father. What have you told the boys?"

His head jerked up. "What can I tell them? Crystal insisted that it would work. I wanted it to work with all my heart. I want Evie to be okay."

"You had to know that you wouldn't get the money right away."

"Crystal said that if I claimed a hardship because of the boys, they'd give me the money faster. Then it all went wrong. When you came to Hawaii and I could tell that you didn't believe me, I panicked. I almost told the truth. I told her you weren't fooled and asked her what to do about it."

"What did she say?"

"She told me to man up. Stick with the story. You had no proof of anything; nobody did." He closed his eyes for a second, then rubbed his chin. When he opened his eyes, he continued. "She insisted that the plan was perfect—if I kept my nerve."

"She tried to run me over."

"I had nothing to do with that. I was angry because of it. Crystal left Hawaii after that. The last words she said to me were that she was sorry she'd wasted so much time on me and that I was on my own. I asked her if Evie was still alive."

"What did she say?"

"She laughed."

Lainie ran a hand down her face. He had so many chances to come forward and tell them about her sister. Instead, he was only concerned about saving his own skin.

"What about Evie? Has Vine contacted you about Evie since you got back? Where is my sister?"

"I don't know. I tried to call Vine; he won't take my calls. I don't have the money. I don't have access to the accounts. Crystal has cut me out of everything. She left enough evidence so I'd be arrested for everything. Now she's gone and I'm in jail."

"I suppose that you had nothing to do with Ms. Abbott, the day shift supervisor who was murdered in your office."

"I haven't been back to my office since I returned from Hawaii."

"You told my parents the other day that you were going to work."

"I didn't go. I was trying to find Crystal. I even sat outside Vine's house for a bit, went to his cigar club. I never found either of them."

Lainie leaned back. Stan sniffled; tears dried on his face.

"All you're concerned about is the money. I'm concerned about my sister."

"I don't know where she is. If I did, I would have gone to get her. *I just don't know.*"

The last sentence came out like a whine. Lainie wanted to get up and run to where Vine was and squeeze answers from him. But there was more information she needed to get from Stan. "What happened to Efren?"

"Efren?"

"Don't be stupid. He worked at the car wash. He was undercover FBI."

He dropped his head and covered his eyes. "FBI? He just detailed cars. I don't know what you mean. Has something happened to him?" His cloying tone was disingenuous.

"He's missing."

He shrugged. "Crystal didn't say anything to me about him."

"You have his badge and gun."

Stan shook his head. "I don't know how that got in my car. Maybe Crystal put it there. Maybe she knows where he is. If she knew that he was FBI, she probably killed him. Crystal is evil. Now I'm her fall guy."

"She's in the hospital."

"What?"

"Coma. She was in a car accident."

"No. I just spoke to her."

"When?"

"Yesterday. She warned me that the cops were after me. She told me to run and not stop or the boys would be in danger. I didn't know where to go. I got as far as Ventura."

That took Lainie by surprise. They knew for a fact that Benton hadn't been talking to anyone for at least three days. Why would he lie about it? Then she recalled training she'd had on artificial intelligence. It would be a simple thing for Vine or anyone to fake a phone call using AI. Telling Stan to run away and try to hide would certainly make him appear guilty.

There was no doubt in her mind that Stan was guilty of a lot. But of being a criminal mastermind? As angry as she was with him, she still couldn't see that.

"The paperwork in your car indicates that you were behind all of this. That you sent money to two hit men to kill Martin Straight a couple of months ago. Nothing in there incriminates Crystal."

His face screwed up in distress and his voice squeaked. "Straight? What motive would I have to kill him? They're framing me. Come on, Lainie. Do you really think that I'm such a monster?"

"My sister is gone, Stan, and you are more concerned about what has happened to you than where she is or what's happened to her. I wouldn't put anything past you. At least have the decency to tell me where her body is so my family can have some closure."

He raised his voice. "I had nothing to do with what happened to Evie, I swear. I had an affair with a liar, I admit that, but that's all I'm guilty of." Tears fell anew.

She stared at him for a few minutes, bile rising in her throat.

"What about all the stuff we found in the safe at your office? Money, IDs, and paperwork for offshore bank accounts?"

"All Crystal's idea." Then he seemed to perk up a bit. "You found all of that?"

"Yeah, we did."

"The bathroom floor safe. That was the only thing I did on my own. Right before I left for Hawaii, I set it up." A slight smile emerged. "At least I put one thing over on Crystal. The money was in case we had to flee from Vine. She pretended that we would flee together. But when he took Evie, no way I could leave. I love my boys; I couldn't lose them as well. Crystal made it sound like the shark attack would work. I really thought that would save Evie and solve all my problems."

"All your problems?" Disgusted, Lainie stood. "I suggest you lawyer up. The evidence all points to you. Not Crystal, not Vine."

The expression on his face was so lost, so perplexed, Lainie almost felt sorry for him.

Almost.

CHAPTER 35

Lainie closed the door to the interview and almost collapsed in the hallway.

"You okay, Lainie?" Shea and Ben hurried toward her.

"No, I'm not. I'm angry. He is so cavalier about my sister." For a few seconds, she leaned against the wall, bent over a bit, hands on her knees.

"Yeah, but I believe him. He doesn't have the chops to be the bad guy here," Ben said. "But why claim he just talked to Benton? We know that's not possible. I do think he was lying to you about not knowing anything regarding Efren."

Lainie straightened up as she got her balance back. "I got that feeling as well. I'm not sure why he would lie about Efren. If he didn't kill him, he might know who did. Why protect them?"

"Maybe a couple more nights in jail will loosen his tongue."

"Maybe. Stan certainly isn't going to like county lockup. The only place we might get more answers is with Benton, if she ever wakes up. She had Evie's jewelry. She must know something about where Evie is. You heard him blame Vine for Evie's disappearance."

"I did," Shea said.

"Can we put any pressure on Vine? Kidnapping Evie sounds like something he would do."

"I agree with you, it sounds exactly like something he would do. But you know as well as I do, it's Stan's word against Vine's. And right now, all the evidence points to Stan."

"Vine still needs to be interrogated."

"You know that won't happen," Ben said. "Vine is not stupid. He'll hide behind his attorneys, and they'll say that Stan is obviously trying to deflect blame. With all the evidence in the car, that's a plausible argument for him to use. There is no incentive at all for Vine to talk to us. We have no leverage. Right now, his fingerprints aren't on anything; the only prints we have are Stan's."

Lainie closed her eyes and leaned back against the wall.

"I know that, and I hate it. He always seems to hold the winning hand. If he did take Evie . . ." She couldn't finish the thought; it was too dark. She changed gears. "Benton's still alive. If Vine knows that, she could be in trouble."

"If Vine is the one who put her in the hospital, you would be right," Shea said. "So far, there have been no problems."

"Is there any kind of guard on her?"

"I asked and was told that since she's in CCU, no one can get to see her without doctor approval. Since she's not in custody for anything and the two guys she was with are dead, no guard."

"I was going to come back to work tomorrow. Now I think I'll wait. You don't mind if I hang out at St. Bernardine, do you?"

"Not at all. But don't do it on your own time. I think we can get the chief to sign off on an out-of-city assignment. This case has a lot of moving parts. And Crystal Benton is an important part of this investigation."

✦

As Ben had listened to the interview, he thought Lainie did as well as she could considering the circumstances. His impression of Stan was that he was a narcissistic personality. Clearly all he cared about was how everything was affecting him. It really galled Ben how he pretended not to know who Efren was. Efren had been to his house for dinner, sat with his wife and kids. Why lie so blatantly about barely knowing him unless he was hiding something? Ben wanted a crack at Moffit. He wanted to shake him and get the truth.

Yet there was always the chance that Stan really knew nothing of substance. Bucshon was certainly no help. Mark had postulated that very thing after the meeting with the ASAC. Packard was convinced that they'd caught their man.

"There was a pile of evidence in the trunk of his car. It looks as if you men were on the right track, just shadowing the wrong criminal. We are going to work with LBPD on finding out what happened to Agent Gomez. We have no reason to believe that he was taken out of state."

"I can't believe this," Ben said to Mark after Packard left. "Stan Moffit a criminal mastermind?"

"I'm blindsided as well. Nothing Efren ever reported would have led us to reach that conclusion. I only hope all the evidence will convince me as much as it convinced Packard."

Ben reread the criminal complaint against Moffit. Perhaps Benton and Vine found the perfect fall guy. Taking all the evidence at face value, one would have to conclude that Vine wasn't the one trafficking people, laundering money, and kidnapping Evangeline. It was Stan Moffit.

"I've got some paperwork to take care of," Mark said. "Call Shea and ask about talking to Moffit."

That was how Ben had ended up at LBPD. He wanted to talk to Moffit, but the man made it clear he'd only talk to Lainie. In spite of her best efforts, he didn't say much of what Ben wanted to hear.

CHAPTER 36

The chief approved Lainie's return to work. He also greenlighted her idea to go back to San Bernardino to keep an eye on Benton. He also had some good news for her.

"This sounds like an easy way for you to ease back into work. I read the report about the shooting at the tow yard. They found the helmet when they found the motorcycle." He held up his phone with a photo of the helmet.

Lainie took the phone and studied the damage she'd done. There was a perfect crease across the top of the helmet.

"The bad guy got his head jerked back and probably a good scare when the bullet hit. And we might just get DNA from the inside."

"That's great to hear." Lainie handed the phone back. "But you know as well as I do that getting DNA back will take time. I really don't want that shooter to get away."

"I'm optimistic that we'll catch him, and whenever the DNA comes back, it will seal the deal. As far as the woman in San Bernardino goes, contact Shea first thing if they wake her up. You don't have authorization to conduct an interview. You're too close."

Lainie didn't mind the admonition. It had been so hard to interview Stan in a controlled environment. She wasn't certain she'd be able to maintain her control with Benton in real life. It would be much better for an uninvolved detective to do the interview.

She left the chief's office and went down the hall to the violent crimes' office. Mike was there and she filled him in on what she planned.

"You're only one person, and you can only be at the medical center during the day. Is that really effective?" Mike asked.

"I'll be there during visiting hours. Hospital security told the chief that after visiting hours end, the Critical Care Unit floor is locked down pretty tight. They agree to keep an extra eye on it."

"How long do you think you can handle being a babysitter?"

"I need to hear what Benton has to say. I can sit tight for a day or two. Call me if you get anything from Bucshon."

"Of course. I'm heading out to Terminal Island now."

They left the department together. Mike to his plain car en route to the federal prison and Lainie to her personal car en route home, to pick up a few things to make hospital duty a little more bearable.

She went home, packed a lunch, grabbed her Kindle, and drove to St. Bernardine.

Dr. Hardin was there when she arrived. Chief Mackall had told her that he would alert the hospital staff and the sheriff's department that she'd be at the hospital for the next few days. Once inside the Critical Care floor, Dr. Hardin met her at the nurses' station.

"Are you certain her life is in danger?" He seemed a little tense. "So far, no one has shown any interest in her at all, other than the police. We would have been happy if we could notify next of kin."

"I'm just covering all the bases. It's obvious that she was a prisoner in the vehicle that crashed. And even though nothing has happened up until now, someone may still appear to finish the job. It won't hurt to sit here for a couple of days. You were optimistic the other night about bringing her out of the coma in a day or two. Does that still stand?"

He nodded. "Swelling in her brain has decreased appreciably. I've been decreasing her medication. We are in the process of reversing the coma. I've arranged for a chair to be outside her cubicle for you. I don't want you inside the cubicle. No excitement or noise that might jolt her awake unexpectedly. It's better if we manage her rousing slowly and methodically."

"Understood. Thanks, Doc."

He introduced her to the two nurses on duty, Cherie and Ava.

Lainie settled in, opening her Kindle to read.

The floor was quiet but for the sound of life-preserving machinery and the Critical Care nurses softly padding from cubicle to cubicle. Since the official waiting room was outside the secured double doors, visitors were not allowed in Critical Care cubicles without a nurse or a doctor accompanying them. There was seldom anyone else in her line of vision.

That changed around five minutes to seven. Hospital visiting hours ended at seven. Lainie stood and stretched, getting ready to call it a night, when the double doors opened. She assumed it would be Ava and Cherie returning. At some point, she hadn't noticed when, they'd both left the station.

She glanced toward the doors, Kindle under her arm. Instead of the two nurses, three men came walking her way. The man in the middle caught her attention immediately. She'd know him anywhere, even after fifteen years. He was older, somewhat smaller, and his hair was grayer, but the scar on his left cheek still stood out like a tattoo.

Dallas Vine.

CHAPTER 37

Their eyes locked and a progression of emotions crossed Vine's features: surprise followed by irritation and then recognition.

Lainie recovered from the shock quickly and spoke up first. "What are you doing here?"

"I could ask you the same thing. This is a long way from Long Beach, Officer Jensen."

"Detective Jensen now. I'm here on official business. Guarding a witness." Her heart still pounded. She hadn't seen him in person for at least ten years. He creeped her out now as much as he did back then. He was an evil murderer as far as Lainie was concerned.

She felt a little uncomfortable being without her duty weapon. She'd left it locked up in her car, thinking she wouldn't need it. And in reality, the last place she wanted to get into a gunfight would be the hospital.

Vine arched an eyebrow. "Detective. I'm here to check up on a faithful employee. You might have heard that she was injured in a horrible traffic accident."

"I have heard. She's been here for four days. You just checking up on her now?"

"I only recently received the message. What did Crystal witness?"

Lainie heard the question; she wasn't immediately certain how to answer. The last thing she wanted to do was give away anything she knew but he didn't.

"I didn't say I was here for Crystal. Why are you here now? Visiting hours just ended. How did you even get in without someone opening the door?" At that moment Lainie realized that Ava and Cherie were still not on the floor. Other than the patients, the only people on the floor were her, Vine, and his two goons.

"As I stated, I was only just notified." He leaned forward. "On another subject, I'm astonished to hear that you're still employed by the city of Long Beach." His tone turned snarky, his lips curled into a smirk.

"I don't really care what astonishes you."

He threw back his head and laughed. The goons with him also smiled.

Lainie seethed inside but she kept her cool. She was fifteen years older and wiser; she would not make the same mistakes she had made when she was green.

When he saw that he hadn't gotten a rise out of her, the laughing stopped. The smirk stayed.

"It's just quite a juxtaposition. I read an article just the other day, and it appears as if you have a serious criminal in your family. The only thing he's not guilty of is having a dead woman in his car. I'd think an officer of the law would have a tighter grip on such things. Amazing how situations turn in time."

His expression told her that he knew something; he was baiting her. The problem was, as Ben had noted, she had no leverage.

"Nothing's turned. You're still a criminal and you won't evade justice forever."

His face darkened; a muscle twitched in his cheek. "You've been a shadow over my life for long enough. You're nothing but a bug I'll squash and then scrape off my shoe. Soon. I've waited too long as it is."

"Are you threatening me?"

Through clenched teeth, he said, "I don't make threats."

Lainie tensed but Vine's attention turned from her when the double doors opened, and Ava and Cherie stepped in. They were chatting, and Lainie caught snatches of their conversation.

"Weird."

"I don't think that's ever happened before."

Vine glanced behind him, then turned back to Lainie. "I guess we'll just have to come back tomorrow." His tone changed instantly to something less sinister and more conciliatory. But darkness never left his eyes.

He turned to leave, and the two goons followed him, but not before each cast a glare toward Lainie.

"You might want to take the stairs," one of the nurses said. "The elevator malfunctioned a few minutes ago."

He waved a hand toward her, and the trio exited through the double doors.

When she was sure they were gone, Lainie looked over at Cherie and Ava.

"Who were those guys?" Ava asked. "Did you let them in?"

"No. They opened the door and walked right in. What's wrong with the elevator?"

"I don't know," Ava said as they exchanged glances. "We were both called downstairs separately, and when we got down there, there was nothing for us. So when we hopped onto the elevator to come back upstairs, it wouldn't work. That's why we came up the stairs."

Lainie walked over to the double doors and peered through the window in the door just as Vine and his men stepped onto the elevator and the doors closed. "It works now. They just got on."

"Weird, huh?" the nurse said.

"Yeah." Lainie didn't like it at all. She would use the word *sinister*. Vine didn't just show up to check on Benton. All her instincts were tingling, telling her that Vine was here because he was up to no good.

Her phone rang, and she saw that Mike was calling. "Hey, partner, what's up?"

"I wanted to let you know how it went with Bucshon. Are you still in San Bernardino?"

"I am. I was just getting ready to leave." She took a seat back in her chair. "What did Hank say?"

"Some interesting things about Benton. Bucshon's attorney allowed me to record the interaction. I'll send it to you in an MP3 file and you can listen to it at your leisure. He offered nothing that we can use in court, but he did give some interesting insight into the relationship between Stan and Crystal Benton."

"I can't wait to hear it."

"Are you heading back to the city?"

"I was, but something weird just happened." She explained to him about Vine's visit.

"Strange. From what I've heard, that guy never comes out in public anymore. If he showed up to try and check up on Benton, wow, something is going on."

"I agree. I'm almost afraid to leave."

"You can't stay there indefinitely. At some point you must trust hospital security."

"I know you're right. I'll call the sheriff's office and give them a heads-up. Send the file."

"You got it."

After about a minute, her phone chimed with an incoming message. Lainie could sit here for a few minutes and listen to the interview. She put her earbuds on and downloaded the file. It took a few minutes, but the hospital Wi-Fi was more than adequate.

The file opened with the normal sounds of people moving around, and Mike announced who was present and that the recording was allowed by Bucshon's public defender.

"Thanks for getting me sent here, Detective Pepper."

"I wish I could take credit for it, Hank. But the Feds put you here."

"Whoever, it's just better here than County."

"Are you ready to answer some questions?" Mike asked.

"I'll answer whatever I can."

"Do you know who Stan Moffit is?"

"Yeah. He was the stooge running Sudsy Place."

"Why do you call him a stooge?"

"He isn't that bright. He doesn't really know what he's doing. Out of his league really."

"League?"

"Yeah, Vine is miles ahead of that guy. And so is that girl of his, Crystal. I think the two of them play Moffit, like an instrument. Especially the girl. Moffit is one of those guys who checks his brain at the door when he sees a pretty face. Just my observation."

"Why do they need to play Moffit?" Mike asked.

There was the sound of fidgeting, whispering. Lainie heard a voice she guessed belonged to the attorney. The sound of someone clearing their throat, then Bucshon spoke again.

"Sudsy Place is a drop. Money comes in and instructions go out. Moffit ain't going to question anything."

"What do you mean by that?"

"He's a compliant guy. He does what he's told. Nothing more."

"The money and the instructions—what is that all about?"

"Vine's business," Bucshon said. *"He moves money, drugs, people, all over the place. Sudsy Place was set up to facilitate all that. Couple of guys there keep the goods moving while Crystal handles the money. Moffit is kind of window dressing, so everything seems legit."*

"How do you know what Moffit would do in relation to Vine?" Mike asked. *"What exactly did you do for Vine?"*

The attorney spoke up. *"My client is not going to incriminate himself. He may have made comments earlier, before representation. I will fight the use of those comments in court."*

"Hypothetically," Mike said. *"What job would a person have where he would be privy to information about what you're saying?"*

There was a sound on the tape, as if someone was playing with a plastic water bottle, tapping it on the table and crinkling the plastic.

Lainie waited, growing impatient by the minute. Hank was self-serving; she wasn't certain they could trust anything he said.

"A runner," he said finally. *"Freelance. Someone who takes a message from one person and runs it to the next. Not knowing what the message said."*

"Taking messages from Vine to the car wash?" Mike asked.

"And the other way. Someone like that might see how the dynamics in a business work."

"Would that person have any proof?"

"Only what he saw and heard."

Lainie closed the file. In a way it lent credence to what Stan had said. Both men hedged their answers, and she'd bet a paycheck neither was completely truthful. Bucshon would not be the strongest witness in court, but he could be put on the stand. Still, they needed a stronger voice.

She glanced toward the cubicle where Benton lay. Crystal Benton could probably bury Vine if she wanted to. If she woke up, would she?

CHAPTER 38

Thinking about court and the type of evidence they'd need to make a solid case, Lainie got up to pace the hallway in the CCU. They'd need a lot to get Vine. And they did have a lot of solid evidence. The trouble was, it only pointed to Stan. DNA from the motorcycle helmet could blow things wide open, but it could be months before they got it. Could the DNA be Stan's? Lainie didn't see it.

She was about to dial the sheriff's department and let them know about Vine's visit when her phone chimed with a call. It was Ben Isaacs.

"I hear you're babysitting Crystal Benton."

"Yeah, I think she's our best bet to get to Vine. If I know that, he knows that. He was just here."

"What? Vine? At the hospital?" Ben's voice rose an octave.

"Yeah." Lainie told him about the visit.

"That is alarming. Someone does need to be watching Benton. His being there says that he doesn't trust her to stay quiet."

"Why should she? It certainly seems like Vine wanted her dead."

"You need a break," Ben said. "I can come down and cover the midnight shift. Can you wait until I get there?"

"Seriously, you'd sit here all night?"

"You bet. I believe Benton might know about Efren. I want to talk to her as much as you do. It's important that she gets well and wakes up to talk."

"Agreed. I will wait. Can I ask you a favor?"

"Shoot."

"My lunch was a long time ago. Can you do an In-N-Out run for me?"

"You got it. I'll be down there in about an hour."

"Thanks."

At the nurses' station Lainie noted that there was a shift change. She watched as two of them entered Benton's cubicle and reviewed her vitals. She saw this happen earlier in the day. The outgoing group would apprise the incoming group of every patient's status.

"Any change?" Lainie asked when they exited.

"She's holding her own. She's a fighter."

Ava and Cherie said goodbye. April and John were the new nurses, and they resumed their duties.

Lainie yawned and rubbed the back of her neck. Staying here overnight would be harder than during the day. The Critical Care Unit was quiet during the day; overnight she bet that it was more like the morgue. With that thought she cast a glance at Benton, praying that she'd wake up and be angry enough with Vine for what he did to her to turn state's evidence.

She remembered Stan claiming that he had just spoken to Benton. Obviously, it wasn't Benton, and who else would call Stan? Someone who wanted Stan to run and look guilty.

The door to the CCU whooshed open and a male dressed in scrubs and wearing a surgical mask strode through, past the nurses' station and toward Benton's space.

"Excuse me, can I help you?" April was at the station while John was in another cubicle with another patient.

She got no response. The man continued straight toward Benton's cubicle as if April had said nothing, and April started after him. Lainie followed. Over April's shoulder, Lainie saw the man pull a syringe out of his pocket and reach for Benton's IV.

"Hey, what are you doing?" April cried.

In one smooth motion, the masked man turned and backhanded her, sending her flailing into the machine recording Benton's heart rate, her feet tangled in cords, and she went down.

"Stop what you're doing." Lainie leapt forward toward the man as he appeared ready to inject something into the IV.

She grabbed his arm and yanked it as hard as she could. The syringe went flying. The man grunted and turned, fist in the air. Lainie dodged the fist and stepped back, her foot landing on and smashing the syringe then slipping on the liquid that squirted out. She lost her balance and fell backward, into the wall.

The man started toward her; all she could see was the anger in his eyes.

Then John entered the room. He was a big guy. "What is going on here? I'll call security."

The masked man cursed and turned toward him. John stood in a square, well-balanced stance. "Who are you? Do you even work here?"

"Don't let him leave." Lainie pushed herself up from the floor, her left palm stung like fire, and she realized that she'd put it down in whatever fluid had been in the syringe. It was caustic and her palm reddened as if burned. "What was in that shot?"

The masked man turned toward Lainie, then back to John, smacking him with a quick right hand, knocking him back into the doorframe and then grabbing him by the shoulders and throwing him at Lainie.

He lurched out of the room, breaking into a run while John fell into Lainie, and they both fought to stay on their feet.

"Ah." John brought a hand to his jaw. "Who was that?"

Lainie wanted to run after the man. But April was still down, obviously disoriented after being thrown to the floor, and she was entangled with John.

"Are you okay?" John steadied Lainie before moving toward April to help her get up from a tangle of cords.

"I think so," April said.

Lainie, still stunned, helped John get April up. The burning in her hand increased. She needed to get it under cold water. Holding her hand up, she hurried to the bathroom where she put the appendage under running water. It was already cherry red, as if she'd burned it on the stove.

"Be careful of the liquid on the floor; it's acid or something," she called out while keeping the water on her hand.

John poked his head into the restroom. "Did you get hurt?"

"My hand. I want to know what was in that syringe. Can you be sure that none of it got into Benton?"

"I'll check."

Lainie turned toward April. "Are you okay?"

"I am. I'm a little angry. Who was that guy?"

Lainie shook her head and looked down at the liquid on the floor. "I think he was trying to kill Crystal Benton with acid." This certainly wasn't the peace and quiet the doctor wanted for Benton.

"I'm going to call security," April said as she left the room.

"He did not manage to violate the IV," John said as he double-checked the IV line. "She's fine. No change in her vitals." He turned to Lainie. "He gave me quite a slug." He rubbed his jaw. "I'd like to catch him."

"You and me both." Lainie flexed her hand that still stung from the corrosive liquid.

"Let me see your hand." John gently took hold of her fingertips. "Hmm, it could be a chemical burn."

"I'm glad he didn't get any of that into the patient."

She looked over at Benton. The bruises on the side of her face were a faded yellowish green now. Her chest rose and fell rhythmically with her breathing. Lainie stepped close to the bed—then she sucked in a breath as if she'd been slapped.

CHAPTER 39

Ben stepped off the elevator, hands full with bags of food from In-N-Out as the double doors of the Critical Care Unit burst open. A man wearing a surgical mask and scrubs slammed the doors open, sprinted out, and rammed the door to the stairwell. Realizing that it was a pull, he then pulled it open and disappeared down the stairwell.

Snapping out of his shock, recognizing something was off, Ben leapt through the double doors before they could close.

"Lainie?" he called out as he hurried onto the floor, fear biting when he realized there were no nurses and no Lainie. Leaving the burgers on the counter at the nurses' station, he started for Benton's room.

Just then a nurse stepped out of the room. She was disheveled, as if she'd been in a fight. "Who are you? You're not security."

"Security is busy. There was a gang fight in the parking lot. Cops and security are all over the place outside the Emergency department. I'm an FBI agent. What happened up here?"

"Some guy tried to inject something into our patient. I need to call security. Did you see the man leave?"

"Yes, he took the stairs. Tried? He wasn't successful, was he? Where's Lainie?"

"We stopped him." The nurse pointed to the cubicle.

"Lainie," Ben called out as he entered the room. She had her back to him. Next to her was a male nurse. "Is everything okay?"

The male nurse turned toward him. "Who are you?"

"I'm Agent Ben Isaacs. What's going on?"

"I wish I knew."

"Lainie?" He stepped next to her. "What happened? Did someone try to hurt Benton?"

She turned toward him, an expression of total astonishment on her pale face. "It's not Benton."

"What? What do you mean?"

"This is not Crystal Benton, this is Evie."

By the time Ben had made all the necessary notifications for Lainie, calling LBPD, San Bernardino, and his own boss, the burgers were stone-cold. He waited at the nurses' station while Lainie sat with her sister. After he got over the shock of hearing that Evangeline Moffit was in the bed and not Crystal Benton, he watched as Lainie talked to her silent, still-comatose sister, held her hand, and apologized for taking so long to find her.

It touched his heart, and it made him want to work so very hard to bring Vine to justice. He found it hard to believe that Stan Moffit ordered his employees to kidnap his wife and hold her somewhere. Sure, it was possible. His gut was just telling him that Moffit didn't really have it in him; he was too much of a weasel. Vine had to be the culprit.

But where was Evangeline held and why?

Was it truly because Vine wanted his money back?

Where were they taking her when the car crashed?

Was Vine planning to kill her?

Too many questions.

His phone buzzed. Mark was uncharacteristically breathless. "I can't believe it, but I'm happy that Evangeline Moffit is alive."

"Yes, it is a great discovery."

"I just got off a three-way call with San Bernardino and Long Beach. We are all working together now."

"That's good news as well. There's some evidence from the crash that needs to go to our lab. There were three damaged phones—"

"Already at the lab. San Bernardino sent them. We're trying to find any connection to Stan and/or Vine. The only bad news is they fear the damage is too extensive."

"Well thanks for that information." Ben glanced back toward Evie's cubicle. Lainie had finished speaking to her sister and stood to confer with Dr. Hardin. He handed her some Kleenex. She blew her nose, and the two of them left the cubicle and walked toward the nurses' station.

"I'll let you go, Mark. Call you when I'm back in Long Beach." He disconnected as Lainie approached him.

"Boy, that smells good." She pointed at the In-N-Out bags, and for a second their gazes locked.

He smiled, glad to see some light back in her eyes. "It's cold, but I'm sure it still tastes good." He handed her a bag with a cold burger and soggy fries in it.

"I'm so hungry the temperature won't matter." The two of them took the food to the waiting room to scarf it down. While they ate, it did his heart good to see the change in her. She was animated, hopeful.

"Thanks for bringing the food," she said, mouth full of her first bite.

"No problem. I was hungry as well. I only wish that I'd gotten here a little bit sooner. Maybe I could have stopped that guy."

She shrugged and swallowed. "He wasn't able to do what he came here for, so that makes me happy."

"Shea and Collins will be here soon; I expect the San Bernardino County detective will be here first. They'll probably want to fingerprint your sister, only to officially verify."

She nodded. "I'm fine with that. I'm fine with just about everything right now. I'm just happy to know that Evie is alive. After my parents get here, I'm sure my focus will shift." She glanced toward her sister's cubicle. "Questions, I have so many questions. If Vine took her when Stan said he did, where did she go? Where did he keep her? Dr. Hardin said that when she was first admitted to the hospital, it appeared as if she'd been restrained for some time before the crash. A lot of her bruises were old, not from the crash."

"I've been asking myself those same questions," Ben said. "If we believe your brother-in-law, Vine took her and held her captive. Why were they on the move? Where were they taking her when they crashed?"

She nodded, chewing.

"What did your parents say when you told them?"

Lainie shook her head. "I didn't have the words. I called Mike and asked that he bring them here. It's too monumental to have them drive all this way."

"I get it."

"You must be thinking about Efren right now."

Again, he held her gaze and saw compassion and understanding in her eyes. He could admit that it hurt right now. This was a miracle for sure, that Evangeline was alive. Was it possible Efren would be found alive through another miracle?

"I am. I pray continually. I have to rest in the knowledge that God is in control, no matter the outcome for Efren. It seems like ages ago when I spoke to your sister about him, and after all this time to—"

"You spoke to my sister?"

Ben swallowed. "I did. When Efren failed to check in, I met with her and asked if she'd heard anything from him. Despite what Stan told you, Efren knew him and your sister well."

Anger built in her eyes, and it was justified. "When was this?"

"If we go by what Stan told you, the day before Vine took her."

A few seconds of silence passed.

"Was this part of your investigation?"

"No. I overstepped."

"You overstepped? You're telling me that you could be the reason Vine targeted my sister? I can't believe that you put her in danger like that."

"It was a lapse in judgment. I was worried about my partner—" Ben stopped talking. There was really no excuse for what he had done.

"I don't even know what to say. Who knows what horrible things happened to her during her captivity. And you're responsible."

She tossed the remainder of her food in the trash and left him sitting in the waiting room.

It crushed Ben that Lainie was probably right.

CHAPTER 40

It was early in the morning by the time fingerprints confirmed what Lainie knew. The woman in CCU in a coma was her sister, Evie. The joy was somewhat tempered by what Ben had told her. His actions were completely unprofessional.

Lainie tried to puzzle everything out. Efren went missing before Evie—most likely because his cover was blown. Then his partner contacted Evie, and Evie went missing. True, Stan had told Lainie Vine took Evie because he found out about the missing money, but there was no way to confirm his story. However, it was a fact that Efren was a federal agent undercover. He got close to Evie and Stan. Stan could be lying because he had something to do with Efren's disappearance.

She'd left Ben in the waiting area, grabbed some coffee, and now sat next to the bed and held Evie's hand, once again whispering to her sister and trying not to let the anger dominate. Was that why Evie had called her, to tell her that she'd been contacted by a stupid FBI agent and she wanted to know what to do?

Lainie took several deep breaths, tried to relax and forget Ben Isaacs. Evie was alive, that was all that mattered. And maybe she now held the key to arresting Vine. She spoke to her sister, wanting to believe that in spite of the coma she could hear.

"I'm so sorry that you're here like this, Evie. I'm sorry that I didn't call you back right away. I'm sorry that I walked away from my faith. I'm sorry for so much."

Then she sat quietly, sipping her coffee and praying.

"Detective."

Lainie turned to find Dr. Hardin.

"We need to do our morning assessment, change her bedding, et cetera. You'll need to wait in the waiting room."

"Of course. I know you started weaning her off the medication that is keeping her in a coma. How long before she wakes up?"

"It's hard to say. Weaning off the drugs is a process. Brain swelling has resolved, so I'm optimistic that she'll start to wake up before the medication is at zero."

"Do you think there will be any permanent damage?" Lainie wondered if her sister would be impaired in some way.

"That's also nothing I can tell you with certainty right now. However, she responded quickly and efficiently to the treatment. That's promising. I will caution you about one thing."

"What's that?"

"While she may wake up and seem normal, she may not be able to help you with the information you're hoping to get out of her. Even if there is no permanent damage, disorientation, memory loss, confusion all are likely to be present for a few days, maybe longer."

Lainie nodded. "I understand."

She kissed Evie on the cheek and left the doctor and nurse to go about their business. She'd felt Evie's pulse—it was sure and strong. And she'd prayed as hard as she could. Her sister was in God's hands, she always had been, and that gave Lainie great peace. Her steps felt lighter as she joined her colleagues in the waiting room.

"Awesome." Shea's face split in a wide grin. He wrapped Lainie in a hug. "I'm glad something has worked out well in this crazy case," he said when he let her go.

"Me too." She nodded to Gardner but noticed Collins was absent.

"Where's your partner?" Lainie wanted all hands on deck now. Except Isaacs. He was absent now, and she wanted it to stay that way. Though she'd grown to like him, even welcome his presence, now she never wanted to see him again.

"He stayed in Long Beach to coordinate with the Feds. There are now three teams working on this."

"Sorry we missed the ID right off the top," Gardner said.

Happy that she had an army in her corner now, Lainie smiled. "There was no way for you to know since you had Benton's physical ID and the resemblance was so close. All that matters is that we know it now and that my sister's prognosis is positive."

Fatigue overtook her and she covered her mouth when a yawn forced its way out, not wanting to slow down now. "What can you tell me about what happened earlier? How did that guy get up here?"

Shea and Gardner exchanged glances and Gardner answered. "In hindsight, what happened downstairs was an obvious diversion. I've reviewed security footage." He handed her some still shots of the would-be assassin, still masked, in various parts of the hospital, making his way to the CCU floor.

"As soon as the ruckus began, he slipped in through the emergency entrance. He had a key card that was stolen from an ER doc. He came straight to this floor and, well, you know the rest. He escaped down the stairs and out through the front entrance where a vehicle was waiting. The plates on the vehicle were covered."

"Vine sent him." She studied the photo of the man running out the front door. "I know that with every fiber of my soul."

"I think you're right," Shea said. "However, we have no evidence of Vine's direct connection. He won't talk to us, and at this point, we have no way to force him to."

"Maybe my sister will be able to give us some evidence when she wakes up." Her hand that had been burned itched and she was tired, dead tired. But Evie was alive and Lainie was prepared to go full speed ahead to put whoever was responsible for Evie's condition in jail.

CHAPTER 41

When Mom and Dad arrived, the happy relief was palpable. The whole floor seemed brighter. Elation pushed away Lainie's fatigue.

She hugged them both and the tears began again.

"You're sure it's her?" Mom asked.

"I wouldn't have had Mike bring you out here if I wasn't."

"It's answered prayer." They all hugged again.

"Where is Archie?" Lainie asked her mother.

"He stayed at home with the boys. We wanted to assess the situation with"—she cleared her throat—"before bringing the boys. They can't visit anyway until she's moved to a normal room."

Lainie nodded. Mom was right. Still, it was the most joyous day Lainie could remember.

She introduced them to Dr. Hardin, then left them so he could explain to them what she'd already heard. After cheerful emotions wore off, she recognized that she needed to get some rest.

Yawning now was fast and furious. Someone tapped her on the shoulder. Detective Shea said, "You must be exhausted."

"I am," Lainie agreed.

He smiled. "Good call you had, coming down to keep an eye on her."

"I thought she was another suspect that I wanted to be certain didn't get away."

"Whatever works. Isaacs was a big help as well."

Lainie stiffened. "How so?"

"He spent a couple hours with security and me before he left, going over all the camera feeds. They sent me a good still with a picture of our guy before he pulled his mask up."

Shea showed her a photo, a clear maskless shot of the man who'd been at Evie's bedside with a syringe.

Lainie felt a jolt of adrenaline.

"That is one of the men who was up here with Vine earlier. I knew he had to be a Vine goon."

"Yep, you were right. We're working on identifying him. Gardner thinks he may be a joker named Tom Thornton, a local ex-cop who was fired for extortion. He's been working private security. Gardner said it would not surprise him to hear that he was working for Dallas Vine. Everyone else missed it but Isaacs. He's got a good eye."

Probably working to assuage his guilty conscience, Lainie thought but said nothing.

"How's your hand?" Shea asked.

"It's not stinging anymore; it's actually itching a little now."

"Quick thinking, knocking the syringe out of his hand. We've got things covered from here on out. You should go get some rest."

"I agree. I'm on my way home, thanks."

Lainie said goodbye to her parents and took the elevator down. She walked slowly, flexing and unflexing her hand, anger at Isaacs still percolating. Why in the world would he endanger Evie like that? It was unforgivable.

She stopped at a convenience store to get some coffee, hoping she could stay awake for the drive home. It helped but so did the fact that her mind churned in anticipation of catching Dallas Vine.

When she got off the freeway, at the last minute, before turning off for home, she decided to stop at her folks' place to check on Archie and the boys. They only lived a few blocks from her. As she turned the corner and drove toward the house, she saw a black SUV parked in front that she did not recognize. Worse, the license plate was covered with black tape.

Instantly alert and awake, thinking of the vehicle that had picked up the man who tried to kill Evie, Lainie pulled over in front of the next-door neighbors' house before she reached her parents' house. Archie's car was in the driveway, so he was home, but that didn't make her feel any better.

Am I too paranoid, or just too tired?

She punched in Archie's number on her phone. It rang five times before he answered. "Lainie?"

"Yeah, what's going on?"

"What do you mean?"

The call sounded as if she'd been put on speakerphone, and Archie's voice was strained. Lainie decided to pretend she was still at the hospital.

"I just wondered how the boys are doing. Seeing Mom in the room with Evie is wonderful."

"You're still at the hospital?"

"Yeah, Evie should wake up soon. I'm praying she can tell us all of what happened to her."

"Me too. Ah, ah, has she said anything?"

"No, technically she's still in a coma." Lainie carefully unlocked her glove box. "She is showing signs of coming out of it. The doctor is optimistic."

She had placed her gun inside the glove box because she didn't think she'd need it in the hospital. Once her gun was in hand, she climbed out of her vehicle.

"As soon as she does wake up, I'm sure Mom or Dad will call you."

"Great, great, I can't wait for that."

Lainie heard sirens in the distance, fire department sirens. There was a subtle but distinct difference between the tones of fire and police sirens. It made her look around, take in her surroundings, but nothing seemed amiss on this street. Other than the obvious black SUV.

"All right, Arch, talk to you soon." Lainie disconnected and walked toward her parents' back gate, cutting across the neighbors' property. The drapes in the back of her folks' house were usually open. Maybe if she got in the backyard, she could see what was going on.

She was about to jam her phone into her back pocket when it buzzed with a call. It was the dispatch center number.

Keeping her voice low, she answered, "Jensen."

"Lainie, thank God, where are you?" Charlie, the dispatch supervisor, asked.

"At my parents' house, why?"

"We just got a 911 call from your neighbor; fire has been dispatched to your house."

"My house, why?"

"It just exploded into flames."

CHAPTER 42

Ben nursed a couple cups of coffee in the hospital cafeteria before going to his car. What he hadn't finished he poured into a to-go cup. He was sleepy and depressed. The expression on Lainie's face when he'd told her about meeting her sister haunted him. He sat in his car and sipped the bitter, stale coffee.

Thinking back to the meeting with Evangeline, he knew at the time that it was dangerous to contact her. That's why what he did was outside of policy. His fear for Efren overrode all of his self-control and professionalism. He'd talked himself into believing that nothing would happen because no one would know about the meeting. Did Vine find out about it and target her because of him, or was it because of what Stan and Crystal did? Obviously Lainie believed the former.

He prayed fervently that the contact with Evangeline was not the reason she went missing, but right now his fear was that yes, he was the reason the poor woman had been abducted and was now in the hospital.

What can I do to make it up to her and her family?

Catching Vine would go a long way toward easing Lainie's anger. Added to all of this was the pain of knowing that while finding Evangeline was a miracle, the odds of a miracle for Efren were minuscule. Saving Efren was the only thought on Ben's mind when he contacted Evangeline. And now it was all for naught.

Ben knew exactly what he needed to do. He'd nearly caused the death of an innocent while violating policy. It was time to resign.

He started the car and left the hospital. First thing in the morning, he would submit a formal letter of resignation. He didn't deserve to be a federal agent.

✦

For a minute, Lainie couldn't think. *My house is on fire?* "What?"

"We took a call from your neighbor. Your house is almost fully involved. Your parents live in Long Beach as well, don't they?"

"They do. Not far from me."

"Good thing you're there. Anyone else in your house?"

"No, no, ahh." She slapped her forehead with her palm, willing her thoughts back to Archie's situation. There was nothing she could do at her house. She had no pets to save, and everything else could be replaced. If Archie was in danger, she had to act.

"Charlie, something is going on here, at my folks' house. I'm not certain what—it's just odd." She gave him the address. "There's a strange car out front. You heard about my sister in the hospital, how she ended up there?"

"Yeah, I did. Strange story—she didn't get eaten by a shark in Hawaii but she did get abducted here?"

"That's about it, and I'm afraid that my brother and nephews may be hostages here now. Send a couple of units to the house, call it unknown trouble. And let Collins know what's going on at my folks' house. I think Shea is still in San Bernardino."

"You have a plate on the vehicle?"

"Ah, hang on a second." She'd have to risk running out to the street to uncover the license plate. There was no way around it; she had to know who the vehicle belonged to.

Frowning, she lowered the phone and jogged to the SUV, keeping an eye on the house. As quickly as she could, she peeled the duct tape off the plate and then recited the number to Charlie as she jogged back to the neighbors' house.

"It may be nothing, but this car does not belong here. And if my house is on fire, something bad is going down."

"Copy that plate, stand by. It's not only yours, but there's also a second house on fire not very far away. What a day in Long Beach."

She heard the clicking of computer keys, and she knew Charlie was relaying information to another dispatcher.

"Lainie, that vehicle returns no want, no warrant, registered to Quartz Enterprises. Do you know that company?"

Vine.

"Yeah, I do. Please, Charlie, get me backup right away. I'll try and see if I can get you more information."

"Shouldn't you wait for backup?"

"I need to know now." Lainie ended the call, opened the gate, and made her way into the backyard. She couldn't hear anything—not a TV or a radio. The back curtains were closed, so she couldn't see into the house.

She backtracked to the window for Evie's and her old room. Mom had long ago turned it into a sewing room. If the window was not locked, she could climb in. Lately the weather had been mild, and since her folks liked fresh air, the windows were likely open. She and Evie had snuck in and out through this window many times when they were growing up.

After silencing her phone, she shoved it into her pocket and then her gun in her waistband. Lainie worked on the window screen. It took some doing and she broke a fingernail, but the screen came off with minimal noise, she hoped.

She set the screen down and away from the window, then put her hands on the window and pushed up, holding her breath. It opened with a grinding squeak, and she winced. When nothing happened, she let out a sigh of relief and pushed it open enough to slip through.

For a moment she listened. She could hear someone talking, but she could not understand what was being said. Praying she would not make a lot of noise, she pushed herself up and over the windowsill, stopping halfway in.

The room was a mess: It had been torn apart. Her mother was a neat freak. She'd have a heart attack when she saw this. Even her sewing machine was on the floor and every drawer was open, with fabric strewn about. The only good thing about the mess was that there was no impediment to her climbing through the window. Nothing was in her way. And the door to the room was closed.

She had plenty of room to set herself down onto the carpeted floor.

After another minute, holding her breath, praying that no one had heard her, she removed her gun, stood, and tiptoed to the door.

CHAPTER 43

Ben was nearly to his freeway exit when his phone rang. It was Mark.

"Where are you?"

"On the freeway, almost home, why?"

"Something's happening in Long Beach. I just got a call from Detective Collins at LBPD. Two house fires just erupted in the city. One house belongs to Stan Moffit, the other to Elaine Jensen."

Ben nearly stomped on the brake. "What?"

"According to LBPD, the fires were called in roughly five minutes apart. Neighbors to both houses reported hearing an explosion and then a vehicle speeding away."

"Where's Lai—ah, Detective Jensen?"

"At her parents' house. She called in an unknown trouble, then went off-air. They can't raise her."

"Can you give me that address?"

A short while later, Ben saw two black-and-white police vehicles on the street when he turned the corner a block from Lainie's parents' home. He also saw Lainie's car parked in front of the next-door neighbors'. As he drove past her car, he noted the black SUV. He continued past the police cars, then parked. He got out and identified himself.

"Who is in charge?" He held up his ID.

A sergeant stepped toward him. "I am. Why are you here?"

"I'm working with Detective Jensen. This incident might be related to our mutual case."

"Do you know what is going on in that house? We can't raise her. All she told dispatch was that it was unknown trouble. Something to do with that black SUV."

"I'm not certain what's happening in that house, but Jensen's own house is on fire—"

"Fire?" the sergeant said. "Does that have something to do with this situation?"

"I don't know every detail, but I'm afraid that if Lainie went into the house, she may be a hostage. My guess is that whoever torched her house is here now. It's just my gut. The black SUV is suspect."

The sergeant nodded. "Yeah, Lainie told dispatch that. We ran the plate. It's registered to Quartz Enterprises. Do you know anything about that?"

"I do. It's a front for Dallas Vine."

The sergeant frowned. "The guy who sued Lainie?"

"Yes."

The officer considered this for a minute. "If this is a hostage situation, we need to notify SWAT and hostage negotiators."

"Do that. In the meantime, do you mind if I get eyes on the situation?"

"How do you plan to do that?"

"I'll go around into the backyard and see what I can see."

"I can't authorize that, Isaacs."

"I don't answer to you. Contact SWAT. Hopefully by the time they get here, I'll have a better idea of what we're dealing with."

The sergeant clearly didn't like what he heard. A uniformed officer stepped up. Ben recognized her—Sara, the officer from the tow yard incident.

"Sarge, I'll go with him. I know the house, the layout. Lainie and I have been friends since we were kids."

"Aren't you afraid that you'll make the situation worse?"

"It's a chance I'm willing to take. We all need to know what's happening," Ben said. "I think it's worth the risk." He turned to Sara. "Do you know who should be in the house?"

"I know that her parents are at the hospital, so it's got to be Archie and the boys—Evie's boys—in the house. They've been here since Stan was arrested."

"All right, Sara." The sergeant nodded. "I think that we have exigent circumstances here. We'll switch to channel four and you keep us apprised."

"Yes, sir." She turned to Ben. "The house is a three bedroom, two bath. The living room is in the middle, the master bedroom on this side, two smaller bedrooms on the other side."

"Where do you think we can get the better eye?" He motioned with his hand, and they began to walk toward the house. She fell into step with him.

"Let's go into the backyard on this side. Knowing Lainie as I do, I would guess she's already in the backyard, if not in the house."

"Is it easy to get in the house?"

She nodded. "It's an older home; the windows are low. When we were kids, we would sneak in and out of the house, you know, to do kid things. Lainie's parents haven't changed much over the years."

"I get it." They reached the neighbors' house. The houses shared a side fence. The neighbors had a gate to their backyard, but there was not a gate to the Jensens' yard on this side of the house, and Ben did not want to cross in front of the house to get to the gate. All the blinds to the Jensen home were closed.

Sara lowered her voice. "We can enter the gate here and climb over the fence, if you're game."

"Let's do it."

CHAPTER 44

Lainie knew help was on the way, and that they would want an update. She had left Charlie hanging. But she dare not risk a phone call until she knew exactly what was happening. She tiptoed to the bedroom door. There was a lot of noise on the other side of the door, and for a time, she simply listened. She could hear things being moved, glass breaking. Then a male voice demanded, "Where is it?"

"I have no idea what you're talking about," Archie said. "I've got nothing to hide. If I knew I'd tell you."

She heard what sounded like a slap.

"H-h-hitting me won't g-g-get you answers." Archie only stuttered when stressed.

More ransacking going on, glass breaking. There was more than one person in the house with Archie. Lainie had to count on at least two and not be surprised. Where were the boys?

"I'm out of patience," the first voice said. "It's here somewhere and you'd better tell me, or it will go bad for you and those kids."

He threatened her nephews.

Lainie found herself out of patience.

She opened the bedroom door and hurried down the hallway, gun up. When she stepped into the living room she saw Archie on his knees, blood streaming from his nose. A man stood in front of him, a man Lainie recognized from the photo she'd just been shown: Tom Thornton.

Gun still up, Lainie said, "Get away from him."

✦

Ben opened the gate and he and Sara slipped into the neighbors' yard. The wood fence was not a huge barrier, and they both scaled it and were in the Jensens' yard in short order.

"The window for the master bedroom is around the corner." Sara kept her voice low and pointed.

"Let's move up there." Ben drew his weapon and they both eased along the side of the house to the corner. Ben peered around the corner. He could see the window and a neatly manicured backyard. No people but sounds of glass breaking and things thumping from somewhere inside the house. The blinds were tightly closed.

He turned to Sara. "Wait here. I'm going to try and open the window. Cover me."

She nodded.

Ben had to step on some plants to get close to the window, and he hoped the Jensens didn't mind. Once next to the window, he listened and heard nothing. He holstered his gun and pulled a pocketknife from his pocket to pry the screen off. Once it was free from the window frame, he set it on the ground under the window.

Carefully he pushed up the window, expecting it to protest and be difficult. Thankfully, he was wrong. The window opened easily. Pushing the blinds up, he peered inside the room. Something was on the bed. He sucked in a breath and squinted.

Two children were on the bed, both bound and gagged. He had to get in.

He carefully stepped back to Sara.

He filled her in on the situation, whispering. "They are bound and gagged. Let your sergeant know that I am going to try and get them."

"Lainie's nephews. You sure that's wise?"

"I think it's the only way to save them."

Sara chewed on her bottom lip, moved away from the house back to the fence. She climbed over, then she keyed her mike and let the sergeant know.

Ben didn't wait to hear his objections. He feared that it would make a lot of noise when he slid under the blinds, but he had no choice. The boys were clearly in danger.

He pushed himself up and in, realizing he'd be an easy target at first. The boys squirmed, and he was certain that he'd scared them. He pushed his body in, landed on his hands, then scooted the rest of the way inside.

Standing as quickly as he could, Ben put a finger to his lips, trying to put the boys at ease and quiet their frightened murmurs. He heard voices in the other room. Someone was searching for something. He couldn't pause to listen. Two pairs of frightened eyes stared up at him from the bed.

He scooped one off the bed and shoved him out the window. Sara was there and ready to take him. Ben was glad she'd come. To her credit, she didn't hesitate. She holstered her weapon and took him. It appeared to Ben that the boy knew her because his body relaxed as Sara took him.

Ben held up his finger to indicate that he would return for the next one. She nodded and disappeared around the corner with the boy.

Ben retrieved the second boy, and by the time he shoved him out the window, Sara was back. With the boys gone, Ben stared at the bedroom door. What should his next move be?

✦

Eyes wide, the man jerked toward Lainie. Over his shoulder she could see the other man staring at her from the kitchen.

Lainie's gun was up and on target.

Thornton threw his hands up. "Whoa, whoa! Don't get excited."

"Excited? You've ransacked the house and you're beating up my brother. You need to step away from him now. Archie, move away."

He scrambled away from the man and toward Lainie.

"And if you think I won't shoot at the slightest provocation, you're wrong. You, come out of the kitchen."

"You might want to put your gun down," the man in the kitchen said. He disappeared momentarily and then appeared around the corner with his gun drawn, pointed right at Archie.

Lainie didn't hesitate. Like shooting a target at the range, she pulled the trigger twice, hitting the man center of mass and he crumpled in the hallway. His gun fired into the floor before it fell from his hand. He grunted in pain.

Though half deaf from the sound of gunfire, Lainie brought her gun around quickly as Thornton reached toward his waistband. "You're dead if you draw that weapon. I'm not playing."

Surprise and fear sparked on the man's face. He brought his hands up and said nothing.

"Where are the boys, Archie?"

"The bedroom—"

There was the whoop of a siren from outside, and a voice came over the PA. "This is the Long Beach Police Department. Exit the house with your hands up."

Lainie didn't take her eyes off the big guy to grab her phone. She needed him unarmed. "You heard that. Backup is here. And your friend likely needs help. With your left hand, take your gun out and drop it on the floor. When he does that, Archie, pick it up and then get the other gun."

The man slowly complied, and once Archie had possession of both guns, Lainie retrieved her phone from her pocket and called Charlie to explain the situation.

"I'm sending my brother to the front door, and he'll let everyone in. Let me know when you've advised them. We also need medics. In here, a bad guy is down."

In a few minutes, Charlie let her know that everyone had been notified.

"Give me the guns, Archie, and then answer the door."

Her brother wiped his nose on his sleeve and did as she asked. Lainie didn't relax until two uniformed officers entered and handcuffed Thornton. As soon as the officers entered, Archie ran toward a back bedroom.

Then he came running back. "The boys are gone!"

"What?" Her adrenaline ramped up at warp speed.

"Relax," one of the uniformed officers said. "We got them out."

"We?"

"Yeah, Sara can explain."

Just then Sara walked through the front door. "When we hadn't heard from you, we did some reconnaissance, snuck into the back, saw the kids tied up on the bed, and got them out to protect them."

Relief flooded Lainie. "Where are they now?"

"Outside getting checked by medics. They are scared but seem okay."

The prisoner was taken out of the house at the same time two medics came in to deal with the man Lainie had shot.

"You did that, Sara? Thanks."

"It was me and that FBI agent, Ben. He was great."

CHAPTER 45

Gunshots jolted Ben.

Who was shooting?

Was Lainie okay?

Part of him wanted to open the bedroom door and run toward the shots, but the other part knew he needed to get the boys far away from the house to safety. They took priority. First things first, he exited the window and helped Sara get them over the fence to officers waiting to grab them. Then he and Sara hopped back over the fence.

"What do you think is going on in there?" Sara asked.

Ben saw fear in her eyes. "I can't guess. All I know is, Lainie is smart and resilient." His words seemed to calm her, and the optimism in them helped him as well.

Sara stepped forward to shepherd the boys to a waiting paramedic. "We need to get them checked out," Sara said, and Ben agreed. Their wrists were red, one was bleeding because the tape had been applied quite tightly. Both boys seemed in shock.

He followed Sara but kept his attention on the house, praying fervently that Lainie was okay. One of the boys whimpered when the medic took his hand. Ben bent down and picked him up.

"You'll be okay," Ben told him as the medic removed all the tape from his small hand. The boy was shaking. "What's your name?"

"O-O-Owen."

"Owen, I'm Ben."

"Will you stay with me?"

He wanted to say no, he wanted to go back to the house and find out what was going on with Lainie. But seeing the little boy and knowing how much he'd been through in the last few days made Ben say yes.

He'd have to kick back and let the uniformed officers handle the situation.

"Let the medics examine your hands," Sara said to the boy she had. He was quiet and seemed more affected by the situation than Owen.

While the boys were tended to, Ben took in the situation on the street now. LBPD blocked off most of the street. A lot more officers were here now than when he'd gone over the fence. The sergeant gave a blast of a siren and then got on the PA.

He tensed with fear and apprehension, praying that Lainie was okay.

✦

As soon as she felt everything in the house was under control, Lainie hurried out toward the paramedic van to check on Owen and Evan. Ben sat on the back of the rig with Owen in his arms.

The boy saw her. "Aunt Lainie."

Ben let him down and Owen ran toward her. She picked him up and held him tight for a moment. Evan's hand and wrist were being treated. She turned to Ben. "Thank you."

He nodded. "Glad I could help. Are you okay?"

She nodded, then turned her attention to her brother. Archie held an ice pack on his face.

"Tell me what happened, Archie."

"They pushed their way into the house a little while ago."

"What were they after?"

"They said that they wanted the ledger."

She frowned. "What ledger?"

"That's what I asked. I hoped maybe you knew. They were certain we had a ledger, and they tore the house apart for it."

Lainie looked back toward the house. The second team of medics was just now wheeling out a gurney with the man she'd shot. There was an O2 mask on his face, so Lainie knew that he was still alive.

She put Owen down and he grabbed Archie's hand. It not only broke her heart what had happened to her nephews, it made her angry.

"Are you really okay, Arch?"

"Yeah, I am. Glad you showed up when you did."

"Did they say anything else, mention any names, anything?"

"No, they just wanted the ledger."

She turned to Ben. "What do you make of this? What is the ledger?"

"I don't know, but for some reason Vine thinks that your family has it. You heard about your house?"

"Yes."

"What happened to your house, Lainie?" Archie asked.

"It's burning down as we speak."

"They also torched Evangeline's house," Ben said.

"You're kidding." Lainie was smacked with another burst of shock.

"No, that's why I'm here. When I heard about both houses, I figured something big was happening."

Lainie leaned against the closest black-and-white, unable to fight the feeling of defeat she felt. "Vine needs to go down. I can't believe all the destruction he's caused."

Her thoughts were still haunted by Vine's voice saying, *"I'm bulletproof."* With all the devastation today, Lainie feared that he was.

CHAPTER 46

Broken glass, bullet holes, and blood.

After all the police activity was over and the house was empty, Lainie, Archie, and Sara, when she ended her shift, worked hard to clean up the destruction left by Vine's two henchmen. They couldn't fix the bullet hole in the floor, but they were able to sweep up the glass and clean up the blood. Lainie didn't want her mother to see the place all busted up.

It was dark before she was able to rest. She'd been awake over twenty-four hours so when she was finally able to lay down and close her eyes, sleep should have been instant, but it wasn't. Her bed was the couch in her folks' house.

Her father had returned home as they were finishing up. Shea had driven him back from the hospital. "Your mother will stay at the hospital until Evie wakes up," he'd said, after Lainie explained everything that had happened. "Tomorrow maybe the two of us can take her a change of clothes."

"Sure. But I hate to be the one to tell her about all the destruction here. They broke a lot of Mom's china, all of her vases, and I'm not sure if her sewing machine still works."

Dad shook his head. "She's not going to care. Everyone is okay, that's all that will matter to her." He'd peered hard at Lainie. "Are you all right? You had to shoot someone."

"He threatened Archie and the boys. Yeah, I shot him. I'd do it again under the same circumstances." Lainie meant what she said. Archie had been more upset about the shooting than she was, and she worried about him.

"I can't believe you did that, Lainie. My goodness, you shot him."

"He didn't give me any choice. You realize that don't you?"

"I do. But it's shocking, nonetheless." His gaze was probing. *"Are you sure that you're okay?"*

"I am. But if you're worried about me, I'll have to talk to the police psychologist eventually. I've prayed about what happened, Archie. I truly had no choice. I can live with my actions."

It didn't surprise Lainie that her mom had stayed with Evie. As soon as she was rested, Lainie planned on returning to San Bernardino. She had to stop by the station and be interviewed about the shooting first. Officers had taken her gun to be examined, standard procedure. Her backup weapon was in her home, and she wasn't ready to dig through ashes to see if it was okay. Her life was clearly in danger, so she hoped to get the gun back soon.

After the station, she planned on driving with her father to join her mother at the hospital. Though San Bernardino was now providing an officer to stay with Evie, Lainie still worried that Vine would try again to get to her.

What did surprise her was the conversation she'd had with Sara and how much it bugged her, how she couldn't get it off her mind. Her friend had fed everyone by bringing a couple of pizzas with her when she returned to the house. While they sat and ate, she amazed Lainie with a question.

"What's up with you and that FBI agent?"

"What do you mean?"

"He saved the boys, and you hardly showed any appreciation."

"What was I supposed to do, kiss his feet?"

"Wow, why so hostile?"

Lainie had to pause for a couple of seconds. Why was she suddenly so irritated?

"You don't understand. He's responsible for what happened to Evie."

"How so?"

Lainie told her what Ben had done.

"He was worried about his partner."

"So that excuses putting Evie in danger?"

"I didn't say that. It does explain why he did what he did."

"Are you taking his side?"

"Why do I have to take a side? He's not the first law enforcement officer to violate policy because he felt passionate about something, is he?"

Lainie ignored the underlying point of that quip. "Evie could be dead. How can I forgive him for that?"

"You're not even sure that's the reason Evie was abducted. Vine is the enemy in this, not Ben Isaacs."

Now, trying to sleep, Lainie wrestled with her conscience. On the one hand she could understand why Ben did what he did because she understood the bond between partners. She trusted and depended on Mike with her life. She'd take a bullet for him and knew that he'd do the same for her.

And she hated to admit it, but she would probably have done exactly what Ben had done if she'd been in Ben's shoes. Her partner's life would have been more important than policy.

So, why couldn't she forgive him?

That was the thought that troubled her as she finally drifted off to sleep.

CHAPTER 47

The next morning Lainie, wearing borrowed jeans and a T-shirt from Sara, drove by her decimated home on her way to the station.

"Do you think he's trying to intimidate you?" Sara had asked.

"If he is, I'm not intimidated, I'm angry. I don't have time to be anything else."

That was doubly true, she thought as she observed what was left of the structure she'd resided in for ten years. She didn't even have time to be sad. Only the garage stood, seemingly undamaged. Maybe her Christmas decorations survived. The rest of the house was flattened, blackened, nothing salvageable.

A fire captain had called her and gone over the preliminary report. He'd said that the fire's cause was an incendiary device thrown through the front window. From the timing he'd outlined, and the description of the vehicle seen fleeing from the scene, Lainie guessed the two guys who terrorized Archie and her nephews were probably the ones who tossed the devices into the houses.

They all lived close, and the reports said that Evie's home went up first, then Lainie's, then the goons went to her parents' home. According to Archie, they tied the boys up first, then started tearing the place up. They were in a hurry to find the book.

Lainie didn't drive by Evie's home, but she figured it was probably the same. She shook her head, heart breaking that her poor sister would not have a home to return to when she got out of the hospital.

She left the shell of her home and drove to the station. Since both cases appeared related, Evie's abduction and the assault on the boys, Shea and Collins were also handling the case concerning the men who'd ransacked her parents' home.

Though preoccupied with current issues, at one point Lainie felt as if she was being watched. It was an odd feeling; the hair on the back of her neck rose.

Stopped at a light, she turned left and right and then looked in the rearview mirror. There was a black SUV behind her, just like the one that had been at her folks' house.

A troubling thought tiptoed through her mind: *Am I being followed?*

The light changed and Lainie accelerated, keeping an eye on the vehicle. It turned right while she continued straight.

Taking a breath, Lainie relaxed. She was still tired and maybe a little loopy.

She arrived at the station and went straight to the homicide office.

"Hey, great work yesterday," Collins said. "You saved the day."

"I only did what I had to. My family means everything to me. What's the status of everything now?"

"Tom Thornton lawyered up," Shea said. "The other guy, we ID'd him as Davis Compton, is in stable condition at County General, but neither is talking."

"They both work for Vine. Doesn't what happened yesterday give you some probable cause to bring him in?"

"Yes and no."

"What does that mean?"

"The men work for Quartz Enterprises. They both denied working directly for Vine."

"Then why were they at my house searching for a journal?"

"Like I said, they are not talking."

"Vine owns Quartz."

"Yes, so we tried to get a hold of him," Shea said, "and we can't locate him."

"You're kidding."

"I wish I was. He's off the grid. Not sure if he left the country. We have the Feds checking into that. The only real good news is that the DA was able to put no bail holds on them both. Maybe if they realize Vine—or Quartz—can't get them out, they'll decide to talk."

Lainie sighed. "I won't hold my breath."

"Humph. How's your sister doing?"

"I'm on my way to the hospital now. I'm optimistic she'll wake up soon."

"Glad to hear it."

"Any chance I can have my gun back?"

"We're way ahead of you." Collins handed her a bag. "Already examined. You just need to reload."

✦

Lainie made it to the hospital around noon. She and her father drove together and brought Mom a change of clothes. Before they'd left, Mom had called and updated them with the news that Evie had regained consciousness in the early morning hours and that she'd been moved to a normal room.

Lainie took the stairs two at a time; she didn't want to wait for the elevator. She beat her dad to the room, and when she got to the door, she stopped. An officer in uniform sat outside the door, and she nodded to him. "Thanks for hanging out."

"Not a problem. Glad to hear that she's improving."

"Me too." Lainie took one step into the room and stopped again. It felt as if her heart would burst. Her mom sat on the edge of the bed, holding Evie's hand. The bed was elevated slightly. Evie was sitting up and there was a healthy color in her cheeks and a smile on her face. Her father stepped in behind her.

Wiping the tears that suddenly formed, Lainie continued into the room. "Evie!"

Her sister's face brightened. "Lainie."

With her father there as well, the reunion was tearful. Evie sounded weak but good, a little muted maybe, but she didn't appear confused or disoriented at all.

"How do you feel?" Lainie asked.

Evie sipped some water from a straw. "I feel tired, but Mom tells me I've been sleeping for a week."

"Not quite a week." Mom patted her hand.

"I'm a little stiff and sore. And I itch a bit. The doctor said he would raise my head slowly. I'd kind of like to stand and go to the bathroom by myself, but they tell me to take it slow." Evie frowned.

"What's the matter?"

"I only just realized: Where's Stan?"

"You don't remember the crash?" Lainie asked.

"Crash? Was Stan hurt?" Evie got agitated.

"Oh no, honey, no." Mom patted her hand again. "Stan is fine. He's . . ."

"He's taking care of business," Dad finished for Mom.

Evie yawned. "I'm so tired. The doctor said I might be in and out."

"You can rest, Evie. We'll be here when you wake up."

Evie's eyes closed and she drifted off to sleep.

"The doctor said this might happen," Mom said. "She still has coma drugs in her system."

"Did she say anything about the crash?" Lainie asked.

"No, I don't think she remembers. She was more confused earlier. I told her that the boys were with Archie."

Lainie gave her mother the change of clothes she had brought. "I'll sit with her if you want to go change and get something to eat."

Mom gave her a hug. "Thank you. I think everything will be all right now."

She stepped into the restroom to change.

"I wish I could be as optimistic as she is about everything," Lainie said to her father.

"Our faith gives us reason to be optimistic, Lainie, don't you agree?"

"I guess I'm getting back to that, Dad. I would feel better if Dallas Vine were in jail."

Later, after Mom and Dad left for the cafeteria and Lainie sat with Evie, she bent her head to pray.

What a roller coaster the last few days had been. She was so very glad Evie was going to be okay, but a killer still roamed free.

Lainie stood and paced for a bit, yawning. She was still bone-tired; she hadn't been this sleep-deprived since she worked graveyard patrol. And she was younger then.

Evie began to stir a little and Lainie went back to the bed.

Her sister frowned and her eyes opened. "Lainie?"

"Yeah, I'm here."

Evie seemed worried, her eyes closed, and the frown deepened.

"What's the matter?" Lainie asked.

"My brain is so foggy. My thoughts are bouncing around. Did I call you?"

"Yeah, you did, but you didn't leave a message."

Her eyes opened again. "I had something to tell you, I just can't remember what it was."

"It's all right. I'm sure it will come back to you in time."

CHAPTER 48

"You can't quit now," Mark pleaded with Ben. He had a file in his hand with all the information they had gathered regarding the crash and the incident at the Jensen house.

"I don't know how I can stay. I saw that woman in the hospital, Mark. Lainie is right; I put her there. Thank God it wasn't any worse. My actions were reckless. Unforgivable."

"You don't know that for sure. Ben, if you quit now, you're quitting on Efren and Candy."

That comment cut Ben to the quick. He ran a hand through his hair and said nothing.

Mark put a hand on his shoulder. "If you want to quit, quit. Just wait until this case is resolved. We are finally seeing some chinks in Vine's armor. The phone records for the man in the SUV passenger seat, Raphael Diaz, show that twenty minutes before the crash he called Vine's cigar lounge."

"We can't link that to Vine directly; he could have called anyone at the lounge."

"Maybe not. But it is still a possible link to Vine. His next move was sending goons to search and burn houses. Vine is obviously desperate to be so heavy-handed."

"I agree with that." Ben nodded.

"Desperate men make mistakes. We've got two in custody, and we know that Vine is searching for a ledger. Help me finish the job, Ben. We can put Vine away for Efren." He held out the file for Ben to take.

Ben stared at it for a minute. In his whole career, he'd never felt more useless than he had when Lainie Jensen called him out about putting her sister in danger. Now he knew what Mark said was true—if he left now, he'd be quitting on Efren.

Efren would never quit on him.

Finally, Ben reached out and took the file. Maybe closing this case the right way would provide some redemption.

"Thanks, bud. Let's get this guy. What else do you have?"

✦

Ben sat at his desk and opened the file Mark had given him. The burner phone was too damaged to retrieve any information. Besides the one call to the cigar lounge on the phone belonging to Raphael Diaz there was nothing useful on the phones. Those men were both dead, and other than the fact that Diaz worked for Stan, Ben saw no way to connect them to Vine.

He moved to the information on the two men caught in the Jensen home. Tom Thornton was a fired cop who worked for Quartz Enterprises. Davis Compton had been an armored truck driver until he got fired when money came up missing. His employer was also listed as Quartz Enterprises, not Dallas Vine.

Vine always built in plausible deniability.

Frustrated, Ben went back to the file containing all of Efren's notes, searching for any mention of a ledger. Nothing. He reread Efren's notes: *I have no clue about the code—how important it is, who knows it. I've found no threads or notes to help with the code, but I will keep searching.*

A couple of items Ben had missed before caught his attention. One was mention of Crystal Benton: *So much going on here—Benton knows where all the bodies are buried, but she is as loyal as they come.*

And the second was a note about Vine's personal bodyguard: *Plug, might be way more involved than I know.*

He wasn't sure why he'd missed those before and why they jumped out at him now. Hank Bucshon had told him he thought Plug and Benton were involved. Did that hold more significance than Ben thought? If Vine had an important ledger, certainly his girlfriend and his bodyguard would have access to it.

But why did Efren never mention a ledger? Everyone knew Vine was averse to technology, but the idea of his keeping important information in a ledger was never considered.

Maybe that's what Efren found at the last minute and what cost him his life. But if so, where was Efren and where was the ledger?

✦

After two days, her mother was finally convinced to go home and rest for a bit.

"Evie is doing so much better," Mom told Lainie when Dad brought her home. Lainie was herself preparing to go for a visit.

"I was able to help her wash her hair and even gave her some lipstick to use. Not only was she up, but she was walking with the aid of a walker."

The news cheered Lainie, and she was excited about what she'd find when she got to Evie's room. By the time she connected with her sister, it was obvious that Evie was more clearheaded and alert. To Lainie, her sister was almost back to normal.

"I'm as weak as a kitten," Evie said. "The first time I stood, I nearly fell. But every time I try again, I get better."

She handled the news about Stan and the crash stoically.

"There were two people in the car with me?" Evie asked Lainie.

"Yes, one of them worked for Stan. Raphael, remember him?"

"The detailer. Sure."

"You were on 330, coming down the mountain."

"Wow, I have no memory of that."

"Don't fret, Evie. I'm sure things will come back to you in time."

"I'm glad you're so optimistic."

"I am."

"When can I see the boys?"

"Dad and Archie will bring them later this afternoon," Lainie said. "Mom is resting."

"Oh, good. Archie is coming. It will be good to see him as well." Evie pulled herself up using the bar above the bed.

Lainie watched her effort, so much emotion swirling inside. Her sister was strong, improving quickly, and she worked hard to get back to normal. The only nagging problem was her cloudy memory.

"Are you up to a jaunt out to the patio?" Lainie asked. "We can have lunch out there."

Evie nodded. "I could use some sunshine."

She sat up and swung her legs off the bed. Lainie helped Evie into a robe and then stepped back to get the walker. Evie got off the bed by herself and walked slowly, limping slightly, across the room to where Lainie handed over the walker. Dr. Hardin had told them that while Evie's brain was healing well, the other bumps, bruises, and strains would probably be sore for a while longer.

They left the room and passed the officer at the door.

"We're just going to the patio. You can take a break."

He nodded.

The patio was in a protected area of the hospital. There was no way to get to it from outside because they were two floors up. They found a table. Evie put the walker aside, and they both sat. It was a few minutes before she spoke up. "Lainie, can I ask you a question?"

"Of course."

"Once I'm released, will I be able to visit Stan?"

"What? Why would you want to?" Lainie couldn't believe what she was hearing.

"He's still my husband and the father of my children. I pray for him every day."

"He almost killed you."

"I don't know that he had anything to do with what happened to me. And neither do you."

"You don't know that he didn't." The rage Lainie had felt toward Stan that day on the beach when he tried to sell the shark attack resurfaced. She worked to calm down.

"I would be the first to say that he's not perfect. I live with him, I know that. But we are all sinners saved by grace, Lainie. I know that you haven't forgotten that."

"Evie, he tried to convince everyone that you were killed by a shark. He knew you were in danger, and he was only concerned about himself."

"I realize all of that. And I am angry and hurt. But I still need to talk to him and hear from him directly about everything."

"Even the affair?" Lainie was immediately sorry she asked the question when pain crossed her sister's face. But Evie recovered quickly.

"Sorry, that was mean."

Evie gave a wave of her hand. "Even the affair. Stan has his faults, and so do I. I can't walk away without talking to him and praying every single day."

"I get it."

"Do you? I worry about you, Lainie. It's been a while since I've seen you in church. Do you really understand my faith?"

Lainie looked away, fighting the shame and guilt that threatened to engulf her. At least it pushed away the anger. She turned back to answer. "I wouldn't have known how to answer that question a week ago. I might have gotten angry. In fact, when you called me before all this mess started and I saw your caller ID, I didn't want to talk to you, because I didn't want a lecture about church."

"Is that what I do, lecture?"

"No, no, that was just how I saw it then. I didn't like being called out for my sin." Lainie took a deep breath and cleared her throat, the pain of that phone call hitting like bricks all over again.

"When I talked to Stan that day, I realized how far I'd moved away from faith. I regret that. I regret that I opened a door for hatred of Vine and closed a door on the love of God. I've prayed for forgiveness. I'm trying to move back."

Evie reached across the table and gripped Lainie's hand. "A sincere prayer is all it takes. God forgives, Lainie. He forgives you. If he asks me to forgive Stan, I will."

✦

He lied.

He cheated.

He almost got Evie killed.

Later, as Lainie drove home, she struggled with indignation. How could Evie forgive Stan after all the hurt and pain he'd caused? Then it hit like a fiery arrow to the chest—*I expect God to forgive me. How am I any better than Stan?*

For a time, I turned my back on God and my family.

I violated department policy and almost lost my job.

I was inches away from a full-blown affair with a married man.

Tears fell as she drove, and Lainie knew she had more soul-searching to do. Her festering anger at Stan was not justified; her sister was right. As someone who was so forgiven, she had no room to withhold forgiveness from Stan.

CHAPTER 49

Two days later, Ben felt like it had been years since he'd had a good night's sleep. He'd been following the progress of Evangeline Moffit tangentially and trying to find Dallas Vine directly. Moffit was recovering quickly, walking and talking. Vine was still MIA.

Ben had gone so far as to drive up to Big Bear Lake and check out Vine's summer home. The place was locked up tight. It didn't seem like anyone had been at the house in quite a while.

The only thing that wigged Ben out was that he'd picked up a tail. He'd first seen the black SUV on the 210 freeway and talked himself into believing he was being paranoid. But after he stopped in Running Springs for gas and a beverage, he saw the vehicle again. The third time was the charm, when the vehicle was also in Big Bear Lake.

Ben could see the SUV three cars back as he started back down the hill. The road leading in and out of Big Bear was a narrow two-lane road. When Ben saw the opportunity, he made a sharp U-turn, causing the vehicle behind him to break and honk.

As he passed the black vehicle, he stared at the driver, who ducked away. But the vehicle did not follow him.

He'd not been able to get a license plate, and it would have been nearly impossible with all the traffic to try and turn the tables on the guy, so he continued on his way. Was it Vine? Was he that desperate? All federal agencies were on the lookout for him. He'd be caught eventually, especially if he was stupid enough to try and tail a federal agent.

Now, Ben was back in the office going over his notes—again. While everyone was happy with Evangeline Moffit's progress, she didn't remember being kidnapped, and she had no idea where she had been for nearly a week.

Ben reviewed what he'd written on the day he'd talked to her before her abduction. She'd seen Efren the Friday he was supposed to check in. In the morning, he'd washed and detailed her car. That night Efren should have checked in with his progress, but all methods they had for contact were silent.

Frustrated, Ben paced. He was missing too many pieces, but how to find them? He kept returning to that Friday. There was no way to know what else happened that day or who else Efren interacted with. Ben wanted to talk to Stan, but he was not sure if that would fly. The guy had lawyered up. Ben had no choice but to review everything he'd reviewed several times already.

A stray thought hit his head like a bullet: What kind of car did Evangeline have? None of the files or paperwork mentioned her vehicle. No one knew exactly when or how she was taken. Was she taken from home or while she was out running errands?

Ben felt energized by this new avenue to explore. He'd hoped to find some kind of message in Efren's car and came up empty. What if he just had the wrong car?

Ben tried to put himself in Efren's shoes. If he had found something, like say a ledger, and he wanted to hide it, where would be the safest place? He couldn't hide it in his car or on his person, nor could he hide it in the car wash.

Then in came Evangeline for a routine detail. The boss's wife. Perhaps Efren thought that her car was the last place anyone would look. Since it was likely that she regularly got her car washed there, he could either plan to retrieve it another day, or if he was going to blow his cover and pull himself out of the car wash, get it later, with the full force of a warrant.

It made sense to Ben. Now he was on a mission to find that car.

✦

"Your progress is astounding." Dr. Hardin beamed as he watched Evie walk without the help of a walker.

Lainie leaned against the wall and smiled. Evie had always been a hard worker and very determined.

"I feel so much better than when I first opened my eyes," Evie told the doctor. "Except for my memory, everything is working. The bruises are fading, and honestly, I'm tired of hospital food."

"Fine. One more CAT scan and then I'll sign your discharge papers. Right now, I don't foresee any issues, so you'll likely be on your way home later this afternoon."

Evie was coming home.

"I'm happy for you, Evie. Mom and Dad will be glad to bring you home. Now I have to go back to Long Beach and get my apartment set up." She gave Evie a hug and then left. Life was finally settling down.

Home for Lainie now was a rented apartment. The insurance company had sent an adjuster to evaluate the ruins of her house. They would settle soon, and hopefully one day she'd be able to rebuild. While she knew that her parents would always welcome her into their home, it was just a little too crowded now with the boys. Since Evie would also move in, Lainie decided to rent temporarily.

As far as the investigation went, Lainie had to step away. She'd been involved in a shooting. It was being handled as an on-duty shooting because of the circumstances. Her handgun had been examined and returned, but she was still required to talk to the department psychologist, who would eventually have to approve her return to work.

The problem was, Lainie didn't really want to talk to the psychologist. Years ago, after the lawsuit, she'd been required to talk to him.

"They just want to be certain that you're right in the head," Beck had said back then.

Even though Beck had said it, Lainie didn't like the idea of psychological probing, the requirement that she do some self-examination. At that time, she hadn't even shot anyone.

On the way home, Lainie got a call from her lieutenant, asking for a meeting. She diverted to the station. Setting up her apartment would have to wait.

"How are you doing?" LT asked.

"I'm still standing. Evie is improving. She's coming home so that is great."

"Glad to hear it. Have you spoken to Dr. Reynolds?"

Lainie sighed. She should have known the LT would want to know about that. There was no way she could get out of it; she just wanted to put it off as long as possible. If the shooting had happened on a regular shift, she would have automatically had three days off. She figured she had time to wait.

"I have not. I will call him. I've just been a little busy. I'm kind of bummed because I'm ready to return to work."

"I understand. But it's your first shooting, and it's possible you hit the guy, though it does not appear as if he was hurt badly. Stuff like that can play with your head, so let's take it slowly. How is everything else going? You found a place to live?"

"I have. I rented an apartment up by the circle. I guess it's a good thing that I'm off work. I'll need some time to finish clothes shopping. Everything burned. I also have furniture being delivered to my new apartment. I feel like a slug making Mike handle our caseload."

"He hasn't complained. And everyone understands your life is crazy right now. Don't hesitate to tell someone if you're having any issues at all."

"I won't. And I appreciate your concern."

After the meeting, Lainie stopped in the violent crimes office to see how Mike was holding up. He wasn't in; he was in court.

"Lainie." She turned to see Detective Shea coming her way.

"I was just going to text you," he said. "Come into my office for a sec?"

"Sure." She followed him to the homicide office. Surprise struck—there sat Ben Isaacs. Lainie had thought of him often over the last few days. Mostly she was ashamed of herself. For how she had treated him. When she faced up to all the hate and unforgiveness she felt toward Stan, she realized she'd directed some vitriol at Ben as well. She'd withheld forgiveness from Ben, and for that she was truly sorry.

"We've been reviewing all that we have on this case. Ben here came up with a good question. Go ahead, Ben."

He nodded toward Lainie. "Good to see you, Lainie. How are you doing?"

"Like I told the lieutenant, I'm still standing. Thanks for asking." She hoped that her tone would telegraph that she was over her snit. "What do you have?"

"It's what we don't have. Do you know where your sister's car is?"

"What? Her car?"

"Yeah, we know that there is a Toyota Corolla registered to her, but we haven't been able to locate it."

Flabbergasted, Lainie sat. "I hadn't thought about it. It wasn't in the garage at her house?"

"No, I checked. I checked the car wash as well. Stan's car is in impound because he was arrested in it, but I don't think anyone is even concerned about Evie's vehicle. Has she been able to tell you anything about when and how she was taken?"

Lainie shook her head. "She still doesn't remember what happened. The last thing she remembers was packing for Hawaii. Then waking up in the hospital. Why is the car important?"

"I'm not certain it is, but we've exhausted everything to this point. She told me when I spoke to her that she'd had her car washed on Friday and had spoken to Efren there, at Sudsy Place."

"The Friday before she went missing?"

"Yes. And it was that Friday that Efren missed his scheduled check-in."

Lainie rubbed her hands together, thinking. "Her memory is so spotty. She remembers that she called me, but she doesn't know why. Doc says maybe with time more memories will return."

"This is the last loose end. Vine has disappeared, and I'm afraid Crystal Benton might have left the country."

"Might have? You're not sure?" she asked.

"Not positive. However, her alias Martha White flew to Barbados from LAX a week ago, before we could flag her. If that was her, right now she's out of our grasp."

"But we have that passport. How could she have used it?"

"Like I say, we're not sure, but she has disappeared as completely as Vine."

"Do you think Vine left the country?"

He arched an eyebrow and held one hand out, palm up. "Nowadays the most convenient way to track people is their digital footprint. Vine does not have one. Notoriously old-school, he doesn't even use credit cards. To leave the country he'd need a passport. Vine has mastered the art of being off-grid."

Lainie considered this information for a moment, trying not to descend into depression because of it. *God is in control* came to mind, and it gave her some confidence and maybe even some optimism.

"He can't stay holed up forever. Everyone gets caught eventually. Evie comes home later today; I'll talk to her again. One more thing, she wants to talk to Stan." Lainie looked at Shea.

"Ah, he's been arraigned and sent to County. She'll need to talk to his public defender, but it shouldn't be a problem. She is his wife."

"Do you think Stan will tell her anything?" Ben asked.

"About the case? I'm not sure. Evie's concern with Stan is more personal."

"Ah, I understand."

"I don't really. I don't think she should put herself through it. Evie is a forgiving person. I think her mission is to confront him with everything she knows and see what he has to say for himself."

"Makes sense. I hope Stan sees the error of his ways and comes clean for his wife. She can't be compelled to testify against him, but maybe he will tell her something that could help us find Vine. Please keep me up-to-date on her meeting." Ben stood to leave.

"Are you going back to your office?" she asked.

"Nope. Lunch."

Lainie checked her watch. "I didn't realize it was that time. Do you mind if I join you?"

Surprise flashed across his face and then disappeared. "Sure. Do you have a place you'd like to go?"

"Someplace down in The Pike?"

"I'll follow you."

They said goodbye to Shea and left the office for the elevator. Once the doors closed, Lainie turned to Ben. Standing here with him, knowing what she had to do, only positive feelings flooded her. Ben was a good guy, a good agent. She liked him. Forgiveness erased all the negativity she'd felt.

"I need to get something off my chest."

"Yeah?"

"I'm sorry I was so hard on you about Evie—"

He held up a hand to stop her. "You were right; I was wrong." His expression was open and friendly, sincere.

"Yeah, maybe you were wrong, but so was I. You made a judgment call, a call I might have made myself if our roles were reversed. There is no reason for me to be angry or for you to feel guilty. Stan is responsible for what happened to Evie, not you. Can you forgive me?"

He smiled. "Hey, if you can forgive me, it's a no-brainer to forgive you a few harsh words."

"Great." Lainie held her hand out. "Friends? Shake on it?"

He gripped her outstretched hand, and Lainie felt great peace settle over her. And something else. Ben's blue eyes were so warm, his grip strong and comforting. This could be dangerous, Lainie thought, but not in a bad way.

CHAPTER 50

Ben found himself smiling, pleasantly surprised at Lainie's change of heart. He'd missed being around her, hearing how she thought, seeing how she responded to different circumstances. It dawned on him that it had been a long time since he'd dated anyone. Most women he met didn't understand his work, and that made relationships hard.

Lainie was different. They'd only known each other for a short time, yet he felt connected. Was it possible she could feel the same way?

They ended up at P.F. Chang's.

"How long have Stan and Evie been married?" Ben asked as they were led to a table.

"Eight years." Lainie paused as they sat. "I confess I'm still working out how I feel toward Stan. He's caused Evie so much pain, physical and emotional. If Stan talks to anyone, it will be Evie. She might even get the truth out of him."

"Do you think Stan would talk to me?" Ben asked.

Surprise crossed her features. "I don't know. I guess it depends on what happens with Evie. My guess is that she'll urge him to confess, come clean about everything. If he listens to her, he may talk to you."

"He was closer to Efren than he admits. At least from what Efren wrote in his notes."

"How so?"

"He was at their house several times for barbecues. He even wrote about spending time with your nephews. When you talked to Stan, he just glossed over his relationship with Efren, acted like he barely knew him."

Lainie nodded. "The vibe I got from him that day is that he was lying. Stan is self-serving at every level. I'll give Evie a call and ask her to drop a hint and suggest he speaks to you."

"Thanks."

"Thank you, again, for what you did for the boys." Her eyes sparkled and Ben felt a little lost in her gaze. "You took a big chance, put yourself at risk."

He took a deep breath, feeling that they had a connection deeper than just colleagues and maybe more than simple gratitude. It wasn't a feeling that he wanted to stifle.

"I did my job, Lainie. I simply thank God that I was in the right place at the right time." He put his hand over hers, and she didn't move it away.

✦

Lainie spent the next morning arranging her new furniture and watching the clock. Evie had called her the night before to let her know that the hope of meeting with Stan was now a firm reality.

"Wow, that was fast."

"His public defender is a woman," Evie said. "She was very helpful in arranging the meeting. She said that Stan is eager to see me and has been asking about me."

"I pray that the meeting is what you need, that Stan is honest with you. If you're able, will you ask him and his lawyer if he will talk to Ben Isaacs?"

"The FBI agent? Of course. I want Stan to be honest and tell the authorities all that he knows. The public defender told me all the charges against him. I can't believe Stan is guilty of all that."

"If it's any consolation, I also don't think he's guilty of everything." *He's guilty enough,* Lainie thought, but she didn't say it.

Even though she could admit to herself that forgiving Ben was the right thing, Stan was another issue altogether. She knew holding a grudge, or harboring anger in her heart concerning Stan, would only damage her; it would never affect Stan. Still, there was a wall between what she knew she should do and what she was doing. Daily in her prayer time Lainie asked for help regarding Stan. Some days it was easier than other days.

Would Stan tell Evie anything important, or would he continue lying and feeling sorry for himself? Evie promised to call when the meeting was over.

Her phone rang. Caller ID said Ben, not Evie. The excitement she felt seeing Ben's number caught her a bit by surprise.

"Hello, Ben." Could he hear the smile in her voice?

"Lainie, sorry to bug you, but have you heard from your sister?"

"You're not bugging me at all. I'm honestly as eager as you are."

"Have you eaten yet? I can bring over a pizza and we can eat and wait together."

"That sounds great," she said, and it did. She was very glad that she and Ben were back in sync.

Lainie finished tidying everything up quickly; she didn't have much to tidy. Once she finished, she sat on the couch and surveyed the sparsely furnished room. She hadn't had time to mourn her home, her things. Lainie had never been overly attached to her possessions, but she had worked over the years to make her house a comfy home.

It hit suddenly that it was all gone—her favorite jeans, the pair of pajamas that were a gift from Evie that she loved, her collection of books, novels, criminology textbooks she'd kept from college, her desk and all the mementos and awards from her police career, all her photographs.

Delayed sadness overwhelmed her, and Lainie felt a lump in her throat, and tears trailed down her cheeks. "Oh, Lord, they were only things . . . Help me to keep it all in perspective."

When the sadness lessened and she blew her nose, Lainie found something to smile about: reliance on prayer was coming back to her. It was beginning to be a habit again, and that was gratifying. By the time Ben knocked on her door, her mood had improved and she was hungry for pizza.

"I have a small table and only two chairs. You're lucky my furniture came yesterday," she said when she let Ben in.

"It's homey with very little. I imagine your house was great." He opened the pizza box and loaded up two plates with pieces.

"I was just thinking about that, how much I lost in the fire. I had kind of a delayed reaction."

He stopped the pizza slice halfway to his mouth, then set it down, his expression serious. "I'm so sorry, Lainie. You lost your whole life." He gripped her hand and gave a reassuring squeeze.

The sincerity in his eyes rolled over Lainie, and pleasure flooded through her. She liked this guy. It warmed her heart.

"I'm okay. I'm sad, but I'm grateful no one was hurt. I realized something recently that really helped."

"What's that?"

"Kind of a confession. Ever since Vine escaped the murder charges for Daphne Sparks, I guess I held a grudge against God. What happened with Evie—" She paused and sipped her water. "Well, it kind of brought me back into the fold. And just now I realized that prayer had become a habit again. It felt good, it gave me peace even though my whole world is falling apart in a bunch of disparate pieces right now."

Ben smiled. Lainie really liked his smile. It lit up his whole face, made him look less federal.

"I get it. I think we've all been there, wondering why something horrible happens, why God didn't stop it. *Why* is a question we rarely get answered. I've asked it enough concerning Efren."

"That's worse than a fire taking my house. I can't imagine losing a partner."

"I just wish—" His voice broke, and he cleared his throat. "There would be some consolation if we could catch Vine. If Efren's work would at least lead to that guy's arrest and conviction."

Lainie's response was interrupted by her phone. Evie. Lainie asked, "How did the visit go?"

"It was hard, harder than I thought it would be, very emotional. I need to talk to you; he had a lot to say. Can I come over?"

Twenty minutes later, Evie was at the door. Her eyes were red and puffy.

"Agent Isaacs, I'm glad you're here. Stan told me about Efren."

CHAPTER 51

Ben learned from Lainie that her sister was not yet cleared to drive. When she knocked on the door, her mother was with her. Considering the accident and the time spent in the hospital, he was amazed at how good Evangeline looked, pale but with life in her eyes.

"Wow, I'd never know that you just emerged from a coma." He reached out his hand and she shook it. Though he could see that she'd been crying. "Are you okay?"

"Thank you, Agent Isaacs. I'm fine, just emotional." She blew her nose.

"The doctor said that because she was in good shape to begin with, Evie should be back to 100 percent sooner than most," her mother said.

"I'm glad to hear that. Thank you for bringing her over today. I want to have this talk. We saved you some pizza. And please, call me Ben."

"I'm not hungry right now."

Lainie gave them both some water, and she and Ben pulled the kitchen chairs into the living room while Mrs. Jensen and Evie sat on the couch.

"Thanks anyway." Evie dabbed her eyes.

To Ben it appeared as if she was struggling for control.

"I'm sorry. It was difficult and more than a little heartbreaking to see Stan. For both of us, really. He broke down and confessed so many things." She paused, and Ben could see this was not easy for her.

"He told me a lot, but I know that you're concerned the most about Efren. He admitted that he was not completely truthful when he talked to you, Lainie."

"Not truthful how? With everything?"

"About Efren. He knew Efren well, and he liked him. But Crystal didn't. She didn't like him, and she didn't trust him the whole time he worked at the car wash."

"Did she say why?" Ben asked.

"She thought that he paid too much attention to everything; it bothered her. In her eyes detailers were stupid, only manual labor. Efren was too smart for his own good. It came to a head one Friday. She caught him snooping in one of the cars. He told her he found a loose handrest and was only fixing it."

"Did Stan say exactly what Friday that was?"

"It was the Friday before the Hawaii trip. According to Stan, Crystal accused Efren of stealing something from the car he claimed he was fixing."

"Did Stan witness this?" Ben asked.

"He heard Crystal confront Efren."

"That same day?"

"Yes. It was after the car wash closed for the day. It was time to go home, and he came out of his office to raised voices—Crystal accusing Efren of something, and Efren denying it. Then Crystal's driver, a guy they call Plug, beat him up."

"Beat Efren up?"

Evie nodded. "Hit him from behind, knocked him to the ground, and began kicking him when he was down." She closed her eyes and rubbed her hands together.

"Stan said Efren swore he didn't know what they were talking about, that he didn't have anything. Stan also says he tried to stop the beating; he pleaded with Crystal."

"Did they stop?"

She shook her head. "Plug threatened him, said it was none of his business. Stan said even though he left the room, he kept listening, He heard Crystal say that she knew that Efren took the book."

"The book?" Ben asked. "What book?"

"Stan didn't know. And he heard Efren deny taking anything. Crystal was hysterical. Stan said he'd never seen or heard her so upset. From what he overheard, Crystal had taken a book from Vine. She wanted something from the book, and then she planned on getting it back to Vine before he knew it was gone. Because she couldn't find the book, she was afraid Vine would find out it was gone before she could return it." Evie paused and drank some water.

"Maybe they guessed he was listening because they both told him to leave, so he did. The next day at work, Efren didn't show up and Stan was told not to ask questions."

"Did Stan ever find out anything about the book?"

Evie shook her head. "Stan has no idea about the book. I believe him about that." She swallowed. "He said that the next day, Raphael had to work hard to get the blood out of Crystal's car." She grabbed a Kleenex.

Ben blinked as emotion hit hard. Blood. Efren's blood.

A feeling of deep loss emerged, then rising fury. They'd beaten his friend. More than anything he wanted to catch everyone involved.

Evie needed time to compose herself. She sobbed and her mother handed her another tissue.

"What happened to me was bad," Evie said after a minute, a sob still in her voice. "But I'm here, alive. I have difficulty processing that Stan knew something bad had happened to Efren and never said anything."

"Do you remember having your car washed and talking to Efren?"

"Washed? No." She frowned. "Well, maybe vaguely. I used to get my car washed once a week. Efren always did the best job."

"Do you remember meeting me for coffee?"

Evie rubbed at her temple. "I met you for coffee?"

Ben nodded.

"Memories are so blurry. I know that I met you at some point. I just can't put my finger on when."

"We met the day before you were abducted. I asked you about Efren. You told me that the last time you saw him was that Friday, when you took your car to have it washed."

She sat up straight, closed her eyes as if trying to remember. "It's coming to me in flashes. I do remember having a conversation with someone about Efren. I also remember being at the car wash and talking to Efren as he was detailing my car." She pressed a palm to her forehead.

"Did anything out of the ordinary happen when you spoke to him?"

"I don't think so. He did a perfect job like always."

"Did he talk to you about anything important?"

"Not that I remember."

"Evie, do you know where your car is now?" Lainie asked.

Her brow furrowed. "It wasn't in my garage? No, I don't. I wish I did."

"Let's try something," Ben said. "I've seen agents conduct hypnosis interviews where they take people back to an incident. I don't particularly believe in hypnosis, but I do think if you consider your routine, think about your normal activities, it might spark a memory."

"My routine?"

"Yeah, you were getting ready for a trip. What would you do to prepare for the trip? You got the car washed, what would be next?"

Evie thought for a moment. "It was going to be my first trip away in a very long time. I was packing, and one of the wheels on my suitcase broke. So I went to the outlet stores in Orange." Her eyes got wide.

"You remember something?" Lainie asked.

"I do. Raphael was there when I came out of the store." She shuddered and her eyes narrowed. "I remember now. He grabbed me, put his hand over my mouth."

"Raphael abducted you from the outlet mall? Did he take your car?"

Evie shook her head. "There was another car." Her face drained of all color.

"Give her a minute," her mother said.

"Oh, oh." Evie shook her hands out. "I'm not sure I'm ready for this. Lainie, can I use your bathroom?"

"Sure." Lainie pointed in the direction of her one and only bathroom, and Evie got up and went there.

Lainie turned to Ben. "We know who took her now, but he's dead. Will this help us at all?"

"Raphael was working on someone's orders. Right now, we need to go to Orange and find that car."

CHAPTER 52

Evie and her mother left after the unpleasant memories resurfaced. Evie wanted to rest, and Mom agreed. She was very protective. Lainie had a tempered excitement about what she'd heard.

"After a week, I doubt the car is still there." She hated to put a damper on Ben's unbridled optimism. In her mind's eye, she remembered what had happened to Efren's car, how destroyed it had been.

"Shea put a BOLO out for it. If it had been impounded, we would have heard from the impounding jurisdiction."

"All the more reason to hope that it's still there," Ben said, countering her negativity.

"Ah, it's a Toyota Corolla. They're easily stolen."

"Let's think positively. You're still up for a drive out there, aren't you?"

"I am. Your car or mine?"

They ended up in Ben's sedan, and he drove to Orange.

"Is this a company car?" Lainie asked. The nondescript Ford sedan reminded her of a rental.

"What, are you saying that it's boring?"

"It's a four-door sedan that could be a low-profile police vehicle," she teased, feeling good today with a lead to follow.

"Ha, ha. Yeah, it's my car. It's efficient."

"It is that."

"Back on subject, I feel bad for your sister," Ben said. "It appeared as if the recollected memories were hard for her to take."

"Maybe, but she needs to know. Buried wounds usually only fester. Maybe she'll remember something that will help us find the ledger if we come up empty on her car."

"I don't believe we'll come up empty." He turned to Lainie and smiled, and his optimism lifted her spirits. For a few seconds, as Ben sped up the freeway ramp, silence filled the car. It was not an uncomfortable silence, but Lainie had questions.

"Why did you become an agent?"

He shot a glance her way and chuckled. "It kind of runs in the family. Dad and Granddad were US Marshals. My way of rebelling was to join the FBI."

"You didn't want to save the world?" Lainie teased.

"Nope, nothing noble here. It was more than what I wanted; it was what I was supposed to do. I thought I'd only last a couple of years, though."

"What happened?"

He didn't say anything for a minute, tilting his head as if collecting his thoughts.

"After Efren and I became partners, we were part of a team that rescued several children and women from traffickers at the border. They were jammed in a shipping container in hundred-degree heat. The traffickers had left because they knew we were coming. If we hadn't gotten there when we did, they all would have suffocated." He paused to check traffic and change lanes.

"It felt good, you know, freeing all of those victims. I guess for a minute I did feel like I could save the world." He turned to Lainie and shot her a half smile. "So now, there isn't anything else I'd rather be doing. Your turn." His blue eyes sparkled with warmth.

Lainie had to look away for a second. This guy was getting under her skin in a good way, and she felt her face flush. "Nothing quite as dramatic. When I was a kid, my best friend was kidnapped off the street, right in front of her house."

"Whoa. Not dramatic?"

"It turned out okay. I mean, the cops found her, arrested the kidnapper, and brought her home. I remember how scared her mother was while we waited and then how wonderful it was when Jaycee came home. The officer carried her up the walk. Everyone was so happy, so relieved. From that moment on, I knew I wanted to be a cop."

"Is it everything you thought it would be back then?"

"Rough patches here and there. Vine almost cost me, but yeah, it's been a good job."

The freeway drive went fast. Before long, Ben exited the 22 freeway and approached the outlet mall. The parking lot was huge. Ben entered from The City Drive.

"Where do you think Evangeline would've parked?"

"She wanted a suitcase, so wherever you see Global Luggage. Let's start there. And Evie doesn't park close; she likes to walk."

As Ben drove up the first aisle of parked vehicles, Lainie's pessimism kicked in. "I find it hard to believe security here would let a vehicle stay parked in the lot for a week and not do anything with it."

"I'm still praying we'll find it."

"We're after an older-model blue Toyota Corolla, four doors."

Ben cruised slowly up and then down several rows of parked cars. There was no blue Toyota near the luggage store. They entered another lot. They'd searched for about ten minutes before they turned a corner, and in the next row of parked vehicles, Lainie saw her sister's car.

"I can't believe it; there it is, the next endcap."

"I see it." Ben sped up and pulled in next to Evie's car.

It was dusty, one back tire was low, but it was Evie's car. There was a ticket under the windshield wiper blade. They both got out and walked around the Toyota.

Lainie pulled the ticket and held it up. "Three-day warning for an abandoned vehicle. Placed by a meter maid. They never would have checked the plate for a BOLO. It's set to be towed tomorrow."

Lainie leaned forward and peered into the driver's-side window. Like their mother, Evie was a neat freak. The inside of the vehicle was spotless, save for a Bible on the back seat. Then again, she'd just had it detailed.

Lainie pulled out her phone. "I'll call for a tow truck."

"Great. I can't wait to get inside this car."

✦

An hour later, the tow truck arrived. To pull the car up onto the flatbed, the driver needed to disengage the brake. He used a Slim Jim to open the driver's door and get inside the car.

"I want to wait until we're inside the yard to do a thorough search," Ben said. "But how about a cursory one?"

"Sure." Lainie popped the trunk, and Ben searched there while she checked the glove box and the car's interior. All she found, besides the Bible, was the manual for the vehicle. She removed the Bible, intending to return it to Evie as soon as she could. Knowing Evie, the Bible was probably well used, marked up, and very important to her. The well-worn case Evie kept her Bible in bore the inscription *His grace is enough*.

"Anything in the trunk?"

Ben shook his head. "Just an emergency road kit, tools, and first aid, that kind of thing."

Once the car was loaded, Ben and Lainie followed the tow truck back to Long Beach. To Lainie it was one of the many incongruities of this case that they didn't have the car keys. For some reason, Evie had Crystal's purse and ID and her own jewelry but not her car keys.

Or any other personal property belonging to Evie. And, of course, the spare keys most likely burned up in the house fire.

Lainie called Shea while Ben drove, explaining the find.

"You're supposed to be off, taking care of your house," Shea teased. "What are you doing out in Orange, Lainie?"

"Evie's car was the last big missing piece. Got to get to the bottom of things. I am an impatient sort, you know that."

"Hugh and I can't get to the tow yard tonight. Have Isaacs record everything."

"Of course. And I'll call you if we find anything important."

✦

It was dark by the time they arrived at the tow yard. Ben followed the tow truck through the gate, and it closed behind them. He parked and they walked to where the tow truck had stopped.

Mel came out of the office. "This car is in better shape than the last one you came here for," he said to Lainie.

"What are you still doing here Mel? Isn't it past your bedtime?"

"Ha. Night guy called in sick. I'm getting a little OT. And I have another call for the driver." He pointed with a piece of paper in hand toward the tow truck driver.

Meanwhile, the driver maneuvered to a relatively uncrowded portion of the lot to place the vehicle, not far from the office. Ben and Lainie watched as he unloaded the Toyota from his wrecker. When it was unhooked and in place, the driver took the paper from Mel and headed out for his next call.

"It's all yours, guys," Mel said. "I'm curious, what are you after?"

"Evidence," Lainie said. "We're hoping there's something hidden in the car."

"I hope you find it." The phone rang. The office had a ringer in the yard so calls would not be missed, and Mel jogged back inside, leaving Lainie and Ben to their search.

"Will you open all four doors, the hood, and the trunk as I record this on my phone?" Ben asked.

"Sure." Lainie hit the unlock button and opened all four doors wide. Then she lifted the hood and opened the trunk. In the trunk she found a black backpack. When she opened it, she saw the roadside emergency kit Ben had mentioned. There were flares, an emergency blanket, a tool kit, and a first aid kit inside. Under the hood was nothing but the engine.

She stepped back while Ben recorded a description of what they were doing and why.

"Is there a flashlight in the trunk?" Ben asked.

Lainie checked and found one. She illuminated the inside of the vehicle. Wide open, brightly illuminated, the inside was spotless. She opened the glove box. Along with some Kleenex was the vehicle's manual. She continued searching the vehicle, shining the light under the seats, flipping down the sun visors, peering into the door pockets.

When she finished, Lainie faced Ben and shook her head. He paused recording. "What?"

"There's nothing here. This is a waste."

"I don't think so. Remember I told you that Vine hid things inside cars? He removed door panels, seat backs. There's something here; I feel it."

Lainie stood back, hands on her hips. "Have at it."

Ben knocked on the front door panel, then the back passenger door panel behind the driver's seat. They both sounded hollow. He moved to the car's other side. The rear passenger door panel sounded different.

Lainie arched an eyebrow, feeling excitement rise. He knocked on the front passenger door; it sounded hollow like the other two doors.

Pointing to the door panel for the back passenger door, he said, "There is something in this panel. I need a screwdriver."

"Tool kit." Lainie went to the trunk and opened the kit. She grabbed the screwdriver and handed it to Ben.

Vehicle lights cut into the dark, and Lainie glanced over her shoulder. The tow truck was back.

He handed her his phone. "Keep recording." Then he knelt and pried at the door panel. One edge came up rather easily, and with a quick pull, Ben removed the panel. There, taped to the metal frame, was a black leather notebook.

CHAPTER 53

Ben sat back on his heels when he found the book. He looked up at Lainie. "Can you believe it?"

"I need to call Shea. We should put this in an evidence bag." She handed him his phone and pulled her own out of her pocket.

Chain of evidence would be important if this ledger got to court. As much as Ben wanted to rip it open, he could wait.

He put the screwdriver down, squatted, and took his phone, recording a close-up of the book. He was a little disheartened by what he saw. The cover was untreated leather. That meant that finding fingerprints was not likely; the surface was too porous. Depending on what they found in the book, they'd want it tied to Vine without a shadow of a doubt. His prints would have helped immensely. It also had a small lock on it, like a diary lock that needed a small key.

I'm getting ahead of myself, Ben thought. *Jumping to conclusions. How can we prove that this was left here by Efren?*

Standing, Ben waited for Lainie to finish her call.

"He'll be in the office if we bring this down. What's the matter? You look disturbed."

"The cover excludes prints. And I guess I'm getting a little worried—what if this book is not what we think?"

"Why would Efren go to the trouble of hiding it?"

"How can we prove Efren hid it? You need to call your sister and make sure she or Stan didn't hide the book."

"I'm sure they wouldn't do that, but I know what you're saying. We're likely to have to prove chain of custody to a jury. This is my sister's car. Without Efren to testify, we need a solid connection to Vine."

"Right. You and I can be convinced that Efren put it here and that it cost him his life, but we need to be able to prove that to twelve people who didn't know him. Well, here goes, I'm going to pull it off."

He stooped over and yanked the book from the doorframe. The book was the size of a diary. Ben turned it over in his hands. "No title."

"If this puts Dallas Vine in prison, I think I'll call it an early Christmas gift," Lainie said.

Ben smiled. "I like that. Let's get to the station."

They bagged it, wanting to open it with Shea and Collins present so no one could imply that they wrote anything in the book or altered it in any way.

I pray this is from you, my friend, Ben thought, again hoping Efren's loss was not in vain.

CHAPTER 54

With the book in an evidence bag, Ben and Lainie got back into his car.

"Hey, are you up for dinner after we drop this off?" Ben asked Lainie as he walked to the driver's side and she walked to the passenger side. As sad as he was about Efren, he was glad he'd met Lainie, and he hoped to get to know her better.

"I'm hungry, that's for sure." She looked at him over the top of the car.

"Great, we'll pick a spot later."

They hopped in and he started the engine. "Even with this find, or maybe because of it, I'd still like to talk to Stan," Ben said as they waited for the tow yard gate to open. "He might know more about this book than he told your sister."

"Sounds like there is a *but* there."

He turned toward her, amazed that she knew he was bugged about something. "I'm thinking about what your sister said about Efren. The idea that Benton was on to him from the get-go bothers me."

"Are you thinking that his cover was blown long before he disappeared?"

Ben nodded. "I am. I'd like to hear more about the situation at the car wash."

The gate opened and he exited the yard.

"If Evie can talk him into talking to you, I'm sure she will."

"Great, I . . ." The next words caught in Ben's throat. He saw a black SUV.

"What's the matter?"

"I think we've got a tail. There's a black SUV behind us. It was parked outside the tow yard. I think that's the same car that was behind me a couple of days ago."

Lainie leaned forward to see what she could in the side-view mirror. They were traveling west on Willow Street, in the middle lane. Ben drove west toward Long Beach Boulevard, planning to turn left there to head downtown to the police station. He sped up and changed lanes.

"Yep," Lainie said, "they are following us. I see two people at least. A man and a woman, I think."

"Well, they can follow us to the station, I guess." As they approached the light at Atlantic, it changed to yellow. Ben punched it and made it through as the light turned red.

The SUV followed on the red light and rapidly caught up with him, now riding his bumper.

"He's not being shy. I'm glad there's not a lot of traffic right now." Ben swerved around slower traffic and then moved back into the left lane.

The SUV pulled up next to Ben on the passenger side. As he concentrated on driving, he asked Lainie, "What's he doing?"

"Driver's-side window is coming down. I think he wants you to pull over."

"Not happening." Gripping the steering wheel, he pressed the accelerator down more.

The SUV dropped back. Then Ben's sedan shuddered when the SUV rammed the bumper.

Ben fought to maintain control as the seat belt locked and kept him from lurching in the seat. Long Beach Boulevard was the next intersection.

"He's trying to PIT maneuver us," Lainie said.

Ben had seen effective PIT maneuvers on TV, the precision immobilization technique was effective if applied correctly. He prayed the guy next to him did not know how to apply it correctly.

"Hang on," he told her as they barreled toward the boulevard, and he decided to make the left turn whether the light was green or not.

✦

Lainie kept her eyes focused on the side mirror and kept a firm grip on her weapon as they sped down Willow Street. She'd drawn the gun when the SUV had pulled next to them, and she held it down between her knees.

She snapped against the seat belt as Ben made a left onto Long Beach Boulevard, the sound of tires squealing and honking horns blaring. When she recovered enough to check the side mirror, she could see that the SUV had followed. The image in the mirror grew as the vehicle pulled up on Lainie's right.

"Look out!"

Ben's sedan was no match for the huge, full-size SUV. The driver rammed into the side of the car, pushing them left over the curb and onto the southbound Blue Line train tracks. They bounced over them and continued toward the northbound tracks.

Lainie watched in horror at the light of a northbound Blue Line train headed right for them.

Ben slammed on the brakes. The SUV driver did likewise, still sliding in front of them, fishtailing a bit as the tires smoked and he laid down rubber.

Ben struggled for control over the car. He jerked the vehicle to the right to get it out of the direct path of the northbound train, but it was too late. Momentum carried them onto the track. He couldn't pull the wheel fast enough.

The train's horn screamed, and the train impacted the side of the car, sideswiping and scraping the driver's side with a sickening squeal of metal on metal. Sparks flew, the driver's side airbag deployed, slamming Ben back in his seat.

The driver stepped out of the SUV and the vehicle blocked traffic. He was just ahead of them and to Lainie's right. He raised a handgun. "I want the book!" he yelled. "Just give me the book."

The train had stopped and she opened her door, knowing Ben was groggy from the airbag and still pinned in by the train. She had to draw the gunman away from Ben. With one foot out, using the door as cover, she pointed her gun at the man. "Drop the gun!"

He ignored her and fired, shots impacting their vehicle's windshield. Lainie returned fire immediately, hitting him twice and he went down.

But the threat was not over. In her peripheral vision, Lainie caught movement. It had to be the passenger from the SUV. Lainie recognized Crystal Benton as the woman began shooting.

She had a better angle than the driver had, and a bullet whizzed by Lainie's face. Fearing for Ben, Lainie went low and moved right, shooting as she moved, her first shots firing off-balance with no aim.

Benton followed her movement, seemingly oblivious to the fact that Lainie was shooting at her. At least two vehicles in the southbound lanes had stopped abruptly, and bullets slammed into the hood and left fender of one.

Lainie had no cover so she had to plant, aim, and shoot. Benton was like a robot, advancing and firing. A bullet struck Lainie's right shoulder and she lost the grip on her gun.

She dropped to her knees and slid behind a second stopped vehicle, twisting back as soon as she was able. Two shots dinged the car, and she felt one whistle past her ear. Once at the back of the car, training kicked in.

Terrified that Ben or an innocent driver would now be shot, Lainie grabbed her gun with her left hand, aimed, and fired.

✦

Ben was stuck. He couldn't open the driver's door because it was jammed against the train, and the airbag was slow to deflate. The pain in his left shoulder told him that his collarbone was likely broken or seriously strained from being whipped against the seat belt. The windshield took two bullets and then spiderwebbed, shattering but staying in place. He heard more bullets hit the side of the car as he struggled to undo his seat belt and draw his weapon.

He heard Lainie return fire and saw the driver go down. He ripped his seat belt off as the second shooter appeared and Ben threw himself across the front seat as more bullets sprayed the car. He prayed that Lainie was okay but feared for her because he no longer heard her firing. He just couldn't risk sticking his head up and giving the shooter a clear shot.

Then two shots rang out. He prayed that was Lainie from behind the car.

Then silence.

CHAPTER 55

Lainie rested on a paramedic gurney while her shoulder was tended to. Stitches were in her future, but the wound was not all that painful now.

Medics checked Ben out and determined that his shoulder was likely separated.

"I'm good with a sling," Ben said.

The medics put his arm in one.

"You okay, Lainie?" he asked. "I'd like to go check out the driver. The coroner just got here."

"I'll be fine. Let me know what you find on him."

He nodded and walked toward the yellow sheet that covered the SUV's driver.

The street was full of emergency lights—police, LA sheriff because the Blue Line was their jurisdiction, paramedics, and fire because Ben's vehicle had begun to smoke. Also, despite the late hour a large crowd encircled the scene. Lainie bet many of them had been on the train and had to disembark.

While the SUV driver was dead, Crystal Benton had been transported to the hospital. The medics had acted in a manner that told Lainie the woman's injuries were life-threatening.

Chief Mackall had arrived on-scene a few minutes ago. After he inspected the Blue Line train, he came over to Lainie. "How are you, Detective?" He was not in uniform, he wore jeans and a department sweatshirt, but he still carried himself like the man in charge.

"My shoulder hurts, but they told me that the bullet went through and through. Have you heard about Benton?"

"Being prepped for surgery, last communication I received." He waved his hand around. "All this over a book?"

"I think so. Ben—ah, Agent Isaacs—thought so. The guy I shot yelled out that he wanted the book, right before he opened fire. Neither one of us can come up with another reason as to why Benton would ambush us like this."

"I'm interested to see what is in that book."

You and me both, Lainie thought. But right now all she wanted to do was go home, clean up, and head to bed. After the adrenaline and shock wore off, exhaustion hit her like a bulldozer. Relieved that she and Ben were okay, Lainie could leave the examination of the book to Shea and Collins.

"We're ready to go," one of the medics told the chief.

"By all means. Lainie, this will be considered an on-duty injury. I'll send a sergeant after you to take an IOD report."

Lainie relaxed on the gurney, wishing that she could talk to Ben. He never came back to tell her what he'd found out about the driver. His boss had arrived and now he was deep in conversation with him near Ben's car, which was completely totaled. With all the bullet holes, it was a miracle Ben had not been struck. She figured he'd be at the scene for a while.

Homicide detectives had taken Lainie's gun, again. They promised to have it back soon. The protocol was in place to be certain the gun had not been modified in any way and that Lainie loaded it with department-approved ammo.

"We know that you're good, Lainie, but we still have to take it," Shea had said.

They'd also recovered her fanny pack and Evie's Bible from Ben's vehicle and gave them to her. Those items rested on her lap.

The medics hoisted her up into the van, and shortly after they were on their way to the hospital.

✦

Ben watched as the paramedic van with Lainie in it pulled away. He was thankful that they were both okay and regretted that he'd not been able to speak with Lainie before she left. The dead guy's ID said that he was Peter Ludwig Grant. Vine's bodyguard, Plug.

"Wow, when you say crash, you don't mess around. You even derailed a train." Mark had arrived to give Ben a ride home. He stood and stared at the wreckage of Ben's car entangled with the Blue Line train. A tow truck had only just arrived to remove the vehicle. He turned to Ben. "You're lucky you're okay."

"I realize that. Don't know about luck. Lainie had a part in saving my bacon, and I feel like there was some divine intervention." As destroyed as his car was, they should both be dead. His collarbone was not broken, just bruised and strained.

Mark put a hand on his right shoulder. "After you finish talking with the locals, you can take me home in the company car, and this will be your ride until you get yours sorted out, okay? That is, if you are okay to drive."

Ben nodded. "As long as no one else tries to run me into a train, I'll be fine."

Just then Chief Mackall walked up. "Agent Isaacs?"

"Yes, sir?"

"Are you certain those two people were after this book?" He held up the evidence bag, and it had been grazed by bullets.

"Yes, sir, that's what the guy was yelling for."

The chief held the book out to Ben. "The evidence bag was destroyed when we recovered it from your car, and gunfire damaged the lock. Can you tell me how any of this would be relevant to a police investigation?"

Ben took the book and opened it, viewing the pages in the glare of emergency lighting. The first page began, "Dear Lord" and then continued with a prayer for husband and children. He flipped through more pages—they were all prayers, for various and sundry things. He flipped to the front again, but there was no name to indicate who the book belonged to, just prayers and Bible verses.

This did not belong to Dallas Vine.

Jaw slack, he looked up at the chief. "We didn't open it. We assumed that this would be the evidence. If I'd have known, I would have tossed this out of the car and let the guy take it."

Mackall shook his head. "Well, let's hope the woman comes out of surgery alive and talking. We still have that." He was called back to his people by the homicide detective who had arrived on-scene.

Ben turned to Mark. "I don't know what to say. Why would Efren hide a prayer book?"

Mark just shrugged.

Ben felt as if he'd been hit by the train all over again.

He phoned Lainie while Mark drove, gratified when she answered. He let her know the dead man's identity and heard from her that her injury was not serious.

"In all the excitement, the evidence bag opened. Guess what?"

"What?" Lainie asked.

"There's no ledger. The book we found is a prayer journal."

Silence.

"Yeah, I need to process this," Lainie said.

"We'll talk soon, and I'll show this to you. Get some rest."

"Thanks, you do the same."

He hung up, gratified that she sounded good and would be fine.

Mark lived about five miles from Ben. After he was dropped off, fatigue hit Ben harder. Not only tired, but he also hurt. When the SUV rammed him into the train, it jerked his neck and jammed his shoulder. Plus, his stitches were bugging him.

He couldn't believe how the joy of finding the book had turned to utter and complete disappointment and dejection.

Ben opened the front door, walked into his house, and kicked off his shoes. He pulled a bottle of water from his fridge and drank half before he set the bottle down. Depressed, he turned to the only thing that ever calmed him: prayer. He grabbed his Bible, then stopped.

Suddenly he knew where the ledger was. He smiled and then rushed to put his shoes back on.

CHAPTER 56

"You were very lucky, Detective Jensen," the ER doctor said as he signed her discharge papers. "The bullet passed through the fleshy part of your upper arm. It will be sore for a while, but I don't see any permanent damage. It should heal up nicely."

"Thank you."

A patrol officer dropped Lainie off at home sometime early in the morning. So much was on her mind. The patrol officer told her he'd heard that Benton was expected to survive.

"She went into surgery and provided she comes through it okay, they're lining up guys to guard her until she can be moved to county jail."

With two shootings under her belt, one fatal, she could no longer avoid talking to the department psychologist. Lainie wasn't certain why she didn't want to talk to psych, she just didn't.

Right now, she was wired and not certain she could get to sleep. Setting her fanny pack and Evie's Bible down, Lainie decided to take a shower, hoping the warm water would relax her nerves and help her get to sleep. She had to keep the stitches dry, but half a shower was better than nothing.

She thought back to her conversation with Ben about the SUV driver.

"He has an extensive record and was also employed by Quartz Enterprises. At one time he was Vine's bodyguard. Bucshon told me he thought Plug and Benton were having an affair," Ben had said.

The whole episode raised so many questions in Lainie's mind. As the hot water ran over her head, she ran through just a few of the big ones.

Why was a prayer journal hidden in Evie's car?

Why did Benton come after it?

Was Benton working for Vine or against him?

Where was Vine?

Shower finished, Lainie dressed in comfortable sweats and a long sleeve T-shirt. She pulled her wet hair back into a bun and settled onto her couch. She didn't have a television set so she thought about streaming something on her computer.

Maybe I should just read instead.

The only books she had were her brand-new Bible and a blank journal. Her old, well-used ones—from years ago—burned up in her house. As kids, Lainie and her siblings had been given blank journals on Christmas Day every year by their folks in the hopes that they would record prayers and important points they learned in church on Sundays. Lainie was faithful for many years to do just that. But when she walked away from church, she walked away from that habit as well.

She got up to retrieve her Bible and noticed Evie's. She was certain that Evie was faithful to keep up a journal. There was probably a lot of wisdom and insight in her journal.

She unzipped the Bible cover and laid it out on the table. On top of the Bible was a plain black notebook. It wasn't anything like the journals their parents used to give them. It was smaller, almost industrial. Lainie frowned. Had her sister's tastes changed so much over the years? She set the notebook aside and leafed through the Bible, smiling at all the notes Evie had written in the margins. Here and there were also prayers and exclamation marks when something the pastor had said touched her heart.

Lainie read several notes and then wondered if this was a violation of Evie's privacy. She decided not and her attention returned to the odd little notebook.

Lainie opened it. Inside the front cover was a sticky note with a handwritten message on it.

Ben, sorry I messed up—if you're reading this, I did. Found this little gem in one of Vine's SUVs. It's got everything: the code legend, names, and involvement of other players, and I only scanned a small portion of it. I pray to God it gets to you. Tell Candy that I love her. Efren

Her heart nearly stopped. This was the ledger, not what they had put into evidence. Efren might have thought that he messed up, but he protected the book.

Lainie grabbed her phone to call Ben just as someone pounded on her door.

CHAPTER 57

Ben winced as he got behind the wheel of his car. His whole shoulder girdle ached. He tried calling Lainie, but she hadn't answered. It took about fifteen minutes to reach her apartment. It was early, and she might not have answered because she was asleep, but he needed to talk to her.

He bounded up the steps to the second floor and knocked on her apartment door, wincing because maybe he'd overdone it a bit and knocked too loudly.

He was about to knock again when Lainie said, "Who's there?"

"Lainie, it's Ben. We need to talk."

She pulled the door open. In her hand she held a black notebook. "The journal must be Evie's because I found the ledger in her Bible."

Ben stared at what she held in her hand. Relief flooded him as he stepped inside. "That's what I came to tell you. I guessed that it had to be in the Bible. Efren must have switched them."

Lainie nodded, closed the door, and handed Ben the book. "I'm afraid I might have muddied the chain of custody, but I had to open it. There is a note from Efren."

Ben held her gaze for a moment and took the book. He opened it and saw the note. Each word pierced him. Though on some level he knew days ago that Efren was gone, this note cemented that fact. Now the question was, where did they put his body?

When he tore his eyes away from the book, he saw Lainie watching him with compassion and understanding in her eyes.

"Did you read any more?"

"Bits. I don't understand the code, but the dates I do. This goes back a good fifteen years. If you can break the code, then I imagine it will tell us a lot. Benton sure was desperate to get it. And she's still alive. I have your optimism now. Vine is going down."

Ben nodded, the connection he felt with Lainie so strong. And he felt tremendous relief. Perhaps Efren would be the end of Vine after all. He held his arms out. "Right now, I just want to give you a big hug for finding the ledger."

She smiled and his spirits soared. He wrapped his arms around her, knowing now, despite the sadness and pain of losing Efren, there was the hope and promise of something special with Lainie.

A knock sounded at the door and Lainie pulled back. "That's Shea, I'm sure. I told him to come get the book."

"Good. It's just as well. We're not going to break the code tonight. We both need to get some sleep."

"Yeah," Lainie said as she stepped toward the door. "I'm not letting you off the hook so easily."

"What do you mean?"

"You still owe me dinner, Isaacs. Better figure out a time and a place."

Ben laughed. "It will be my pleasure to do that."

CHAPTER 58

"Lainie, are you all right?"

Lainie had slept until midday, waking up only when her phone rang. It was Mom.

"You were in a shooting yesterday."

"I'm fine, Mom." She yawned. "It was actually early this morning."

"I'm coming over. I'll bring some pastries with me. We need to talk."

The call ended without Lainie having the opportunity to object. Mom saying "we need to talk" was not a good sign. What had she done to upset her mom?

There was nothing she could do but get up, get dressed, and wait for her mother. Wincing, Lainie stretched. Her arm was sore, and she swallowed some Advil. After starting a pot of coffee, she pulled up the news website to see what her mother had read.

Callen West had the headline story about the Blue Line crash and the shooting. The press-information officer gave out everyone's names, which surprised Lainie; they normally waited a couple of days. It didn't bother her. The shooting would be in policy in any city in the country.

What bothered her was the last paragraph of what was supposed to be a news story.

> Crystal Benton is currently in the hospital in critical but stable condition. It is notable that Benton is employed by Dallas Vine. Considering Detective Jensen's history with Vine, this shooting incident deserves scrutiny.

West hated cops, and Lainie was used to barbs being shot in her general direction, but this was a first for him to go directly after her. *"It is what it is,"* Beck would say. *"You can't fix stupid."*

Her mom arrived with a box of sweet-smelling pastries—cheese Danish and bear claws—Lainie's favorites.

After a hug, her mom inspected her. "Oh, Lainie, you were shot. Why didn't you call us and let us know? Why did we have to find out from the news?"

"Mom, it wasn't serious. I didn't see any reason to wake up you and Dad. In retrospect, I should have and I'm sorry. So much has been going on lately. I never want you to worry about me and my job."

Mom gave her the "mom look."

"What?" Lainie held her hands out. "That was the reason. Please don't overthink this."

"It wasn't because all of our energy lately was for Evie? And maybe you were feeling a little ignored?"

Lainie laughed and grabbed her mom in hug, ignoring the pain in her arm. "No, Mom, not at all. Evie deserves all the attention and more right now. I'm fine with that. I hate being fussed over; you know that."

Mom hugged her back. "I love all my kids, very, very much. They all deserve my attention."

She pushed back and looked Lainie in the eye. "Pour me some coffee and let's eat these sweets."

Lainie did just that, getting the plates and coffee mugs. They sat at her small kitchen table.

"How is Evie doing today?" Lainie asked.

"She improves every day, physically. Emotionally it's much harder for her. She wants to visit Stan again."

Something in her mother's tone caught Lainie's ear. "You don't approve?"

"It's not up to me to approve or disapprove. It's a battle. I struggle to forgive him."

Her mother's admission surprised her. "I do too. Evie amazes me."

"It's difficult for her as well."

"I didn't think so. Evie's a saint."

"She's that. Still, it's a minute-by-minute choice for her, and for all of us. Sometimes I can forgive; sometimes I can't," Mom said. "Forgiveness is the right thing, I know that, but I don't feel it all the time. Evie has the boys to worry about. She doesn't want them hating their father, and neither do I, for that matter."

Lainie finished a bear claw and started in on a Danish. Thinking about Stan still made her blood boil. She knew that Evan and Owen loved their dad; they were too young to recognize what a flawed failure of a man he was. Did she really want them crushed by such knowledge?

No, I don't.

She remembered what Ben had said when she asked him if he was a believer. She'd admitted her failure, and his response had stayed with her.

"We're all failures at some level. That's why we need a Savior."

I don't want to forgive him. The thought pierced her considering the truth Ben had shared.

"A lot of life is about doing things we don't want to do," Beck had said to her once. They'd been dispatched to a dead-body call, a person who had been dead for a week. The beat car had weaseled out of it, and Lainie was not happy when Beck answered up to take the call.

"Don't be the cop who shirks your clear responsibility. Do your job, the best you can all the time, no matter the call."

There was a lot of wisdom in Beck's training that applied to other areas of life, not just police work.

"Mom, how do I forgive Stan? I never liked him. And honestly, a part of me doesn't want to forgive him."

Mom sighed. "I think we'll have to work on it together, Lainie. Remind each other every day that as we are forgiven, we need to forgive. Forgiving Stan will help Evie, and Evie deserves our support."

✦

Lainie's mom hadn't been gone long when her phone rang again. The caller ID said Callen West.

Why on earth would he be calling me? His story was already written; it's not like he was asking for a comment.

She picked up the phone but didn't answer it. West didn't leave a message.

The next call was from Ben, and she answered.

"I wondered how you were doing," Ben asked.

"I'm tired, but overall, okay. How about you?"

"About the same. Did you read the article about the incident?"

"The one with the jibe at me?" Lainie nodded. "Yeah."

"What was up with that?"

"Callen West doesn't like cops. I guess he decided to pick on me today."

"Did he have some connection to the Daphne Sparks case?"

"No, he's probably twenty-five years old. He would have been ten when she was killed. Why do you ask?"

"The old reference to Vine," Ben said.

"He's a reporter. I'm sure he's read the old stories."

"Well, I hope he doesn't take any more shots at you."

"You and me both," Lainie said.

CHAPTER 59

The next morning, Lainie woke up with a smile on her face. Finally feeling rested and thinking about the promise in her relationship with Ben, her mood was better than it had been in days. They'd chatted a bit the night before. He'd told her that the ledger had already given them some good information on some out-of-state criminals. The code was still proving difficult, but they were optimistic about cracking it.

A phone call from Dr. Reynolds's office couldn't even dampen her mood.

"We have an opening in the office this morning if you feel up to dropping by."

"I'm fine. I'll be there in a couple of hours."

She'd already planned to go into the station to check on the status of the investigation and pick up her gun again. She could not put off talking to Reynolds anymore, so she was glad to get that over with. Most of all, injured arm notwithstanding, Lainie wanted to get back to work. She felt like she'd been away from her caseload for a year.

Thinking of Ben had Lainie whistling in the car as she drove to the office. Evie being rescued and meeting Ben Isaacs were the two positive things to come out of a very negative situation. Putting Vine behind bars would be the next positive, she was certain.

✦

"The Feds are working hard on that book," Shea told Lainie when she popped into the homicide office. "How are you? I'm surprised you're here now. Your arm okay?"

"I'm good. It's sore but healing. I need to talk to the psych today. I kept putting it off. When his office called to see if I was okay, they said they had an opening this morning."

"A little nervous about it, are you?"

"Yeah, a little. You shot a man before. What does he want to know?"

"He just wants to make sure you're not having nightmares, that you're sleeping okay, and that having to shoot someone hasn't messed with your head," Shea said. "I shot a guy we attempted to arrest. He was wanted for murder, and he drew down on me. I did what I was trained to do, so did you."

"I know that, and I'm sleeping okay. Have you heard anything about Benton? Her status?"

"Ah, you don't know?" He and Collins exchanged a glance.

"No."

"She'll live, but the bullet severed her spine. She'll never walk again. She was transferred to County last night. She's being held in the hospital ward. Not sure when she'll be arraigned."

Lainie stared at him, unexpectedly shocked by this new development. Benton's driver was dead, and that knowledge hadn't tweaked her as much as this news did. "I'm not sure how I feel about that."

"She shot at you, you shot back. End of story."

Lainie shrugged. "You're right, I guess. Any luck locating Vine?"

"Not so far. We've served warrants at his home, his cigar lounge, and his office with no luck. The Feds are almost 100 percent sure he hasn't left the country. He has to surface soon."

"That's certainly my hope."

✦

Dr. Reynolds's office was on the third floor. Lainie left the homicide office and took the stairs. She wasn't sure why she'd procrastinated talking to the man. He wasn't a bad guy. She guessed it was just because she, like most cops, didn't like people digging into their psyche and maybe finding weaknesses. Most cops she knew didn't like to admit they had any weakness, much less have some doctor probe them.

Would the doctor find her weakness? Before all this happened with Stan, Lainie thought, like Vine, that she was bulletproof. But nearly losing Evie, believing for days that she was dead, had changed Lainie. But the change was good because she had her foundation back. Her perspective on life was no longer tunnel vision on her career aspirations. There was so much more to life than working toward a spot on homicide.

"Detective Jensen?" The doctor's receptionist opened the door. "Dr. Reynolds is ready for you."

Lainie stood and walked through the open door. Dr. Reynolds was about sixty years old, short with a potbelly and a big smile. He had a comfortable demeanor about him.

"Detective, you're looking well, considering all you've been through the last few days."

"I'm feeling well. A lot better than when we last talked."

He gave a head tilt. "I remember our last meeting well. I consider you a success story."

"Really?"

"Really. I recall you were ordered to talk to me as part of the settlement with Dallas Vine. You were very angry back then. I feared you'd implode and destroy your career. You didn't. You followed everyone's advice and you dug yourself out of a deep hole. I consider it a great success when we had no opportunity to sit down and talk again in all these years. You've done well."

His praise surprised her. She'd never thought what she'd done to stay a cop was heroic, but the doctor made it sound like it was. "Thanks. I have tried to do my job and keep my nose clean."

He laughed. "Good for you. How are you doing with the recent incidents? Two in a relatively short time."

"I did what I was trained to do. I'm a good shot, Dr. Reynolds. I'm glad I was able to respond quickly and effectively."

"I sense a *but* in what you're saying."

"It kind of set me back on my heels when I heard about Benton being paralyzed. I don't know why."

"She'll live with her handicap for the rest of her life and the reality that you shot her. Most likely in prison. That bothers you?"

"I guess. I mean, I think she's evil, and maybe in my anger I wished something horrible would happen to her, and it did. To some extent, I feel guilty."

"Understandable. And human, to feel guilt. But, Detective, you didn't shoot her in anger; your life was threatened. What would have been the outcome if you hadn't shot her?"

"Ben and I would be dead."

"You have a conscience, good for an officer of the law. But don't let it torment you over actions that were lawful and necessary."

Lainie let his words sink in. She'd done what was necessary, nothing more, and she could live with that.

CHAPTER 60

Ben returned to work stiff and sore but rested. He was met with very good news. The little black book proved invaluable. Analysts and agents had pored over the book, and the information already resulted in multiple arrests all over the country. However, here in Long Beach, no one knew where Dallas Vine was.

"How's the shoulder?" Mark asked.

Ben rolled his shoulders and tried not to wince. "I'm good. What's new?"

"Just talked to Shea. Stan Moffit is angling for a plea. He wants to turn state's evidence."

"Does he have anything we can use?"

"Don't know. Shea and Collins will talk to him. We, on the other hand, get to talk to Crystal Benton."

Ben didn't hide his surprise. "She's able and she wants to talk?"

"Her surgery went well; they repaired what they could. There is no repairing her spine. The doctors at County General had approved a visit, and she didn't argue. The DA prepared an agreement that we will keep her in protective custody." Mark held up a document. "Her public defender will be at the hospital to witness her signature and the interview."

"That's all she's asking for?" Ben asked.

"Yep. We're heading up there now. You ready?"

"You bet."

✦

County General Hospital was a sprawling facility off the 5 freeway. It took a while for Mark and Ben to be admitted. There was ID verification, then they had to stow their weapons, and finally they were admitted to Benton's floor.

Ben was curious about what they'd find. He'd been a bit shocked at her prognosis. Lainie's bullet had severed her spinal cord. Would that injury make her more or less likely to talk with them truthfully? They were about to find out.

When they entered the room, Benton had just been served lunch. Her bed was raised, so she was sitting up, but she wasn't eating. Her eyes were closed, and Ben thought for a minute that she was sleeping. But when they reached the edge of her bed, she opened her eyes. She appeared small and pale lying in the hospital bed, but there was light in her eyes. They knew she was on pain meds, but the doctor said that she should be able to answer questions.

Before they spoke, a woman dressed in business attire came out of the restroom and identified herself as Benton's attorney. "This is your show. My client has instructed me to butt out. I will be recording this interview." She held up her phone.

"Not a problem," Ben told her. "So will we."

"Afternoon, Ms. Benton," Mark spoke to her. "I'm Special Agent Mark Gentry and this is Agent Benjamin Isaacs."

"Feds. I expected locals."

"We are the ones with the protection agreement." Mark set his briefcase down on a chair and took the form out, then handed it to the attorney.

She took a few minutes to read it, then moved Benton's food to place it on the small table. "It's what they promised, and what I advised against."

"Doesn't matter, I told you that. My life is over," Benton said as she signed the paper. The attorney handed it back to Mark, who put it in his briefcase.

Mark turned back to Benton. "Do you feel up to answering questions now?"

"I know I'm facing local charges. I'm foggy on the federal ones."

"Efren Gomez."

Benton looked away and Mark continued. "The charges against you continue to shape up. You could help yourself out, though."

"How? Gomez was a federal agent. You guys aren't going to let me off on that. If you have the book, you have the key to everything."

"Is that why you wanted the ledger?"

"Yeah, that's why I took it in the first place," Benton said. "It would have given me charge of the whole operation. You have it, you should know that."

Mark advised her of her Miranda rights.

"I understand and I'll talk to you. I've got nothing else to lose. It'll take some getting used to, not feeling anything below the waist. I don't want to worry about being knifed in prison. You guys will have to keep me safe."

"As per the agreement, we will."

"What happened to Efren?" Ben asked.

She sighed and toyed with her food. "I knew Stan never should have hired him. My instincts are usually spot-on."

"You knew he was an agent when he was hired?" Ben asked.

"Not an agent. I just knew he didn't fit in at the car wash. Proving my suspicion, he ruined my plans. I got Plug to steal the book. He'd hidden it in the SUV Raphael was supposed to detail. Somehow,

Efren got it first. I knew it was missing right away. He wouldn't tell me where he put it. Plug got a little overzealous."

"Where is Efren now?"

"Weighted, in Big Bear Lake, not sure exactly where. Plug took care of it." She relayed the information coldly, dispassionately. Ben was sick to his stomach and let Mark continue.

"It's easy to blame a dead guy."

"Blame me. I don't care. I'm going to need medical help for the rest of my life. Right now, there isn't much I really care about."

"What about Evangeline Moffit? Who abducted her? Was that you as well?"

She laughed a weak laugh. "No. Stan angered Dallas, that's why he snatched Evie. I was pretty much over Stan by then. At first he was useful. He helped me in a lot of ways. I'd never kill over him; he wasn't that important. I'd spent months siphoning money; Dallas had no clue. Mostly, I needed Stan because he was a convenient scapegoat if Dallas ever found out."

"None of the money would ever go to Stan?"

"I'd give him a hundred here and there." She waved a hand dismissively. "He was easy to manipulate. Then he did something stupid."

"What was that?"

"He took money that wasn't his and then spent it all for a Hawaiian vacation. Dallas put two and two together. Stan didn't make that kind of money, and it was a blip on the radar. Dallas saw the money was gone, and Stan might as well have put a sign on his chest: *I did it.* So he snatched Moffit's wife."

"Where did he take her?"

"Probably to his place in Big Bear. I hate that place. Not a decent restaurant in the whole dreary village."

"You had nothing to do with the abduction of Evangeline Moffit?"

"No. No reason for me to lie about that. Why Dallas kept her alive, I have no idea. Maybe he's getting soft in his old age."

"If you had nothing to do with her abduction, why help Stan cover it up?"

"I keep telling you, I was desperate for the book. The longer it was out there, the sooner Dallas would discover it missing. My helping Stan pull off a con was a way to keep Dallas distracted."

"How can that be true?" Ben tried to keep the anger out of his voice; he wasn't sure if he'd succeeded. "Evangeline Moffit had your purse, your ID. If you had nothing to do with her abduction, how can you explain that?"

"That's where my purse was?"

"You want us to believe that you didn't know?"

"I didn't. I had her passport—that was still in the house after Dallas grabbed her. Stan gave it to me. Maybe he knows more than I thought. Maybe he was trying to pin that on me."

"There was an attempt on her life in the hospital," Ben said.

"I had nothing to do with that."

"Where were they going when they crashed?"

"That's all Dallas. You guys have to believe me. I don't care enough about Stan to get rid of his woman."

Ben and Mark exchanged a glance. She sounded as if she was telling the truth, but nothing made sense.

"So, the trip to Hawaii, the wild story about the shark attack was simply a con to keep Vine engaged?"

"Yes. I was stalling for time. I wanted the book. Dallas hadn't missed it at that point. Plug never got your man to tell us where it was. Plug destroyed Efren's car searching for the ledger. Nothing."

Ben froze as he realized what she was saying. Efren was probably tortured. He had a brief inkling at that minute of how hard it had been for Lainie to interview Stan. He swallowed and fought the anger that simmered. Benton kept talking.

"When I realized the shark thing was not going to pan out—Detective Jensen put a wrench in that—Plug had already gotten rid of Efren and his car. Then Dallas realized the book was gone. He called me and threatened me. What could I do? I planned to cut my losses and flee the country. But I couldn't find my extra passports."

"You ransacked the car wash office."

"Yeah, I guess Stan pulled one over on me. I knew there was a second safe, but I couldn't find it."

"Why kill the morning supervisor?"

"She got in the way."

Ben wondered at how cold-blooded this woman was.

"Anyway, when I got back to Long Beach, I convinced Dallas he was wrong about me, that Stan was the problem. For a little while, he believed me."

She laughed again. "Men are so easily manipulated. I told Stan to run, to make him look even guiltier while I kept trying to find the book."

Ben found his voice. "Why did you shoot at me at the tow yard?"

She shook her head. "That was Plug being protective. He was shooting at Jensen. She messed up the whole shark attack. Sure surprised him when she clipped his helmet. She's a good shot. I guess I can attest to that now."

"Where is Dallas hiding?" Mark asked.

She gave a low, mirthless chuckle. "Dallas? I don't know where he is. Plug's dead, right?"

"Yes," Ben said.

She shrugged and winced. "Then he knows Plug was with me. He knows I conned him. He'll go somewhere I don't know. All I can tell you is that Dallas is terrified to fly. He won't be flying anywhere."

"You've been with him for years and you don't know where he'd hidc?"

She closed her eyes. "If I were looking for him, I'd go to Big Bear or the cigar lounge."

"The place in downtown Long Beach?" Ben asked.

"Yeah. That's his second home. He has an apartment there. A secret room. I've never been there, but Plug used to talk about it. The house in Belmont Shore is my place really. Dallas never cared for it."

"Smokey Dreams doesn't strike me as a good hiding place," Mark said.

"The staff is completely loyal to him. You go in during business hours, and they'll never give him up. I've heard that the place has been searched before, and you guys never found the room. This is the problem I had with Dallas. He's basically a cave dweller. He doesn't like to go anywhere, do anything. That's why I hate Jensen."

"Detective Jensen?"

"Yeah, the stiff who shot me. When she arrested Dallas fifteen years ago, she changed him. He used to be fun. We'd go to Vegas and take the yacht out on the water a lot. The *Havana* was a great boat. I was furious when he got rid of it. After that, he became a hermit. I was more a babysitter than a girlfriend."

"You stayed with him a long time."

"Good money. But I got tired of the rut. I wanted to fleece him without having to face him. Plug and I would have left the country, and Dallas never would have found us. Stan and his sister-in-law messed all that up."

"Why would Vine burn down her house? And Moffit's house?"

"Well, the last conversation I had with him when he realized I took the book was a bit unhinged. He hates Jensen, hates Stan. I told him that it was possible Stan had the book, and he probably gave it to her. He went a little nuts. Guess he did a little payback."

Ben bit his tongue and tried to beat back the disgust he felt for this woman. Efren was dead. An innocent working woman was dead. She didn't even seem to care about her paramour. All she was concerned about was herself.

Lord, please help me to keep from strangling her.

CHAPTER 61

"You're cleared from me to return to work," Reynolds told Lainie after the interview finished. "It's now up to the medical doctor to sign off on your arm." He handed her back her duty weapon.

"Thanks." She took the gun and left his office knowing that the workers' comp doctor would probably not sign off on her return until the stitches were out. She didn't want to wait that long. Could she persuade him to let her return with some conditions? Like no field work, something like that?

She checked in at her office. Mike was out on a call. She sat at her desk to leave him a note and listen to her voicemail. Fifteen were waiting for her.

She pulled out her message pad and a pen and listened. A couple were from the local DA, asking about a case; some were from old victims whom she'd helped, offering condolences about her sister. Some were wrong numbers, and then there was a message from Callen West. From the time stamp, he'd called the office after trying her on her cell.

"Detective Jensen, I'd like an interview with you about Dallas Vine. I understand you just shot two of his employees, one of whom is now deceased. It was my understanding that you were ordered years ago to stay away from him. Is this a vendetta on your part? I believe that this is a valid question, and I would like your side of the incident."

He left his phone number, and Lainie stared at the phone in amazement that he could believe the shooting the other night was a vendetta on her part.

She remembered Ben asking if West had some connection to the Daphne Sparks case. Frowning, she tried to think. It had to be impossible. West was too young.

Lainie logged on to the computer and pulled up a file she hadn't pulled up in years. Of course, she had to click a reason for wanting to view the file, and she chose "for investigation."

"Lord, I hope this doesn't get me in trouble," she prayed under her breath. Soon, the file on the death of Daphne Sparks showed up on her screen.

She skipped her report on finding the body because she remembered it so well, even after all this time, and went straight to the reports filed by the handling investigators. Both were gone now. One died only a few years into retirement; the other died last year, if she remembered right, so there was no way for her to talk to either of them.

They were respected and seasoned investigators in their day, and Lainie had no reason to doubt that they had done their best to find Daphne's killer. She began reading through the interviews. The original investigators had talked to everyone they could down in the harbor where Daphne worked. They also interviewed everyone who worked at the Barn and everyone who worked with Dallas Vine.

Lainie really didn't know what she was looking for. Callen West would not have been interviewed in any capacity regarding the crime. All the reading brought back so many memories of that time. All the frustration she'd felt back then resurfaced almost fresh.

Her phone rang. She picked it up and nearly fell out of her chair. It was Beck. Search forgotten, she answered. "Hey, stranger."

"Lainie, sorry I took so long to get back to you. I've been in the backcountry for three weeks. Only got back yesterday. It took me a while to catch up on newsy things. I saw a story about your shooting. Are you all right?"

Relaxing in the chair, Lainie filled him in on everything that had happened. It felt great to talk to her old, trusted mentor.

"You did good, kid. I told you when you're trained right, your training will save you. When do you go back to work?"

"I hope soon. They'll probably make me wait until after the stitches are out. I just got finished with Dr. Reynolds. I'm sitting here in the office going back over the Sparks file."

"Are you hoping that when you get Vine in custody, you'll be able to revisit that case?"

"Wouldn't that be great? No. Right now I'm not sure what I'm doing. It's Callen West, a local young reporter who hates cops. He wrote a story about the shooting and brought up the Vine case. He seems to be insinuating that I'm violating the settlement to go after Vine. Not sure why he brought up such an old case."

"West, you say?"

"Yeah, why? There is no way you would know him."

"I remember a reporter named Avery West. He was retired by the time you joined the force. He got beat up during the riots and wrote a book about how evil cops are."

There had been city-wide riots when Lainie was in high school. She remembered watching them unfold on TV. Buildings were torched. In some instances, cops went toe to toe with rioters. The National Guard had been called up to calm things down.

"Cops beat him up?" Lainie asked.

"No, rioters did. He blamed the police for not acting fast enough to save him. It was pure chaos that night; I was there. He was covering the chaos when the rioters jumped him. By the time we got to him, he was barely breathing. I think he lost an eye, had some other injuries. Probably has no bearing on your case. The name just jogged my memory. I felt sorry for the guy. You'll figure it out; I have faith."

"Thank you, Beck. So good to hear from you. Take care."

She disconnected, glad he'd called but wishing that he were here. Mike was great, but Beck would always be her best partner.

She looked back at her computer screen. Could Callen West be related to Avery West? Maybe all of his hatred of cops came from that relative. On a hunch, she put *West* into the search of the document. It took her to another interview and an arrest report. Avery West had been brought in for questioning regarding Daphne's case.

Lainie frowned. Why didn't she remember this? Then again, she'd been fixated on Vine the whole time. She never considered that there could be another suspect. Tunnel vision was a bad thing. She'd learned so much from all the mistakes she'd made back then.

West worked part-time at the Barn when Daphne was murdered. He had been uncooperative and then arrested. He was released the next day. He'd been working when Vine was there. Another patron saw Avery and Daphne talking, but there was nothing in the arrest report that said West was connected to Sparks. If he'd cooperated in the first place, he would not have been arrested. He'd been a minor blip, which was probably another reason why Lainie had not remembered him.

If Callen was related to Avery, would that information help the current investigation in any way?

CHAPTER 62

Ben sat silently as Mark drove them back to Long Beach from County General. He'd known Efren was probably gone, but without a body, there had still been a shred of hope. That shred was now shattered. Benton had been clear and cold about Efren's death. Mark had already notified the San Bernardino Sheriff's Department. They would conduct a search of the lake for Efren's remains.

"That was not an easy interview," Mark said when they were about halfway to the office.

"Do you believe her?" Ben asked.

"I'm leaning that way. She has nothing to lose."

"I guess if the sheriff finds Efren's body, we'll know a lot better."

"I'm so sorry, Ben. Do you want me to tell Candy?"

"No, no. I'll go by her house. We should wait until we have confirmation, though."

"Probably wise."

✦

"What are you doing here?" Mike walked in while Lainie was still searching old files.

"Hey, partner. I had my psych interview today."

"Oh, and he confirmed that you're crazy?"

"Ha. Nope, he cleared me. I'll just have to wait for the medical doctor to do the same. I feel bad leaving you on your own for so long."

He sat at his desk. "Don't rush back on my account. I think I'm going to take a little vacation. My father-in-law needs some help with a home improvement project. I have some time to take off, and we don't have anything pressing." He pointed at her monitor. "What's up?"

She told him about Callen and Avery West.

"I've always known that West had an axe to grind. Did you look up Avery West?"

"I was about to." She returned to her search. "I wanted to find out if Callen was related to Avery." After a few keystrokes and searching Callen's bio, she found out that they were, in fact, related.

Mike glanced over her shoulder. "Avery is his uncle. He even listed Avery's book on police brutality in his bio. No wonder Callen hates cops."

Lainie nodded in agreement. Should she call Callen back and talk to him, now that she understood exactly where his animosity came from?

Her phone buzzed with a text. It was Shea in homicide. Instead of answering, she decided to walk back to their office on the way out.

"See you, Mike. Have a great working vacation."

"Thanks, Lainie. You take it easy and heal."

✦

By the time Ben and Mark arrived in Long Beach, Ben's mood had lifted. Though their interview with Benton had netted them sad news, it had also given them a probable location for Dallas Vine. The case was breaking open, and Ben wanted to be with the PD when Vine was arrested.

They'd begun to tell Shea and Collins about the interview when Shea stopped them.

"Let me see if Lainie is still here. She should hear all of this." Shea sent a text and a few minutes later, Lainie walked in. Ben smiled when he saw her, glad that she was still in the station despite her injury.

"Lainie, we just interviewed Crystal Benton. She opened up, gave us some good information," Ben said.

Surprise crossed her features. "I'm amazed that she talked to you."

"It was not an easy conversation. We promised her protection. She was cold and pragmatic." Then Ben let Mark detail the interview they had with Crystal Benton.

"You're sure your agent is gone?" Shea asked.

"San Bernardino is dragging the lake."

"I'm so sorry, Ben." Lainie placed a hand on his forearm, and he appreciated the gesture and genuine care behind it.

He nodded. "What we really wanted you to hear was when we asked her where Vine would go to hide." They played that portion of the interview.

Collins shook his head. "I was there with the team that searched Smokey Dreams, his cigar lounge. Secret room? I don't think so."

"Well, he's afraid to fly," Ben said. "We're reasonably sure he's not left the state, as sure as we can be without any kind of digital footprint. Maybe we should take another shot at the club."

"And if the staff of the club is hiding him," Mark added, "there's no telling how long he could stay holed up there."

"She doesn't give you any hints at all about where the secret room is. Maybe Vine pulled one over on her, and there is no secret room."

"Lainie, any suggestions?" Shea asked.

"I can't see him hiding in the cigar lounge no matter how much of a hermit he is. Secret room?" She waved her hand. "Benton was playing you. We should dig deeper into Quartz Enterprises, or maybe work on his men who are still in custody."

"I wouldn't doubt that she was manipulating us," Ben agreed. "And we have been over the company with a fine-tooth comb. Tracking a man who is completely off-grid is near impossible."

Shea laughed.

"What's funny?"

"It's the twenty-first century, and a man can evade everyone with a nineteenth-century attitude. It just struck me as funny."

CHAPTER 63

"I'm not supposed to be here working. As much as I want to beat my head against a wall, wondering where Vine is, I'm tired. I'll pray for you guys." Lainie got up to leave.

"I'll walk you out," Ben said.

"It's funny," Lainie said as she and Ben walked toward the elevator. "I want Vine caught more than anyone, but now I feel like I can wait. He can't stay hidden forever. He will be found."

The elevator doors opened and they stepped on. "I agree, and I have other things to attend to right now."

Lainie caught his eye. "I'm sorry, I should have realized. You're waiting to hear from San Bernardino." They exited into the lobby and walked toward the parking lot.

"Yeah, I am. And I have to tell Efren's wife. That won't be easy."

Lainie started to say something then stopped. Callen West was leaning against her car. "What do you want, West?"

"I've been calling you, Detective. You don't return my calls."

"You going to be okay, Lainie?" Ben asked.

"Yeah, this is Callen West, reporter for the local paper."

"Oh, the one with the Vine obsession."

"I'm not the one with the obsession." Callen raked Ben up and down with disgust in his eyes. "The only thing I want is true justice."

The reporter was built like a marathon runner, skinny, with sunken cheeks, bony hands. He also sported a nice tan, so Lainie guessed he didn't spend all day inside on his computer.

Lainie saw concern on Ben's face. West sounded a little off. She'd only ever talked to him on the phone, though she'd seen him often at crime scenes.

"Callen, I'm officially off duty. If you want an interview, you'll have to talk to the PIO or wait until the doctor says I can return to work."

"You're not trying to find Dallas Vine?"

"The department is, so are the Feds, but me personally? I just got shot, and my sister went through a trauma, so I have other things to take care of."

West frowned. "I need to talk to you about Dallas Vine. You're all wrong about him. I don't want to see another miscarriage of justice. Dallas is a good man."

Ben stepped up. He was at least a head taller than West. Lainie wasn't certain if he was trying to be intimidating but it seemed to work on West.

"I think Detective Jensen was clear; she's not on duty."

West puffed up his chest, and for a second, Lainie thought he was going to argue. But he backed down. "Fine, please call me when you are back on duty." He stalked away.

"What was that all about?" Ben watched West leave.

Lainie told him about Avery West. "You were the one who thought maybe he was connected to Vine somehow. That's the only connection I could find."

"It's an interesting one. Let's hope West leaves you alone until you're ready to talk to him." Ben turned his attention back to Lainie. "I think I still owe you dinner."

"I think so too."

"Will tomorrow night work? I've got too much paperwork today."

"Tomorrow would be perfect."

✦

Lainie picked up Chinese takeout on her way home. She was ready to relax, but she still didn't have a TV. It would be takeout food and streaming entertainment on her computer and then early to bed. Lainie felt such peace at the moment. Her faith was back, her sister was alive. Even though Lainie had lost her house, she had a positive attitude about the future.

Settling in at her kitchen table, Lainie set out her food, said grace, and began to eat. Her phone rang, and she answered immediately. "Evie! How are you?"

"A lot better. I remembered something. I'm not sure what it means, but I thought I should tell you. I don't remember the drive up to the mountains. I do remember being on a boat."

"A boat?"

"Yes, I remember the rolling and the sound of water. It smelled like the marina. I also remember being blindfolded, pulled along, but nothing else specific. Does that help you at all?"

"I'm not sure, but I'll let everyone know." Lainie disconnected.

She thought back to the time she'd watched Vine. She remembered the yacht; it was docked by his home. It was called *Havana*, if she remembered right. "I wonder if Vine still has the boat."

Quickly, she typed out a text to Shea. Maybe they missed the yacht. Yawning, Lainie had lost her appetite. It was a good thing she'd bought Chinese food. The little cartons would store well, and she didn't have any other containers.

Just as she stood to step to the refrigerator, a knock sounded at the door. Lainie saw the clock. It was a little after six, and she wasn't expecting anyone.

"Detective Jensen, it's Callen West. Please, can we speak?"

Irritated, Lainie got up and opened the door. It wasn't Callen West. Two men stood at her door: one was big and muscular; the other was Dallas Vine.

"Vine."

The big guy pointed a weapon at her. Before she could react, he fired. The Taser prongs hit their mark, and the jolt paralyzed Lainie. By the time she regained control of her muscles, she was tied up, covered in a blanket, and thrown into the trunk of a car.

CHAPTER 64

Ben got the call the next morning—they'd found a body in a deep section of Big Bear Lake, weighted down. They needed someone to make a positive ID, and if that wasn't possible, they would test the DNA.

He had to be the one to try and identify Efren. He couldn't let Candy do it. After the body had spent over a week underwater, Ben wondered if he would be able to make the ID. The sheriff said that the water was cold enough to preserve the body. They were reasonably certain it was Efren; they simply wanted confirmation.

Ben headed out to San Bernardino early.

As sad as this day was, there was some comfort in knowing they could put Efren to rest.

The morgue was like every morgue he'd ever been in—cold, strong odor of formaldehyde, and depressing. The deputy in charge led him to the viewing room. He pulled back the sheet down to mid-chest. There was not much bloating, decay, or slippage. He was discolored, and it was obvious he'd been beaten.

Ben nodded, swallowed a lump, and wiped the tears forming from his eyes.

"I'm so sorry, buddy," he whispered. After a few minutes he nodded to the attendant and the sheet was put back in place.

His next stop was Candy. He dreaded that interaction more than this viewing. But she needed to hear it from him in person. During the drive to Efren's house, Ben rehearsed what he would say. In truth, there was nothing that he could say.

Candy collapsed in his arms when she opened the door. She sobbed and Ben's heart broke.

"Where is he?"

"With the coroner in San Bernardino. I'll let you know when we can plan a funeral."

"And the guy who did it?"

Ben sighed. "He's dead."

"Why, Ben, why did Efren have to die?"

"He was doing his job. And his last act has helped us to arrest some really bad people. He died a hero, Candy. I know that doesn't help much, but it's all I've got."

He held her until the sobbing eased. Then he called her mother to come and stay with her. By the time he left, he was tired and emotionally drained.

He still looked forward to having dinner with Lainie, but his sad mood weighed him down. She energized him, and she would understand what he'd just gone through. He planned to pick her up at six and had plenty of time to get home and shower and change. Being in the morgue always made him feel as if the smell of death hung on him like a necklace of garlic.

He sat in his car for a moment and then pulled out his phone to let Mark know that he'd notified Candy. He had three unread text messages. He clicked on them in turn.

Shea: **Have you spoken to Lainie today?**

Mark: **Shea is trying to get ahold of Lainie. Have you talked to her?**

Shea: **I need to talk to Lainie if she is with you.**

Ben hit Lainie's cell number. It immediately went to voicemail.

Fear spiked and Ben started the car. He hit Shea's number as he pulled away from Candy's house.

"Ben, is Lainie with you?"

"No, I haven't spoken to her. What's going on?"

"We can't find her. She's not at home and she's not answering her phone."

"I'm on my way to the station. I'll be there in a few minutes."

"Oh, Lord," he prayed as he drove, "please let this just be a matter of a dead phone battery."

CHAPTER 65

Lainie fought but it was futile. She feared she'd pulled out all her stitches and could feel a sticky wetness on her shoulder. She was not certain how long she stayed in the trunk. At some point, she fell asleep because she woke up in confusion with a nasty headache.

Where am I?

Blinking in the dark, momentarily disoriented, she tried to remember what day it was.

When she realized that her hands were bound, memories came roaring back. Vine forced her to go with him, and the big guy with him had tasered her.

She wiggled herself to a seated position and saw she was in a small, dark room. Thin light showed at the bottom of the door and along the sides. A closet maybe? The room rocked gently. She was on a boat. But where?

Slowly her eyes adjusted to the dark. It looked as if she *was* in a closet. Every so often there was a bump, like the boat was hitting the dock. That brought some relief; they weren't out in the open sea.

She tensed when she heard footsteps. They passed by the door, and she relaxed. Her shoulders were cramped and stiff, and when she tried to pull her arms free, she could tell the ropes around her wrists were well tied.

On the positive side, her legs were not bound. She was able to push herself to a sitting position. The effort made her shoulder ache, and for a few minutes she sat still, trying to get her bearings.

She frowned. How much time had passed since Vine showed up at her door?

She would be missed, she was sure, but it was a given that no one knew where she was. *Did anyone see me taken out of my apartment?*

Lainie heard voices and again tensed, but again, no one opened the door. She could not make out what was being said.

She strained at the ropes, realizing that she'd never be able to pull them apart. Blowing out a breath, she squinted as her eyes adjusted to the darkness. She needed something sharp. There wasn't much, but there was a cabinet with an edge.

Bracing herself against the throbbing pain in her head, Lainie pushed herself to a standing position. The wall creaked and the floor groaned. There was nothing she could do about the noise. After backing up to the cabinet, she began to rub the rope around her hands up and down on the edge. It was not sharp, but it was an edge. Lainie prayed as she moved up and down that the friction would be enough to weaken her bonds.

It wasn't long before sweat dripped into her eyes. And then the boat lurched. A motor roared to life.

The boat would soon be moving.

She redoubled her efforts on the ropes around her wrists. Her shoulders and thighs ached from the effort, and the stuffy air in the small space was stifling. She heard voices close by and stopped, holding as still as she could. They were coming from above her. Lainie knew nothing about boats. She could only guess that she was down below deck in a storage cabinet. She paused to listen to what was being said.

"This isn't what I meant." A male voice Lainie did not recognize, sounding as if he was right above her head.

"It's what needs to happen." Vine.

"I'm not behind this, not at all." The first voice again.

"Then get off the boat. You can have it back when we're finished."

"Please don't do this."

"You owe me," Vine said. "Don't ever forget that. Off. Now."

The sound of feet against the deck. The boat creaked and groaned, something slammed.

"I beg you, don't . . ." The first voice sounded farther away now.

More footsteps, something else slammed.

"Clear the lines, let's get underway." Vine one more time.

Now there were more sounds, steps, bangs, and the boat shifted. Lainie almost lost her balance, then they were moving.

Oh, Lord, help me get out of this.

She continued to work on the ropes. Her head kept hitting the ceiling, and she could barely stand up straight in the tight space. Her wrists ached and she felt blood dripping, but she couldn't stop. Right now, the boat was going slow. Once it started going faster, it would mean that they'd left the marina and were in the open ocean.

Finally, when the pain in her wrists was almost unbearable, she felt the bonds loosen. Gritting her teeth, with all her strength Lainie pulled, and the ropes broke apart.

Her hands were free. She brought them around to the front, and her shoulders stopped screaming in pain. Blood dripped down both wrists, but there was nothing she could do about that now. Flexing her hands, she turned her attention to the door. She tried to open it, but it was locked.

Next, she tried to find any type of weapon. There were rags and brooms and paper towels but nothing that could be used as a weapon. Just then, the boat's speed increased.

CHAPTER 66

Ben took the stairs two at a time to the homicide office, bursting in breathless, halfway hoping he'd see Lainie there and that this was all a false alarm.

She wasn't there.

"You haven't found Lainie?" Ben asked Shea. The distress on his face gave Ben an answer he didn't want.

"I was hoping she'd be with you. When was the last time you talked to her?"

"Yesterday, when we left here." Ben shoved his hands in his pockets and struggled to maintain his composure. He was worried and a little scared for Lainie. Those emotions would cloud his judgment. He needed to maintain a professional detachment in spite of his feelings.

Could he?

"She sent me a text last night, telling me that her sister remembered being on a boat," Shea said. "She asked me to check into Vine's yacht."

"Did you?"

"I did. He sold the yacht about ten years ago. It's a dead end."

"Did you talk to Evie and sec if there was more to that memory?"

Shea nodded. "She couldn't elaborate. Did Lainie indicate that she was going somewhere, talking to someone?"

"No, but something happened when she got to her car." Ben told them about Callen West.

"West?" Shea frowned and turned to his computer. Tapping keys, he pulled up a document. "Vine sold his yacht to an Avery West. He any relation to Callen?"

"It's his uncle. Do you know where he keeps the boat?"

"Alamitos Bay Marina."

"Let's go and check out the boat."

They took two cars, Ben followed Shea and Collins across town to Alamitos Bay Marina.

Once they arrived at the marina, Shea made an interesting observation. "West's slip is right across the bay from Vine's house on Appian Way." He pointed across the water.

The slip belonging to West was at the end of the dock. Ben followed. As they approached, he could see that the slip was empty. An old man was sitting on the dock.

"That's Avery West," Shea said. "I saw his picture in the file." They walked up on the man.

"Mr. West, Long Beach Police. Where is your boat?"

The old man looked up at Shea. His vacant expression was not unlike someone who was lost in the confusion of Alzheimer's. One eye was gone; there was simply an empty socket. He feared they would get nothing useful from the man.

"Mr. West, can you hear me?"

"I hear you."

The words were clear. Ben had hope now that he'd be able to talk to them. "Where's the boat?"

"He took it."

"Who took it?"

"Dallas. He's going to kill that woman."

✦

Detective Collins radioed for the police boat, and Ben called the Coast Guard. Cementing Ben's fear, Avery West had said that Vine had taken Lainie aboard his boat and planned to dump her out in the ocean.

"He don't have anything left to lose," West said. "He says that she ruined his life. He wants revenge. I tried to talk him out of it, but he's set."

"Has he been living on your boat?"

West nodded. "He came to me a couple of weeks ago, said Crystal had betrayed him, and he had nowhere else to go. I owed him."

"Why do you owe him?"

West said nothing.

"Don't you talk, Uncle. Don't say anything without a lawyer."

Ben turned to see Callen West jogging toward them.

"What do you have to do with this?" Ben stepped between Avery and Callen.

"I'm protecting my uncle."

"Your uncle is protecting a murderer."

"Dallas Vine is not a murderer. He's helped my family my whole life. He's a good man, and you people are trying to frame him. You guys have him cornered. He's reacting, but he's not a killer."

"Callen, Dallas Vine kidnapped a police officer. If you know something that will help us rescue her, now is the time."

"What? You're crazy, he would—"

"He would." Avery stood. "It's time for all the lies to stop."

"Uncle, don't talk."

"Quiet, I need to talk. I should have talked a long time ago. He's gonna take her far out, somewhere between here and Catalina, and dump her. It's a fast boat. You need to hurry if you're going to stop him."

Just then the police boat zoomed into the marina.

Ben knew that their jurisdiction ended where the harbor ended. They needed the Coast Guard, but would they get to Lainie in time?

He turned to Shea. "Your boat can't leave the harbor because of jurisdiction issues, but can it get me to the Coast Guard boat before it leaves the harbor?"

"I'll ask." Shea pulled out his radio. After a short conversation, Shea apprised them of the situation. "They'll take you on board."

Ben then turned to Avery. "Is there more you want to tell me?"

West began to talk.

Ben listened, amazed at what he was hearing, soaking it all in until the police boat arrived and took him on board.

The Coast Guard Base Los Angeles/Long Beach was located at Terminal Island, so the guard did not have far to go. When the police boat reached the harbor mouth, the Coast Guard cutter waited. The 175-foot ship was impressive, and the sight invigorated Ben with hope. In a few minutes he was on the deck, bracing against the wind, and they motored into open ocean.

He was glad to be on the ship and moving forward, but he felt useless. Yeah, Catalina was only twenty-six miles away as the crow flew, but finding Vine and his craft between here and there could prove difficult in the open sea.

There was nothing he could do but pray that they found Vine's boat in time.

CHAPTER 67

The yacht picked up speed quickly. As it bounced over the swells, Lainie fought her rising fear. She'd been through every square inch of the closet, and there was nothing she could use for a weapon. The only thing she had working in her favor was the element of surprise. They would not be expecting her to be free.

She picked up the rope she'd dropped. When they came to the door, she'd have her hands behind her back like she was still tied up. She hoped they didn't have the Taser with them. That was something she could not fight against.

She'd barely gotten the ropes back when she heard footsteps. Hands behind her back, leaning back against the closet wall, Lainie waited.

The door opened and Lainie squinted as light assaulted her eyes.

It was the big guy. She didn't see the Taser in his hands this time, but he had a pistol on his person in a shoulder holster.

He reached in and grabbed her upper arm. She tensed to keep her arms back and not give away her freedom.

"Come on. We're going up top." He pulled her out into a narrow hallway. The boat rocked and he fell off-balance but caught himself quickly.

Lainie stayed alert. This was what she needed, him distracted. She prayed for another pitch as he pulled her into what looked like a galley, with steps that led up top. If she was going to make a move, it had to be down here, while they were one on one. There would be less of a chance of success if it was two against one. She stayed observant, hoping her chance would come.

Her goal was to apply a control hold, a twist lock, the first basic weaponless defense tactic officers learned. If she could land the hold properly, the size and strength difference would be negated, and she could use his tightly muscled strength against him.

They approached the stairs. She pretended to lose her balance, at the same time the boat pitched again and he did stumble. Lainie braced one knee against the counter, whipped the loose rope from her wrist around his at the same time she grabbed his hand, twisting it back into a twist lock while bracing his elbow into her midsection. She knew that she would only have one chance, and she nailed it. She had him.

"Ahh." He rose on his tiptoes and tried to break the hold, but Lainie increased the pressure on his wrist tendons. Holding his wrist in this position took away his power. He moaned in pain.

"Stay quiet or I'll break your wrist."

He didn't obey and Lainie applied more pressure. It took very little strength to hold his wrist back—it was all about leverage, and Lainie had the advantage.

"Okay, okay."

As Lainie considered her next move, she caught sight of the Taser. It would be difficult to try and tie his hands. She'd have to let up on the tension, and she needed to have him secure before Vine knew what was happening.

She nudged him forward as if they were going up the stairs. At the last minute, she shoved him loose and grabbed the Taser. He turned, she fired, and he went down with a thud. Knowing she had seconds, minutes at most, she rolled him over and tied his wrists together as tightly as she could. It took all her strength, but she did it. When she stepped back, her heart pounded, and he was just starting to come out of the shock.

He had a gun in a shoulder holster and Lainie grabbed it as he started to yell.

"Dallas! Dallas! She's loose!"

CHAPTER 68

"Shut up, would you? I'm sure he heard you," Lainie said.

"You got nowhere to go, lady."

"Neither does he."

Lainie had braced herself against the galley counter as the boat bounced along. She couldn't tell if she heard footsteps or if it was just the water slapping against the side of the boat. Lainie couldn't shut him up unless she tasered him again, and she decided instead to take the fight to Vine. She brought the gun up, expecting him to appear at the top of the stairs. He didn't. The big guy kept yelling.

A flash caught her eye and she dove to her knees.

Bang, bang, bang—three bullets came from behind and smashed into the counter above her head.

Lainie rolled and turned to return fire, landing on the big guy's legs. She fired twice and heard a surprised grunt.

The big guy kicked his legs to get her off of him, but she was already moving.

The shots had come from behind, so she bounded up the stairs and swung around, wobbling on the bouncing deck.

In two steps, she saw Vine. He'd lost his balance and slipped through the railing. He hung on as the boat bounced along. Lurching forward, Lainie shoved the gun into her waistband and grabbed him, pulling with all her might. There was no way he was going to escape her arrest and then the eventual trial for the murder of Daphne Sparks.

The fear in his eyes gave her no pleasure. When he was on deck, she saw that she'd hit him in the shoulder. He moaned in pain. She dragged him to the top of the stairs, no easy task with the boat bouncing along on the ocean, and then she went below and found a first aid kit.

By the time she returned, Vine had passed out; he'd lost a lot of blood. When she stopped the bleeding, she talked to the big guy. He'd sat up by now, and his face was streaked with sweat, but he couldn't get free of the knots she'd tied.

"Do you want to tell me how to stop this thing?"

✦

The Coast Guard commander told Ben that they were taking the most common route to Catalina.

"Detective Shea told me that the *Havana* is not equipped with AIS, an automatic-tracking system, so without an eye in the sky, I'm not optimistic."

"I hope that I have enough optimism for the both of us. We will find her."

The commander nodded and went back to his station while Ben stayed at the rail. He searched the sea ahead of them, praying for a sighting. The ocean certainly was a huge place when a person was trying to find a single vessel.

They'd been traveling for about ten minutes when the cutter changed direction. Ben turned and looked back toward the commander, who smiled and gave a thumbs-up. "We're getting a Mayday from the *Havana*."

"What?"

"Your officer. She's got control of the boat. She read us what the instruments are telling her. We'll be with them shortly."

Ben couldn't say that he was surprised. He fought a smile. "What happened?"

"The Mayday says there's been a shooting on the *Havana*, and she didn't know how to slow things down, but we talked her through it. One injured, one restrained, per her report."

Who was injured? Ben wanted to ask, but the commander returned to his duties.

After what seemed like forever, but he knew was just a few minutes, Ben saw the yacht. It bobbed on the swells in front of them, and the cutter slowed.

It wasn't until he saw Lainie waving at them from the deck that he relaxed.

CHAPTER 69

Ben followed the Coast Guard team off the cutter and onto the *Havana*. It gave him a start to see Lainie so bloody—but her eyes were sparkling and alive. There was victory in that gaze, so fear fled.

"Ben, I didn't expect to see you."

"I hitched a ride—are you okay?" He pointed to her wrists.

"Dirty, sore, and tired but okay." She pointed and stepped aside for the Coast Guard medic. "These guys snatched me from my home."

"Vine and who is the other guy?"

"Bodyguard, I guess. Maybe I didn't get Vine for Daphne's murder, but he won't skate on this."

With the rise and fall of the stopped vessel, Lainie stumbled and Ben stepped up to steady her. He put an arm around her waist as a medic approached to treat her wounds.

She looked up at him. "I'm a mess; you'll get dirty."

"I have good cleaners. Besides, I have a surprise for you."

"What?"

"I met Avery West. He was baring his soul to Shea when I left them at the dock. I heard quite a story."

While her bleeding wrists were bandaged, Ben recounted for Lainie what he'd heard Avery West tell Shea.

"He witnessed the murder of Daphne. It happened at the Barn like you thought, Lainie. And it happened because Sparks had discovered Vine was embezzling. She'd threatened to go to the police, and he shot her."

"West saw that?"

"Yeah. Vine used West's hatred of cops and money to keep him quiet. At the time, West had just been evicted from his apartment. He was living at the Barn. Vine let him move to the *Havana*, later giving it to him outright. And over the years, he provided a lot of support to the family. Even putting Avery's favorite nephew through college."

"Callen?"

"The boy had no idea how evil Vine was. He saw him as a benevolent friend of the family."

"And he was on his way to put her body in the foundation of the house he was renovating," Ben said. "You were right about everything."

They stepped aside as the Coast Guard medics carried Vine by on a stretcher.

"Will he make it?" Lainie asked.

"He lost a lot of blood. Right now he's stable."

Ben took her hand and helped her from the *Havana* to the Coast Guard cutter. "Sorry justice was delayed."

"I'm just glad to finally see it."

When the cutter got underway to head back to Long Beach, Lainie leaned into Ben at the rail, and he encircled her waist with his arm to make certain she was safe and protected.

Next to Lainie was a place Ben decided that he wanted to be for a long time.

CHAPTER 70

"It only took you three days to figure out a place and time." Lainie teased Ben as he appeared at the door to pick her up for their much-delayed dinner date.

"We federal agents are a little slow sometimes." He led her to his newly purchased vehicle.

"New truck, no car?" Lainie admired the shiny red four-door Ford Ranger.

"I felt like I needed a change. Something a little beefier. Too ostentatious?"

She laughed. "It's beautiful."

Lainie sat and he closed the door, then walked around to the other side.

"This is nice, good choice."

"Glad you approve. We're having dinner at Parkers' Lighthouse. You okay with that?"

Lainie smiled. "Another great choice."

They chatted about their physical condition; both were healing.

"I hope to be back to work in a few more days," Lainie told him. "Mostly, I feel relieved and a little vindicated now that Dallas Vine is behind bars."

"Everyone is amazed at how spot-on your theory was. I'm very glad Avery West came clean."

"I am too. When I got the chance to talk to him, he told me that the load just got too heavy."

"The load?"

"Yes. The load of anger and bitterness he'd carried over the years. Once he told the truth and trusted the police, he said it made him feel ten years younger. I get it. Anger, bitterness, unforgiveness—they weigh a ton."

"Sounds like you've done some letting go as well."

"It's a process, but yes, I forgive Stan. He's working with investigators to put as many nails in Vine's and Benton's coffins as they can. He'll still see jail time, but I've seen a change in him, real change."

"I hope that goes for Callen West as well. It's sad to think that Avery's bitterness over the years so infected that kid. I hope that Avery finally telling the truth will turn things around for him. Accepting the truth could change his whole life."

Ben pulled into the parking lot of Parkers' Lighthouse. It was a beautiful, clear night, the lights of the *Queen Mary* shining in the distance.

As they walked to the restaurant, Ben took Lainie's hand.

"Speaking of changed lives, Lainie. How do you feel about dating a federal agent?"

She squeezed his hand. "I like the idea. There should be more cooperation between agencies."

"Agree."

DISCUSSION QUESTIONS

1. After witnessing so much injustice in her career, Lainie felt as though God had let her down. How can "seeing gross injustice firsthand" cause us to doubt God's goodness? How can it also strengthen our relationship with God?

2. Lainie has a longstanding obsession with bringing Dallas Vine to justice for the murder of Daphne Sparks. That experience with Vine "infected Lainie with a bitterness that ate at her soul." Can you relate to her feeling of bitterness as it has grown over time, like an infection in the soul? How does bitterness do this?

3. As Lainie considers how much God has forgiven her, she realizes she needs to forgive Stan. Do you agree? Have you ever decided to forgive someone even though they had not asked for your forgiveness? What was the result?

4. Lainie initially hesitates to see the police psychologist. Why do you think that might be? How do you think the visit to Dr. Reynolds ends up being helpful to her?

5. We see a deep care and respect between law enforcement partners in this story: Lainie and Mike, Ben and Efren. What do you

think creates the bond between these characters? Have you experienced a bond like this?

6. Ben thinks about resigning from his position when he's filled with guilt over possibly causing Evie's death. Do you resonate with the emotion behind his decision? Do you think resigning would have been an appropriate action to take?

7. As she looks for the truth of what happened to Evie, Lainie has "instincts screaming inside her that something wasn't right." When have you experienced a similar gut feeling? Did it turn out to be accurate?

8. Although Ben felt pressure from his family to go into law enforcement and was sure he would hate it, he has ended up loving it and feels like he's found his calling. Have you ever felt *called* to something? Like you were meant to do it?

ABOUT THE AUTHOR

A former Long Beach, California, police officer of twenty-two years, Janice Cantore worked a variety of assignments, including patrol, administration, juvenile investigations, and training. She's always enjoyed writing and published two short articles on faith at work for *Cop and Christ* and *Today's Christian Woman* before tackling novels. She now lives in Hawaii, where she enjoys ocean swimming, golfing, spending time on the beach, and going on long walks with her Labrador retriever, Tilly.

Janice writes suspense novels designed to keep readers engrossed and leave them inspired. She has penned more than a dozen novels including the Line of Duty series, the Cold Case Justice series, and several standalones.

Visit Janice's website at janicecantore.com and connect with her on Facebook at facebook.com/JaniceCantore and at the Romantic Suspense A-TEAM group.